Can't Wait to Get to Heaven

FANNIE FLAGG

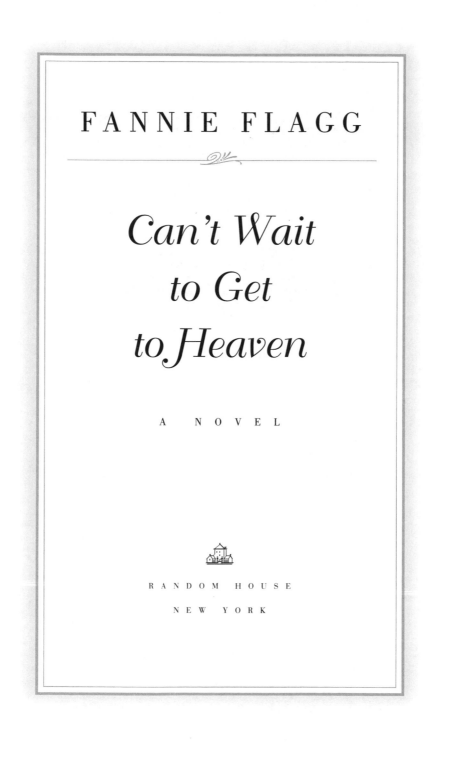

Can't Wait to Get to Heaven

A NOVEL

RANDOM HOUSE

NEW YORK

Copyright © 2006 by Willina Lane Productions, Inc.

Published in the United States by Random House, an imprint
of The Random House Publishing Group, a division
of Random House, Inc., New York.

RANDOM HOUSE and colophon are registered
trademarks of Random House, Inc.

ISBN 1-4000-6126-1

Printed in the United States of America on acid-free paper

www.atrandom.com

2 4 6 8 9 7 5 3 1

First Edition

To my good friend
Peggy Hadley

There are two ways to live your life.
One is as though nothing is a miracle.
The other is as though everything is a miracle.

—Albert Einstein

Can't Wait
to Get
to Heaven

Elmwood Springs, Missouri, Monday, April 1

9:28 AM, 74 degrees and sunny

After Elner Shimfissle accidentally poked that wasps' nest up in her fig tree, the last thing she remembered was thinking "Uh-oh." Then, the next thing she knew, she was lying flat on her back in some hospital emergency room, wondering how in the world she had gotten there. There was no emergency room at the walk-in clinic at home, so she figured she had to be at least as far away as Kansas City. "Good Lord," she thought. "Of all the crazy things to have happen this morning." She had just wanted to pick a few figs and make a jar of fig preserves for that nice woman who had brought her a basket of tomatoes. And now here she was with some boy wearing a green shower cap and a green smock, looking down at her, all excited, talking a mile a minute to five other people running around the room, also in green shower caps, green smocks, and little green paper booties on their feet. Elner suddenly wondered why they weren't wearing white anymore. When had they changed that rule? The last time she had been to a hospital was thirty-four years ago, when her niece, Norma, had given birth to Linda; they had all worn white then. Her next-door neighbor Ruby Robinson, a bona fide professional registered nurse, still wore white, with white shoes and stockings and her snappy little cap with the wing tips. Elner thought white looked more professional and doctorlike than the wrinkly, baggy green things these people had on, and it wasn't even a pretty green to boot.

She had always loved a good neat uniform, but the last time her niece and her niece's husband had taken her to the picture show, she had been disappointed to see that the movie ushers no longer wore uniforms. In fact, they didn't even *have* ushers anymore; you had to find your own seat. "Oh well," thought Elner, "they must have their reasons."

Then she suddenly began to wonder if she had turned off her oven before she had gone out in the yard to pick figs; or if she had fed her cat, Sonny, his breakfast yet. She also wondered what that boy in the ugly green shower cap and those other people leaning over, busy poking at her, were saying. She could see their lips moving all right, but she had not put her hearing aid on this morning, and all she could hear was a faint beeping noise, so she decided to try to take a little nap and wait for her niece Norma to come get her. She needed to get back home to check on Sonny and her stove, but she was not particularly looking forward to seeing her niece, because she knew she was going to get fussed at, but good. Norma was a highly nervous sort of a person and, after Elner's last fall, had told her time and time again not to get up on that ladder and pick figs. Norma had made her promise to wait and let Macky, Norma's husband, come over and do it for her; and now not only had Elner broken a promise, this trip to the emergency room was sure to cost her a pretty penny.

A few years ago, when her neighbor Tot Whooten had gotten that needle-nosed hound fish stuck in her leg and wound up in the emergency room, Tot said they had charged her a small fortune. On reflection, Elner now realized that she probably should have called Norma; she had *thought* about calling, but she hadn't wanted to bother poor Macky for just a few figs. Besides, how could she know there was a wasps' nest up in her tree? If it weren't for them, she would have been up and down that ladder with her figs, making fig preserves by now, and Norma would have been none the wiser. It was the wasps' fault; they had no business being up there in the first place. But at this point she knew that all the excuses in the world would not hold much water with Norma. "I'm in big trouble now," she thought, before she drifted off. "I may have just lost ladder privileges for life."

The Nervous Niece

8:11 AM

Earlier that morning Norma Warren, a still pretty brunette woman in her sixties, had been at home thumbing through her Linens for Less catalog, trying to decide whether or not to order the yellow tone-on-tone floral design chenille bedspread, or the cool seersucker 100-percent-cotton-with-plenty-of-pucker in sea foam green with ribbon stripes on a crisp white background, when her aunt's neighbor, and Norma's beautician, Tot Whooten, had called and informed her that her Aunt Elner had fallen off the ladder again. Norma had hung up the phone and immediately run to the kitchen sink and thrown cold water in her face to keep herself from fainting. She had a tendency to faint when she was upset. Then she quickly picked up the wall phone and dialed her husband Macky's cell phone number at work.

Macky, who was the manager of the hardware department at The Home Depot out at the mall, glanced at the readout of the number calling and answered.

"Hey, what's up?"

"Aunt Elner's fallen off the ladder again!" said Norma frantically. "You'd better get over there right now. God knows what she's broken. She could be lying over in her yard, dead for all I know. I told you we should have taken that ladder away from her!"

Macky, who had been married to Norma for forty-three years and was used to her fits of hysteria, particularly where Aunt Elner was concerned, said, "All right, Norma, just calm down, I'm sure she's fine. She hasn't killed herself yet, has she?"

"I told her not to get on that ladder again, but does she listen to me?"

Macky started walking toward the door, past plumbing supplies, and spoke to a man on the way out. "Hey, Jake, take over for me. I'll be right back."

Norma continued talking a mile a minute in his ear. "Macky, call me the minute you get there, and let me know, but if she's dead, don't even tell me, I can't handle a tragedy right now. . . . Oh, I could just kill her. I knew something like this was going to happen."

"Norma, just hang up and try to relax, go sit in the living room, and I'll call you in a few minutes."

"This is it, I am taking that ladder away from her as of today. The very idea of an old woman like her . . ."

"Hang up, Norma."

"She could have broken every bone in her body."

"I'll call you," he said, and hung up.

Macky walked out to the back parking lot, got in his Ford SUV and headed over to Elner's house. He had learned the hard way; whenever there was a problem with Aunt Elner, having Norma there only made matters worse, so he made Norma stay at home until he could get to Elner's and size up the situation.

After Macky hung up, Norma ran into the living room like he had said to do, but she certainly could not calm down or even sit down until he called to tell her everything was all right.

"I swear to God," she thought, "if she hasn't killed herself this time, not only am I taking that ladder away from her, I'm going over and personally chopping down that damn fig tree, once and for all." As she paced up and down the living room, wringing her hands, she suddenly remembered she should be practicing the positive self-talk exercises she had just learned in a program she was doing, designed to help people, like herself, who suffered from panic attacks and anxiety. Her daughter, Linda, had seen it advertised on TV and had sent it to her for her birthday. She had finished step nine, "Put an End to 'What If' Thinking," and was now on step ten, "How to Stop Obsessive, Scary Thoughts." She also tried to do her biofeedback deep breathing technique that she had been learning from a woman in her yoga class. As she paced, she breathed deeply and repeated a list of positive affirmations to herself: "It's nothing to worry about," "She has fallen out of the tree twice before and it has always been all right," "She's going to be fine," "It's just catastrophic thinking, it is not real," "You will laugh about this later," "There's nothing to be afraid of," "Ninety-nine percent of the things you worry about never happen," "You are not having a heart attack," "It's just anxiety, it's not going to hurt you."

But as hard as she tried, she couldn't help but be anxious. Aunt Elner was the closest living relative she had left in the world, besides Macky and their daughter, Linda, of course. After her own mother had died, her aunt's well-being had become the main focus of most of her worries, and it had not been easy. As she passed by the photograph of a smiling Aunt Elner she kept on the mantel, she sighed. Who would have thought that this sweet, innocent-looking, rosy-cheeked old lady, with her white hair pulled back in a bun, could cause so much trouble? But then, Aunt Elner had always been stubborn; years ago when Aunt Elner's husband, Uncle Will, had died, it had taken Norma forever to get her to move into town so she could keep a better eye on her.

Finally, after years of begging her, Aunt Elner had agreed to sell the farm and move into a small house in town, but she still was hard to handle. Norma dearly loved Aunt Elner, and *hated* to have to nag at her all the time, but she was forced to; Aunt Elner was deaf as a post and would not have gotten a hearing aid if Norma hadn't nagged at her. Aunt Elner *never* locked her doors, she didn't eat right, she would not go to the doctor, and worst of all, she wouldn't let Norma straighten up her house for her, something Norma was just dying to do. Aunt Elner's house was a disaster, with pictures hung all over the wall helter-skelter, in no particular order, and her front porch was a mess. She had all kinds of things strewn everywhere: rocks, pinecones, shells, birds' nests, wooden chickens, old plants, and four or five old rusty metal bulldog doorstoppers that her neighbor Ruby Robinson had given her. It was appalling to Norma, whose house and porch were always kept as neat as a pin. And it was only getting worse; just yesterday when Norma had gone over, there had been yet another new addition to the clutter: a hideously ugly jar of plastic sunflowers. Norma had cringed when she first saw it, but had asked sweetly, "Where did these come from, honey?"

As if she didn't know. It was Aunt Elner's neighbor across the street, Merle Wheeler, who was always bringing over the most horrendous-looking objects. Merle was the one who had brought that ratty, old fake brown leather office chair with the wheels, a chair that Elner had put on the front porch for all the world to see. At the time Norma had been head of the Beautify

Elmwood Springs Committee and had tried every way possible to make her aunt get rid of it, but Elner had said she liked to roll around in it and water all her plants. Norma had even tried to talk Macky into going over there in the middle of the night and stealing it off Elner's porch, but he wouldn't do it. As usual, he stuck up for Aunt Elner, and told Norma that she was making a mountain out of a molehill, and that she was beginning to act just like her mother, which had not been true! Wanting to get rid of that chair had not been snobbism on her part, simply a matter of civic pride. Or at least she had hoped so.

Norma had a complete horror of being anything like her mother. Ida Shimfissle, Elner's younger and prettier sister, had married well and had never been very nice to Elner. She had refused even to visit Elner after she'd moved to town, as long as Elner kept chickens in her backyard. "It's so country," she had said. But yesterday when Aunt Elner pointed at the sunflowers and announced with pride, "Aren't they pretty, Merle brought them over, and you don't even have to water them either," it had been all Norma could do not to grab them and run screaming to the nearest trash can. Instead, she had just nodded pleasantly. Norma also knew where Merle had gotten the flowers. She had seen some exactly like them at Tuesday Mornings. Unfortunately, the local cemetery was just full of similar arrangements. Norma had always been appalled that people would actually put plastic flowers on a grave; to her, they seemed as cheap-looking as black velvet paintings of the Last Supper, but then, she never understood why anyone would want aluminum sliding glass windows, or keep a television set in the dining room either.

As far as Norma was concerned there was no excuse for having bad taste anymore, or at least, none that she could think of, when all you had to do was look in magazines and simply copy what you saw, or watch the design shows on the Home & Garden Channel. Thank God that Martha Stewart had come along when she had and introduced a little style to the American public. Granted, she was a jailbird now, but she had done a lot of good before she went. But it wasn't only home and entertainment matters that bothered Norma, she was constantly dismayed at the way people dressed out in public. "You owe it to your fellow human beings to try and look as nice as you can, it's just common courtesy," her mother had always said. But now all anybody ever wore, even on planes, were tennis shoes, sweat suits, and baseball caps. Not that Norma dressed up all the time like she used to. She had been known to run out to the mall in her orange velour jogging outfit, but she never went anywhere without earrings and makeup. On those two points, she could never compromise. When Norma looked up at the clock again it was almost eight-thirty! Why wasn't Macky calling? He had had plenty of time to get there. "Oh, God," she thought. "Don't tell me Macky has had a wreck and been killed in an accident on the way over there, that's all I need this morning. Aunt Elner falls out of a tree and breaks her hip, and I become a widow on the same day!" At 8:31 she could not stand it another second, and was just about ready to dial Macky's number, when the phone rang, and she almost jumped out of her skin.

Macky began by saying, "Norma, now listen to me. I don't want you to get excited." She could tell something was terribly wrong by the tone in his voice. He had always started conversations with "She's fine, I told you not to worry," but not this time. Norma held her breath. "This is it," she thought. The call she had been so terrified of receiving was actually taking place.

She felt her heart begin to pound even harder than before and her mouth go dry as she tried to remain calm and brace herself for the news.

Macky continued, "I don't want you to panic, but they've called an ambulance."

"AN AMBULANCE!" she screamed. "Oh my God! Has she broken something? I knew it! Is she badly hurt?"

"I don't know, but you better come over here and go with us, you'll probably need to sign some papers."

"Oh my God. Is she in pain?"

There was a pause, then Macky answered, "No. She's not in pain, just get on over here as soon as you can."

"She's broken her hip, hasn't she? You don't have to tell me, I know she has. I knew it. I've told her a thousand times not to get on that ladder!"

Macky cut her off, saying again, "Norma, just come on over here as soon as you can." He had not wanted to be rude to Norma, and hated to hang up on her again, but he also did not want to tell her that Aunt Elner had knocked herself out cold and was still out like a light. At this point, he really had no idea what was broken, or even how badly she was hurt. When he had arrived at her house a few minutes before, Aunt Elner had been lying on the ground under her fig tree, with Ruby Robinson sitting beside her, taking her pulse, while her other neighbor, Tot, was standing there beside them engaged in a running commentary.

The Eyewitness

Earlier, at exactly 8:02 AM, Tot Whooten, a thin and wiry redhead who always wore pale blue eye shadow, even though it had been out of style since the seventies, had been on her way to work at the beauty shop because her client Beverly Cortwright was coming in for a dye job today, and she needed to get to the shop a little early and do some mixing. As she walked by Elner Shimfissle's house, she just happened to look up, in time to see her neighbor topple backward off an eight-foot ladder, with what looked like a hundred wasps buzzing all around her and following her right down to the ground. After poor Elner landed with a thud, Tot yelled at her, "Don't move, Elner!" and ran up her other neighbor's front porch steps, screaming at the top of her lungs, "Ruby! Ruby! Get out here quick! Elner's fallen out of the tree again!" Ruby Robinson, a diminutive woman of about five-foot-one, in clear bifocals that made her eyes look twice as big, was having her breakfast, but the instant she heard Tot, she jumped up, grabbed her small black leather doctor's bag from the hall table, and ran as fast as she could. By the time the two of them reached the side yard, about twenty angry and upset wasps were still flying all around the

· 13 ·

tree, and Elner Shimfissle was lying on the ground, unconscious. Ruby immediately reached in her bag, pulled out the smelling salts, and snapped it under Elner's nose, while Tot relayed what she had just witnessed to the other neighbors, who had started to come out of their houses and gather around the fig tree. "I was headed off to work," she said, "when I heard this loud buzzing noise . . . buzz . . . buzz . . . buzzzzz, so I looked up, and saw Elner hurl herself backward off the top of the ladder, and then . . . Whamo! Bang! She hit the ground, and it's a good thing she's so bottom heavy, because when she fell, she didn't flip or anything; just went straight down like a ton of bricks." Ruby quickly popped another smelling salts under Elner's nose, but still she did not come around. Never taking her eyes off of her patient for a second, Ruby suddenly started barking orders. "Somebody call an ambulance! Merle, bring me a couple of blankets. Tot, go call Norma and tell her what's happened." Ruby, who at one time had been head nurse at a major hospital, knew how to give orders, and everybody scattered and did exactly what she said.

Norma Hits the Road

8:33 AM

The second she hung up with Macky, Norma ran to the kitchen again and threw cold water in her face, then flew through the house frantically gathering up her purse, Aunt Elner's insurance papers and Medicaid information, a toothbrush and toothpaste, and anything else she thought her aunt would need for the hospital. Norma had been waiting for years for something like this to happen, and now that it had, she was glad she'd had the foresight to plan for it. Ten years ago she had prepared a file marked HOSPITAL EMERGENCY, AUNT ELNER.

She also had an earthquake kit in the garage, where she kept bottled water, matches, six cans of Del Monte chili, a small supply of her hormones, thyroid medicine, aspirin, a jar of Merle Norman cold cream, and fingernail polish remover and an extra pair of earrings. Although it was not very likely that an earthquake would hit Elmwood Springs, Missouri, she felt it was better to be safe than sorry.

After Norma had gathered all the things for Aunt Elner, she ran out of the house and yelled to a woman in the yard next door, "I'm on my way to the hospital, my aunt's fallen out of a tree again," and jumped in the car and took off. The woman, who did not know Norma very well, stood there and watched her leave, wondering what in the world Norma's aunt was doing up in a tree. After Norma rounded the steep corner and steered out of the complex, she drove across town as fast as she possibly could without breaking the law. The last time Aunt Elner had fallen and Norma had rushed over, she had been pulled over by the highway patrol and given a speeding ticket, the first one in her life, and to make matters worse, when she had driven away, she had backed up over the officer's foot. Thank God he had been a friend of Macky's or she might have wound up in jail for life. She knew she had to be careful not to get another ticket: she was obeying the speed limit, but as she drove, her thoughts were racing a hundred miles a minute. The more Norma thought about the events of the past six months, the madder she got and the more she began to blame Macky for Aunt Elner's present situation. If they had stayed in Florida instead of coming back home, this would not have happened. When Norma reached the intersection out on the interstate and had to wait for the longest red light in the history of man to change to green, her mind flashed back to that fateful day just six months ago. . . .

It had been a Tuesday afternoon and Aunt Elner had been at her bingo game over at the community center. Norma had just come home from her Weight Watchers meeting, and had been in such a good mood because she had lost another two pounds and received a happy-face sticker from the leader, when Macky had dropped the bomb. When she opened the front door, he was in the living room waiting for her, and had that funny look on his face, the one he always had when he had made up his mind about something, and sure enough, he told her to sit down; he wanted to tell her something. "Oh God, what now?" she thought, and when he told her, Norma could hardly believe her ears. After Macky had gone through what she had dubbed his "middle age crazy period, ten years too late" and they had already sold the hardware store, their house, and most of their furniture, and had all moved, including Aunt Elner and her cat, Sonny, lock, stock, and barrel, all the way down to Vero Beach, Florida, he was now sitting there telling her that he wanted to move back home again! After only two years of living in their mint green concrete-block three-bedroom citrus view patio home in "Leisure Village Central," he now said that he had had it with Florida—with the hurricanes and the traffic and the old people who drove thirty miles an hour. She had looked at him in total disbelief. "Are you going to sit there and tell me that after we have sold practically everything we own and spent the last two years fixing this place up, now you want to move back home?"

"Yes."

"When for years all I heard out of you was, 'I can't wait until we move to Florida.' "

"I know that, but—"

She cut him off again. "Before we moved, I asked you, 'Are you sure you want to do this now?' 'Oh yes,' you said. 'Why wait, let's go early and beat the baby boomers.' "

"I know I did, but—"

"Do you also recall that it was at your behest that I gave away all our winter clothes to the Goodwill? 'Why take all those old coats and sweaters to Florida,' you said. 'I'll never have to rake another leaf or shovel another sidewalk of snow, who needs heavy coats?' you said."

Macky squirmed a little in his chair as she continued. "But beside the fact that we now have no home, and no winter clothes, we can't go back."

"Why not?"

"Why not? What will people think?"

"About what?"

"About what? They will think we are a bunch of flibberti-gibbets, that's what, moving here and there, like a caravan of gypsies."

"Norma, we've moved once in forty years. I don't think that qualifies us as flibbertigibbets or gypsies."

"What will Linda think?"

"She doesn't care, it's perfectly normal for people our age to want to be around familiar settings and old friends."

"Then, Macky, why in God's name did we leave in the first place?"

This was an answer he had thought about and rehearsed. "I think that it was a good learning experience," he said.

"A good learning experience? I see. We now have no home, no winter clothes, no furniture, but it's been a good learning experience. Macky, if you weren't going to be happy here, why did we come?"

"I didn't know I wouldn't like it, and tell the truth, Norma, you don't like it here any more than I do."

"No," she said, "I don't, but unlike you, Macky, I've worked very hard trying to adjust, and I would hate to think I wasted two years of my life adjusting for nothing."

Macky sighed. "OK, OK, we won't go, I don't want to do anything to make you unhappy."

Then Norma sighed and looked at him. "Macky, you know I love you . . . and I'll do what you want, but my God, I just wish you had thought this thing through. After they gave us that big going away party and all, then to crawl back home and say, 'Surprise, we're back.' It will just be so embarrassing."

Macky leaned over and took her hand. "Sweetheart, nobody

cares. A lot of people have moved somewhere and then moved back again."

"Well, I haven't! And what does Aunt Elner think, I'm sure you two have discussed it."

"She said she's happy to go back home, but that it's up to you, she'll do whatever you want."

"Oh great, as usual it's two against one, and if I don't say yes, I'm the dirty shirt."

She sat and stared at him, blinked her eyes a few times, then said, "All right, Macky, we'll go, but promise me that a couple of years from now, you won't get another wild hair and move us again. I can't take another move."

"I promise," said Macky.

"What a mess. Now you've got me so upset I'm going to have to have some ice cream."

Macky jumped up, happy the thing was settled. "Don't get up, honey," he said. "I'll get it. Two scoops or three?"

She opened her purse and felt around for a Kleenex. "Oh . . . make it three, I guess, there's no point in me going back to Weight Watchers if we are leaving."

Thankfully they sold the citrus view patio home in three days, with a thirty-day escrow. But still, it had been very upsetting to move again, and thank God she had not sold all of her knickknacks. She had kept her ceramic dancing storks music box, and her milk-glass top hat. They had been such a comfort to her in her time of need.

Driving back home to Missouri, with Sonny the cat yowling all the way, she'd tried not to continue to complain like her mother used to do, but when Aunt Elner quipped from the backseat, "Norma, look at the bright side, at least you didn't sell off your cemetery lots," it set her off again. "Just when I was starting a new life, here we are going back home to die, like a bunch of old elephants headed back to the burial grounds," she'd said. And to make matters worse, in the two years they had been in Florida, with the new software companies opening up and all the new people moving in, the price of real estate in Elmwood Springs had almost doubled. What had once been a small town, with only two blocks of downtown, was now experiencing suburban sprawl. And with another huge shopping center opening up out on the four lane, most of the town had moved to the outskirts, and their pretty four-bedroom brick house that had sat on an acre had been torn down to make room for an apartment complex.

Elner had been the smart one. She had not sold her house but had rented it to friends of Ruby's, who were gone now, so she could go back to her old house. But when they got back, all Norma and Macky could afford to buy was a two-bedroom two-story town home in a new development called Arbor Springs, and even then, Macky had to go to work at The Home Depot to help pay for that. At the time, Norma had begged Aunt Elner to move in with them, or to at least consider moving to an assisted living facility, but she had wanted to move back to her own house, and as usual, Macky took her side. And thanks to him, Norma was now headed over to see her oldest living relative, who had probably just broken a hip, an arm, or a leg, or worse. For all Norma knew, her aunt could have broken her neck and could be completely paralyzed, and she was probably going to be in a wheelchair for the rest of her life.

"Oh no!" she thought. "Poor Aunt Elner will be miserable not being able to move around." Hopefully, they would be able to get her one of those new motorized chairs, and of course, this would have to happen *now,* when they had just moved into a house with stairs with no wheelchair access. Well, she guessed Macky was just going to have to build a ramp, because the three of them could not possibly live in Aunt Elner's small one-bathroom house, not with Linda and the baby coming to visit all the time.

"I hope you're happy now, Macky!" she said. "If you had listened to me, this would never have happened!"

The three people in the car that waited next to her at the red light looked over at Norma, who was now talking out loud to herself, and wondered if she was a crazy person. By the time she reached the next red light, and as her mind continued to race, Norma wondered if maybe Macky was not entirely to blame. Maybe this whole thing could have been avoided if she had just put her foot down and had not agreed to move to Florida in the first place. At the time she had told Macky that she'd had a bad omen about them moving, but then, she had bad omens about so many things, she couldn't be sure if it was really a bad omen, or just another symptom of her anxiety disorder. It was very frustrating, to not know when she should put her foot down and when she should not. The result was that she never really put her foot down about anything. By the time Norma was a block away from Aunt Elner's house, Macky was completely off the hook, and now she was blaming herself entirely for Aunt Elner's fall. "It's all my fault," she wailed. "I should never have let her move back into that old house!"

Just then, Norma happened to look over and see the same three people in the car who had been at the last stoplight staring at her. She put the window down and said, "My aunt fell out of her fig tree" just as the light changed and they took off as fast as they could.

Verbena Gets the News

8:41 AM

Verbena Wheeler was already at work down at the Blue Ribbon Cleaners and Fluff and Fold Laundromat when her husband, Merle, called and told her that Elner had fallen off the ladder again and this time had knocked herself out cold.

"They are waiting on the ambulance right this very minute," he said.

"Ohhhh, Norma is going to have a fit, you know how she worries about Elner. Call me back and tell me as soon as you know something."

Verbena, a tight-lipped woman with a tight little gray permanent, was a Church of God, no-nonsense, strict Pentecostal, "I'm a Bible-beater and proud of it" kind of person who could quote from Scripture to fit any occasion. She had also been very worried about her neighbor, not only about her falling off a ladder, but about her rapidly changing belief systems as well. In her opinion, Elner Shimfissle had gone quite radical as of late, and Verbena was convinced she could trace the changes right back to the day Elner had gotten cable television, and had started watching the Discovery Channel. Verbena, who only watched TBS and religious channels, had been extremely concerned.

"Too much science, too little religion," if you asked her. To prove her point, only about a week after it had been hooked up, she had received an alarming phone call from Elner.

"Verbena," Elner said, "I'm just not so sure about the Adam and Eve story anymore."

Verbena had been stunned upon hearing such a thing coming from a lifelong Methodist in good standing.

"Oh, Elner," Verbena said, while holding on to the counter for support, "that's a terrible thing to say. . . . Next you'll be telling me you have become an atheist!"

"Oh no, honey, I still believe in God, it's just the Adam and Eve part I have a question about."

An alarm bell went off as Verbena suddenly grasped the real implications and the dire consequences of the word "question." She gasped, "Don't tell me that you're thinking of throwing in with the evolutionists, not at this late date, I'm just shocked, you of all people." Elner agreed, "Well, I'm kind of shocked at myself, Verbena, but if you ever doubted that we didn't come from monkeys, then you need to see the show I saw on television last night, about those little snow monkeys they have over in Japan. They sit around all winter in hot tubs, and I swear to you, there was one that looked so much like Tot Whooten, I half expected it to talk. I'm telling you, honey, if you put a dress on it, put a comb in its hand, you'd be hard-pressed to tell them apart. The thing even had on blue eye shadow just like Tot's . . . had her expression and everything!"

Verbena had been very upset by the phone call. She knew that once a person had even the slightest doubt about Adam and Eve, the stories that followed—Cain and Abel, Noah and the Ark, on down the line—began to fall apart like a stack of dominoes. She had wanted to call Norma immediately and tell her that her aunt was being dangerously influenced by those so-called educational shows, and if she wasn't careful, the next thing you know, she might wind up subscribing to *The New York Times* or joining the ACLU! Verbena knew it was just this kind of thinking that had led to taking prayer out of the school, and Christ out of Christmas. Verbena would have called, but was not quite sure just where Norma stood on the creation issue anymore.

Norma's mother, Ida, had been a strict Presbyterian, but after her mother died, Norma had joined one of those new age, nondenominational, one-size-fits-all, do-it-yourself churches that had moved so far away from the Bible that they hardly ever read it. And even when they did, their interpretation of the Scripture was far too loose to suit Verbena. She tried to warn Norma that joining that new age church was taking a mighty big chance with her immortal soul. Norma had not been rude, she had listened, and thanked her for her call, but she hadn't gone back to a good Bible-based church either. A lot of the new people in town whom she tried to guide back to the Bible *had* been very rude, had even gone so far as to tell her to mind her own business. Some had even canceled their charge account down at the cleaners. She had taken a hit in her pocketbook and learned the hard way, it was best not to tinker around with matters of religion, not if you want to get along with your neighbors. But another reason she had not called Norma was that shortly after talking to Elner, Verbena had gone on the Internet. There was just no two ways of getting around it; Tot Whooten did look exactly like a snow monkey. It had surprised her at the time, but it had not shaken her faith; it stated quite clearly in Genesis 1:27, "So God created humankind in his image," and there was just no way in this world Verbena would ever believe that God looked anything like Tot Whooten, or any of the Whootens, for that matter!

Verbena had not been aware of it at the time, but the snow monkey incident was not the first question Elner had concerning Adam and Eve. Years ago, when Elner still lived out in the country, long before she had watched the Discovery Channel, she had been listening to the Bud and Jay early morning farm report on the radio, when Bud had announced the question of the day. "Which came first," he asked, "the chicken or the egg?" After the show, Elner had gone on about her chores for a little while, then right in the middle of feeding her chickens, she stopped dead in her tracks, put the pan down, and went inside and called Norma.

Norma picked up. "Hello."

"Norma, I think there is a mistake in the Bible, who do I tell, Bud and Jay or Reverend Jenkins?"

Norma looked over at the clock. It was five-forty-five and still dark outside. "Hold on a minute, Aunt Elner. Let me go and pick this up in the kitchen, Macky's still asleep."

"Oh, did I wake you up?"

"That's all right, hold on." Norma got up out of bed and stumbled to the kitchen, put the light on, and plugged in her percolator. Now that she was awake, she might as well fix the coffee. She picked up the phone. "Here I am, Aunt Elner. Now what?"

"I think I may have discovered a serious error in the Bible. I don't know why I hadn't figured it out before."

"What error?"

"Which came first, the chicken or the egg?"

"What? That's not in the Bible."

"I know that, but just answer me this, which came first, the chicken or the egg?"

"I have no idea," Norma said.

"Well, don't feel bad, they say it's the age-old question that nobody's been able to figure out, but the answer just came to me a minute ago, just as clear as a bell and here it is. . . . Are you ready?"

"Yes." Norma yawned.

"The chicken came first, no doubt about it."

"Ahh . . . and how did you come up with that?"

"Simple! Where does an egg come from? A chicken; so the egg had to come after the chicken, the egg *couldn't* lay itself. But then I got to thinking, if the chicken came before the egg . . . then how could Adam get here first, when Eve was the only one who could give birth?"

Norma reached for a cup out of the cabinet. "Aunt Elner, I think you may have forgotten that according to the Bible, nobody gave birth, God made Adam, then took a rib from Adam, and made Eve."

"I know it *says* that, Norma, but the sequence is off. . . . It's the hen that lays the egg with the rooster inside . . . the rooster doesn't even lay eggs."

Norma said, "Yes, honey, but there has to be a rooster to fertilize the egg."

There was a long silence on the other end. Then Elner said, "Well, you've got me there. I guess I need to do some more thinking about it. Oh, shoot. Here I was thinking I'd just solved one of the great mysteries of the world, but I still think there's a chance that Eve came first and the men who wrote the Bible changed it around at the last minute so they could be first, and if that's so, we may have to rethink the entire Bible."

At around seven-thirty, when Macky had come into the kitchen, he found Norma sitting at the kitchen table wide awake.

"What are you doing up so early, couldn't you sleep?"

She looked at him. "I could have . . . if the phone hadn't rung before the crack of dawn and woke me up."

"Oh," said Macky, getting his cup. "What did she want to know this morning?"

"Which came first, the chicken or the egg."

Macky laughed as Norma went over to get the cream out of the refrigerator.

"You can laugh, Macky, but she was just about to call the radio station and tell them that there was a mistake in the Bible, thank God I stopped her."

"What does she think is a mistake?"

"She's convinced Eve was created before Adam. Can you imagine the uproar that would have caused?"

Macky smiled. "Well, at least she has an open mind, you can say that for her."

"Oh, it's open all right," Norma said. "I just wish it would open a little later in the day. Last week she woke me up wanting to know if I knew how much the moon weighed."

"Why did she want to know that?"

"Who can tell? All I know is, she can ask more questions in one day than most people do in a year."

"Yeah, she can."

"And you wait, once she's off and running with this Adam and Eve thing she's going to be calling me all day."

As predicted, around ten AM, just as Norma had finished applying her special Merle Norman facial mask for dry sensitive skin, the phone rang for the fourth time that morning. "Norma, if Adam and Eve were the only two people on earth, then where did Cain and Abel meet their wives?"

"Oh, I don't know, Aunt Elner . . . at Club Med? Don't ask me. I don't even know why the chicken crossed the road."

"You don't? Well I do!" said Aunt Elner. "Do you want me to tell you?"

Norma gave up and sat down. "Sure," she said. "I'm just dying to know."

"To show the possum it can be done."

"Aunt Elner, where do you hear these silly things?"

"From Bud and Jay. Did you know that another name for the potato bug is the Jerusalem grasshopper?"

"No."

"Did you know there are forty-seven trillion cells in the human body?"

"No, I didn't."

"Yes, that was the correct answer yesterday. It won somebody an electric knife."

Norma had just put the phone down and was headed to the bathroom when the phone rang again.

"Hey, Norma, you just wonder who had the time to count all those cells, don't you?"

To Believe or Not to Believe

8:49 AM

Norma was driving as fast as she could, and just missed the last red light by a second and had to slam on her brakes, causing Aunt Elner's insurance files to spill all over the floor of the car. She was so upset by this time, and wanted to pray for help with her nerves, but she knew she either had to pray or drive carefully; she couldn't do both, so she decided to pay attention to the road.

Besides not wanting to have a wreck, she was also not 100 percent sure that praying would help. Norma had struggled with her faith all her life, and wondered why believing had not been easy for her, like English or speech had been in high school. She had made all A's in both subjects; everyone said she had a lovely speaking voice, and to this very day, she could still conjugate a sentence. But she of all people needed to have faith in something. Macky was absolutely no help; he was as sure there was nothing out there as Aunt Elner was sure there was, contrary to what Verbena thought. Aunt Elner had called her just last week and said, "Norma, since I've been watching my science shows, my opinion of the Maker has shot up, I knew he was great, but I didn't know how great, how anybody could

· 29 ·

think of so many things to create is beyond me, why just your different species of tropical fish alone are a miracle."

Aunt Elner had no doubt whatsoever, but Norma was stuck right in the middle, fluctuating back and forth. One day she believed, the next she was not sure. Norma wished she could talk to someone about it, but she couldn't confide in her minister, who was just starting out, and needed all the encouragement she could get. But even though Norma was not sure who or what she was praying to, she often did pray for help in overcoming her character flaws: not to notice when people put the ketchup bottle on the dinner table, or kept their garage full of junk and left the doors wide open, not to recoil at the sight of Verbena's solid oak toilet seats, but she failed miserably, disappointing herself over and over again.

Norma was convinced her inability to not be offended by people with bad taste, terrible manners, or those who used incorrect grammar and said "went" instead of "gone" was directly related to the fact that she was unsteady in her faith. She hoped that one day she might get a sign, some kind of revelation, to prove that *something* was out there. Verbena said she was always on the lookout for "signs, wonders, and miracles," and Norma would take anything at this point, but so far she had seen nothing. If she died in a car crash right now on her way to Aunt Elner's, her tombstone would have to read:

HERE LIES NORMA WARREN
DEAD, BUT STILL CONFUSED.

The Newspaper Woman

The moment Cathy Calvert heard the loud siren of the ambulance as it sped past her downtown office, she knew she would have a story to write. Cathy, a tall thin woman in her early forties, with dark brown hair, was the owner-editor of the small weekly newspaper. She did most of the reporting herself, and from past experience, whenever an emergency vehicle was called to Elmwood Springs, it was either an accident or a serious mishap of some kind. She walked outside to see if it was a fire engine or an ambulance, but missed seeing it, and was surprised to hear the screaming siren cut off so close to town. Usually when an ambulance or a fire engine had been called, it was headed on out to the new four-lane traffic stop, where people were always crashing into each other, or else it was headed on out to the mall. Since Weight Watchers had moved next to the Pottery Barn, people trying to walk off those few pounds before they weighed in had sometimes overdone it and fallen out with heart attacks.

She went back into the office and grabbed her camera and her pad, and ran over to the spot where she thought the siren had stopped. As she came around First Avenue North, she saw that it was an ambulance, and it was parked right in front of Elner Shimfissle's house. "Oh no," she thought, "don't tell me she's fallen off the ladder again." When Cathy reached the scene, Tot was standing on the sidewalk looking very distressed, and ran up to her. "She's done it this time. She fell clean off the ladder and knocked herself out, and Norma is going to have a fit. Macky just called her to come over."

Cathy suddenly forgot about writing her story and became just another concerned friend of Elner's standing around feeling helpless. After a while, when so many neighbors had gathered and there was nothing she could do to help, she suddenly felt funny about being there with a camera. She didn't want anyone to think she was there as a reporter, so she asked Tot to call her and keep her posted about Mrs. Shimfissle's condition, and walked back up to the office. Although she was concerned, she was not overly concerned, because Elner Shimfissle was a pretty hearty old gal, who had fallen off things before and lived to tell the tale. Cathy knew firsthand Elner was a tough old bird in more ways than one.

Some years ago, after Cathy had graduated from college, she had taught a class in oral history at the community college, and Elner Shimfissle had attended with her friend Irene Goodnight. Both had been excellent students with interesting histories. Cathy had learned from that class that looks could be deceiving. For instance, at first glance, you never would have suspected that Irene Goodnight, a plain-looking, quiet grandmother of six, had at one time been known as "Goodnight Irene," and with teammate "Tot the terrible, left-handed bowler from hell" had won the Missouri State Champion Lady Bowlers title three times in a row. And if a stranger were to meet Elner for the first time, they never would have guessed that underneath that old lady façade she was still as strong as an ox.

In exploring Elner's history with her, Cathy had learned that during the Great Depression, when her husband, Will, had been bedridden with tuberculosis for over two years, Elner had risen at four every morning and with nothing but a mule and a plow had single-handedly kept their farm going. She had somehow managed to survive one of the worst floods in Missouri history, plus three tornadoes, had taken care of her husband, and had grown a crop large enough to feed them and half their neighbors. The most amazing thing about it to Cathy was that it had never occurred to Mrs. Shimfissle that it had been anything extraordinary. "Somebody had to do it," she said.

Before she had taught oral history, Cathy had always wanted to be a writer, even dreamed of one day writing the great American novel, but after a few semesters she ditched the idea completely and went into journalism. Her new philosophy was "Why write fiction? Why read fiction?" Scratch any person over sixty, and you have a novel so much better, certainly more interesting than any fiction writer could ever make up. So why try?

Oh No, Not That Robe!

8:51 AM

When Norma finally got across town and pulled up to the house, the ambulance was already there. She had arrived just in time to see Aunt Elner, to her great dismay wearing that old brown plaid robe she had begged her to throw away years ago, being shut into the back of the ambulance. Norma jumped out of the car with her purse and all the papers and ran over, but before she could get to Aunt Elner, they had already closed the doors and were driving away. Then Norma and Macky both got into his car and started down the street, following behind the ambulance. As they drove the forty-five minutes to the Kansas City hospital, Macky, who was very concerned, didn't say much, just an occasional "I'm sure she's going to be fine, Norma, it's just better that they take a good look at her and make sure nothing's broken."

But Norma wasn't listening and did most of the talking all the way there. "I don't know why they didn't let me ride with her, I'm her closest family member, I should be with her, she's probably scared to death, and why is she still wearing that ratty old brown robe? It has to be at least twenty years old, and it's falling apart at the seams. I got her a brand-new one out at Target last week. When she shows up at the hospital in that thing, they are going to think we are just plain old white trash, I don't know why she has to always act as if she didn't have a dime in the world, I said, 'Aunt Elner, Uncle Will left you plenty of money, there's no reason in the world you should run around in the yard wearing that ratty old robe,' but would she listen to me? No . . . and now this."

Norma sighed. "I should have just taken it and burned it, that's what I *should* have done. I just pray she hasn't broken her hip or her leg. I knew she should have moved in with us, but no, she has to stay in that old house, and she won't lock her doors. The other night I went over to leave her suppositories on the porch and her front door was standing wide open. I said, 'Aunt Elner, don't come running to me when you are murdered in your bed by some mass murderer.' "

Macky made a left turn. "Norma, how many mass murders have there been in Elmwood Springs?" Norma looked at him and said, "Well that's no guarantee it won't happen in the future. . . . You thought she would be all right back living in her house all alone. See . . . you don't know everything, Macky."

"Norma, try not to worry yourself into a fit, until we find out anything, OK?"

"I'll try," she said, but she couldn't help but be mad at Macky, and the more she thought about it, the madder she became. The fact that Aunt Elner had fallen off the ladder in the first place was entirely his fault. He was the one who spoiled her and thought everything she did was *so* funny. Even when Aunt Elner had let her friend Luther Griggs park his huge, ugly eighteen-wheeler truck in her side yard for six months, Macky had taken her side, and if he hadn't let her keep that ladder, had taken it away from her like she had asked him to do, Aunt Elner wouldn't be lying up in the hospital right now.

Norma suddenly turned to her husband and said, "I'll tell you one thing, Macky Warren, this is the last time I let you and Aunt Elner talk me out of anything, I *told* you she was too old to be living alone!"

Macky did not say anything. For all he knew, at this point, she might be right. He wished Aunt Elner had not gotten on that ladder by herself as well. He had just been at her house earlier that morning, having coffee with her before he went to work. She hadn't mentioned anything about figs. All she'd wanted to know was, what good was a flea, and where was it on the food chain. Now he was in trouble with Norma and worried sick over Elner himself. He just hoped she had not broken anything major, or he would never hear the end of it.

Norma suddenly reached up and felt the top of her head. "My God," she said, "I think I feel my hair turning completely white! I hope you're happy, Macky. Now instead of just touching up a few spots, Tot will probably have to do a complete dye job on me."

And if things weren't bad enough, when they were within ten minutes of reaching the hospital Macky decided to take a short-cut, and of course the first thing that happened was they got caught at a railroad crossing and had to wait while a freight train passed by. With every fiber in her being Norma wanted to scream, "I told you to just follow the ambulance! Now look!" But she didn't. It never did any good. He always said the same thing. "Norma, don't start the blame game," and his saying that always made her madder, so she quietly stewed and did her deep breathing as they sat and watched one railroad car after another rattle by.

"Why won't people listen to me?" she wondered.

She had been right about her daughter, Linda. She had told Linda *not* to marry that boy she was dating. She had even been modern about it and had advised her to live with him for a while, but no, Linda wanted the big wedding and the honeymoon, and then what did she do? She ended up with a big divorce as well. "Why don't they listen? It's not as if I like being right all the time, being right is certainly not fun for me." Being right, especially about your husband, can be painful; and sometimes you would give your left arm to be wrong. As she sat there waiting for the end of the train to pass, she thought about the events of the last few days. She had been feeling a little more anxious than usual, and now wondered if she had not been having some kind of premonition that something terrible was about to happen.

As she ran over it in her mind, she remembered she had started feeling a little anxious Wednesday morning, right after her regular ten-thirty hair appointment down at the beauty shop. "What could have set it off?" she wondered. She thought back to that morning. . . . She had been in the chair as usual, having her hair set, when Tot Whooten, the snow monkey look-alike, reached across to pick out a medium-size roller from her plastic tray, and dropped it on the floor.

"God dog it!" Tot said. "That's the second time I've dropped something this morning. I tell you, Norma, my nerves are all ajingle. It seems like after 9/11 happened, everything has turned upside down. I was doing just fine, had gotten over my breakdown, came back to work ready to go, and then, wham, you wake up and find out that the Arabs just hate us to pieces, and why? I've never been mean to an Arab in my life, have you?"

"No . . . never met one, really," said Norma.

"And, then you find out people all over the world hate us."

"I know," sighed Norma, handing Tot a bobby pin. "I'm completely baffled, I thought everybody liked us."

"Me too, I just don't get it. How could anybody hate us, when we're so nice? Anytime there was a problem anywhere in the world, haven't we always sent money and help?"

"For as long as I can remember we have."

"Aren't we supposed to be the most generous people in the world?" she said, sticking a pin into a roller.

"That's what I've always heard," said Norma.

"Now I read that even Canada hates us . . . Canada! And we just love them, everybody's always wanting to go up there and visit. I never knew Canada hated us. Did you?"

"No, I didn't," said Norma. "I always thought Canada was our friendly neighbor to the north."

Tot took a drag off her cigarette and put it back in the black plastic ashtray. "It's one thing when somebody you know hates you, but when perfect strangers hate you, it just makes me want to put a rope around my neck and jump out a window, doesn't it you?"

Norma thought about it and said, "I don't think I want to kill myself over it, but it's certainly very upsetting."

Tot picked up a hairnet. "I say forget trying to help the whole damn world, because they sure don't appreciate it."

"They don't seem to," said Norma.

"Hell . . . look at France, after we went over and saved them from the Nazis, and now they say all those ugly things? Shoot, I'll tell you, Norma, this whole thing has really hurt my feelings."

Norma agreed. "It does almost make you not want to even try and help people, doesn't it?"

"You got that right!" she said, stuffing cotton behind

Norma's ears. "All my hard-earned tax money going around the world, and do I even get a thank-you? I used to have faith in the world, but it's turned out to be as bad as my own children, nothing but gimme, gimme, gimme all the time . . . and it's never enough."

Tot's daughter, Darlene, who was as wide as her mother was thin, was working in the next booth and heard her last statement. "Well, thanks a lot, Mother!" she said over the partition. "See if I ever ask you for anything again!"

Tot rolled her eyes in Darlene's direction, and said to Norma, "I can only hope."

Although Norma did not like to think about it, Tot was right of course. After the terrorist attacks on 9/11 everything had changed. Even in a small town like Elmwood Springs, people had been so shocked, they had become a little crazy. Right after it happened Verbena was convinced that the Hing Doag family that ran the little market on the corner might be part of a terrorist sleeper cell. Norma told her, "They're not Arabs, Verbena, they're Vietnamese." But Verbena had not been convinced. "Well, whatever," she said, "I still don't trust them."

But mostly people were just sad about the shape of the world their children and grandchildren had to live in. And for those like Norma and Macky, born and raised in the forties and fifties, it was such a drastic change from that era when everyone felt safe, and your only knowledge of the Middle East was a picture on a Christmas card of a bright star shining down on a peaceful manger, not the place full of hate and rage they saw daily on the television and read about in the newspapers. All Norma knew was she couldn't take it anymore. She didn't want to, so three years ago she just stopped reading the newspapers and watching the news. Now she only watched the Home & Garden network and the *Antiques Roadshow* on PBS, and more or less just stuck her head in the sand, and hoped that somehow things would work out.

About forty minutes later, after Norma had been brought out from under the dryer, Tot continued the conversation.

"You know me, Norma, I always try to put on a happy face, but it's getting harder and harder to keep up a good attitude. They say civilization as we know it is done for, doomed."

"Who says that?" asked an alarmed Norma.

"Everybody!" she said, removing Norma's hairnet. "Nostradamus, CNN, all the papers, according to them, we are on the brink of total annihilation at any second."

"Oh Lord, Tot, why do you pay attention to all that stuff? They are just trying to scare you."

"Well, Norma, Verbena said it was in the Bible that this is the end of times, and the way things are going, I think it's just around the corner."

"Oh, Tot. I've been hearing things like that all my life, and they've always been wrong."

"So far," said Tot, pulling a roller out of Norma's hair. "But one of these days they are going to be right. Verbena says all the signs point to the apocalypse. All the earthquakes, hurricanes, floods, and fires we've been having lately, and now that turkey flu thing—there's your pestilence right there."

Norma felt herself starting to hyperventilate and, trying to use her "Replace a Negative Thought with a Positive One" exercise, said, "People can be wrong, you know, remember when rock and roll came out? Everybody said it couldn't get worse, but it did, so there you go."

"I don't see how it could be any worse. But if the end of the world *does* come before I can collect my social security, then I'm really going to be mad, after I've been looking forward to retiring for years, shoot . . . Life isn't fair, is it? Aren't you worried about the end of the world?" she asked, picking up a brush.

"Of course," said Norma. "I don't want it to happen just when a little style is finally coming back. Go out to Restoration Hardware, or to the Pottery Barn, they have the cutest things now, and for great prices. I just try not to worry about it."

"Yeah," Tot said. "It doesn't do any good. Verbena said she's not worried one whit. Of course, she thinks she's going to disappear, right before the end of the world comes and the rest of us all burn to a crisp. She said if she ever misses her hair appointment, it's because she's been taken up to heaven in the rapture. I said, 'Well, *thanks a lot, Verbena,* if you were really a good Christian you would at least offer me a ride up to heaven, instead of leaving me here to fry.' "

"What did she say?"

"Nothing."

"Well, Tot, if it makes her happy to think that, let her. I've given up trying to figure out why people believe what they do. Look at those suicide bombers that blow themselves up thinking they are going to wake up and have seventy virgins or something."

"Yeah, well, they may be in for a big surprise when they wake up and find out they are just plain old dead and they blew themselves up for nothing. What's that song Peggy Lee sang, 'Is That All There Is?' "

"Yes, well, unfortunately nobody knows if this is it, or if there is life after death," said Norma.

Tot suddenly stopped brushing Norma's hair. "God, I hope not, this one has wore me out. I just want to sleep."

"Oh, Tot, you don't mean that. What if you had a chance to see your family again?"

"Hell no, I didn't want to see most of them when they were alive."

Tot then picked up a can of Clairol hard-to-hold hair spray. "What's life all about anyway, that's what I want to know, and I don't want to have to wait until I'm dead to find out either," she said, spraying Norma's hair with a vengeance. "Is that too damn much to ask?"

After she finished, Tot looked at Norma's hair in the large glass, rearranged a few curls, then handed Norma a hand mirror and spun her chair around so she could see the back. "There you go, hon, pretty as a picture!"

After her hair appointment, Norma felt a little uneasy, so when she arrived at Aunt Elner's house, she was happy to see her sitting on her porch with a big smile on her face. As she came up the stairs, she said, "You look mighty cheerful today."

"Oh, I am, honey. I just saved a butterfly! I walked out here a little while ago and saw the prettiest butterfly caught in a spiderweb and I was able to set it loose. I'm sorry that spider missed out on his lunch, but butterflies only have one day to live, now at least he'll have the rest of the day."

Norma cleared off a chair and sat down. "I'm sure he'll be happy about that."

Elner said, "Did you know a turtle lives to be a hundred and fifty years old and poor little butterflies just get a day? Life doesn't seem fair, does it?"

"No," said Norma. "Tot was just saying the same thing a few minutes ago."

"About butterflies?"

"No, that life was not fair."

"Ah . . . what brought that up?"

"She's worried about not being able to collect her social security before the end of the world."

"Poor Tot, as if she didn't have enough to worry about with those children of hers. What else is she carrying on about this morning?"

"Just her usual this and that, and she's mad because she doesn't know what life is all about."

Aunt Elner laughed. "Well, join the club, who does? That's one of those sixty-four-thousand-dollar questions, isn't it, I'd say it's right up there with the chicken or the egg, wouldn't you?"

"I suppose."

Elner said, "You tell Tot if she finds out, to let me know."

Suddenly, as loud bells began dinging, Norma was abruptly jerked back into the present moment with a start. Back to the horrible present moment at hand, when only five days ago, Aunt Elner had been happy and laughing, and now she was in the emergency room at a strange hospital in God knows what kind of condition. As Norma sat there and waited for the bells to stop clanging and the red and white arms of the railroad cross stoop to finish lifting, she too joined the club and wondered, "What is life all about anyway?"

The Waiting Room

9:58 AM

Because of the delay at the train crossing Norma and Macky arrived at the hospital about eight minutes after the ambulance. The woman at the admittance desk told them that Elner was in the emergency room and she had no information on her condition, but the doctor would meet them in the waiting room and give them a report as soon as he knew something. Meanwhile Norma had to fill out a bunch of insurance forms and answer all the medical questions as best she could. Her hands were shaking so badly she could hardly write.

Of course she never really knew what to put down as Aunt Elner's age. Like most people back then, she had been born at home and the only evidence of her birth date had been recorded in the family Bible, but the Bible had disappeared years ago. Norma's mother had always lied about her own age, and was most likely the one who had gotten rid of the Bible, so now there was no telling how old Aunt Elner was, so she just put down eighty-nine.

She turned to Macky. "Do you think she's allergic to any medications?"

He shook his head. "No, I don't think so."

She went down the list of all past or present ailments and was able to check off no on every one. As far as she knew, Aunt Elner had never really been sick a day in her life, although she didn't know why. Most people her age had already had something, and with how she ate, and cooked everything in butter, she should have had diabetes or a heart attack years ago, but she was still in good health, as far as Norma could tell. She was certainly not frail. Norma knew that she was always lifting twenty-pound bags of birdseed even though she had asked her not to. After she finished filling out all the forms, Norma turned again to Macky. "Should we call Linda and let her know what's happened?"

"No, honey, let's just wait and see what's going on, there's no need to get her upset for nothing. She's in good hands, everything will be fine, you'll see." Norma took a deep breath and reached over and squeezed Macky's hand. "Thank God I have you. I don't know what I would do without you, just go completely insane, I guess."

Yoo Hoo!

10:09 AM

When Elner woke up from her nap, the room was pitch black and she had no idea what time it was, but she knew she was still in the hospital, because she could hear those beeping sounds and people walking around outside the door. She figured she must be all right, though, because she was not in pain and she could move all her fingers and toes. No broken bones, that was good. She lay there for a few more minutes and wondered where Norma and Macky were. "Oh, well," she thought. Norma might have had another one of her fainting spells and that had waylaid them getting to the hospital. They would be here pretty soon, she guessed, but in the meantime, she hoped those people in the green smocks had not stuck her in some room and forgotten where she was. "I hope they didn't lose me." It would be pretty hard to lose a big fat old woman like herself, but if by any chance they had lost her, she knew Norma would be fit to be tied.

Poor little Norma had inherited her good looks and bad nerves from her mother. Elner had always been a pleasant-looking woman but never a beauty like her youngest sister, Ida. She had never been a nervous or high-strung person either, and pretty much took things as they came, but Ida had been a nervous child growing up and so had Norma. Although Elner loved Norma like her own child, she could be hard to deal with at times. Norma, for example, was a clean freak. Macky used to say that he was scared to get up in the middle of the night to go to the bathroom because by the time he got back, she would have made the bed. He said she must have come out of the womb with a can of Lysol in one hand and a rag in the other. But with all of her little quirks, Norma had a heart of gold. Her biggest problem was that she cared too much about people and wanted to take care of the whole world. If there was anything in town that needed to be done, Norma did it. There wasn't a single old person that didn't have a hot meal or a visit from someone once a day, thanks to Norma. So with all of her little faults and her nervous fits, underneath she was one of the most loving people around.

After about another half hour went by, and nobody came to get her, Elner suddenly thought of something. Maybe Norma didn't even know she was here. Maybe the green-smock people didn't know who *she* was or who to contact. That had to be it, or else they would have been there by now, so Elner figured she better get up and go try and get somebody to call Norma to come get her and take her home. She sure did not want to stay overnight. Elner sat up and slowly and carefully got out of bed. "That's all I need, to slip and break my neck after I survived the first fall." But after she stood up, she was surprised at how easy it had been, and how light she felt. She figured she must have lost a little weight while she was waiting. "Norma will be glad of that." Norma was always worried about the fact that Elner was a little on the heavy side, and Norma ran over to her house every day to take her blood pressure. Norma had even cut off Elner's bacon, to no more than two pieces at breakfast, and none at night. Of course, when she had gone over to Merle and Verbena's for dinner the other night, and had had liver and bacon, she had not mentioned it. No use to get Norma upset.

Elner was now standing by the bed, but the room was so dark that she could not see a thing and had to feel her way around the room. She headed in the direction of the voices, and located the door, groped around, found the handle, opened it, and walked out into the bright light of the hall. She looked up and down, but she didn't see a single person anywhere.

She walked down the corridor past a lot of empty rooms. "Yoo hoo!" she called out, but not too loudly because she didn't want to disturb any sick people trying to sleep. She had wandered all the way down to one end and then down to the other end when she saw the elevator. There wasn't a soul on this floor, as far as she could tell, so she guessed she'd better go to another one and try to find somebody. She pushed the button, and after a moment the elevator stopped with a jerk and the doors opened. She stepped inside and turned around, but before she could push another button, the doors closed, and up she went.

The Doctor's Report

10:20 AM

Norma and Macky had been in the hospital waiting room for over twenty minutes, and they had been told nothing yet. Three other people, two women and a man, were there in the waiting room as well, waiting to hear news of their mother's hip replacement. Norma informed them in great detail who she and Macky were, where they were from, why they were there, and how she had warned her aunt over and over again to be careful on that ladder, a fact Macky was sure the hip-replacement family couldn't have cared less about. And that may have been the reason all three decided to go to the cafeteria for a cup of coffee. After another anxious ten minutes a young doctor walked in with a chart and looked around the room. "Is there a Mrs. Norma Warren here?" Norma jumped up. "Yes, that's me."

"Are you Mrs. Shimfissle's next of kin?"

Norma was a complete wreck by this time and began to babble uncontrollably. "Yes . . . she's my aunt, my mother's sister, is she badly hurt, Doctor? I've told her a hundred times not to get on that ladder, but she won't listen to me, I said, 'Aunt Elner, wait until Macky gets off from work.' "

Macky knew she was never going to shut up, and cut her off. "How is she, Doctor? Is she conscious yet?"

Norma, who still didn't know that Aunt Elner had been knocked out cold, turned and looked at Macky. "What do you mean, is she conscious yet?"

The young doctor sized up the situation and said, "Let's go sit down."

"What do you mean, is she conscious yet?" asked Norma again.

When they were seated, the doctor looked first at Macky, then at Norma. "Mrs. Warren, I'm sorry to have to tell you this, but your aunt"—he glanced down at his chart—"uh, Mrs. Shimfissle, died at 9:47 AM. We tried our best to revive her, but by the time she got here, she was already in bad shape, and considering her age and the circumstances, there was nothing we could do. I'm sorry."

Norma collapsed and slowly slid off the chair, and Macky and the doctor were just barely able to catch her, a second before the back of her head hit the floor.

Bad News Travels Fast

9:59 AM

Back in Elmwood Springs, Elner's neighbors Ruby Robinson and Tot Whooten had received the news about Elner, even before Norma and Macky. Earlier that morning, after the ambulance left with Elner, Ruby and Tot had gone inside and Ruby had called her nurse friend, Boots Carroll, who worked at Caraway Hospital, and told her that her neighbor Mrs. Shimfissle was on the way and to be on the lookout for her. As a professional courtesy, Boots had called her back and informed her that the word had just come out of ER that her Mrs. Shimfissle had officially coded at 9:47, and Boots read her the report over the phone. When Ruby put the phone down, she turned to Tot, who was sitting at the kitchen table, and shook her head. "She didn't make it."

"Oh, no. . . . What happened?"

"Anaphylactic shock. That many wasp stings all at once, her heart just stopped."

"I don't believe it. Are they sure?"

"Oh yes, Boots said she was practically a DOA, never had a chance from the get-go. I knew her pulse was weak, but I thought she would pull through, poor old Elner, but at least she didn't suffer, that's something, I guess."

"So she's really dead?" said Tot, not believing it.

"Yes." Ruby walked over and sat down. "Sad to say, but she's really dead."

"I'm just glad if it had to happen, she didn't die down there in Florida, around a bunch of strangers."

"Yes, thank God, she was in her own yard when it happened."

They both just sat for a moment staring into space trying to come to terms with the fact that they had just lost their friend and neighbor for good.

After a while Tot breathed deeply and said, "Well . . . it's the end of an era, isn't it?"

Ruby nodded and said solemnly, "Yes, it is. I've been knowing Elner Shimfissle all my life. . . ."

"Me too," said Tot. "I won't know what to think anymore, not to see her out on her porch every day, waving at everybody. She was one of the oldies but goodies, wasn't she, Ruby?"

"She was that," said Ruby.

They sat there and thought of all the ways their lives were going to be affected now that Elner was gone for good. Not only had they seen her every day, but for years, every evening the same group had all brought their lawn chairs over to Elner's yard and sat and talked and watched the sun go down.

Tot said, "What's going to happen to the Sunset Club now?"

"I don't know," Ruby said.

"And who's going to do the Easter egg hunt this year?"

"I haven't a clue. I guess somebody will."

"Easter just won't be the same without Elner."

"No it won't, I tell you one thing, Luther Griggs is going to be very upset when he hears about Elner . . . and poor Norma, you know she is going to take it hard."

"Oh . . . don't you know it?" said Tot. "She'll probably just fly all to pieces and have a running fit."

"She'll be beside herself, you know that. I think she was closer to Elner than she was to her own mother."

"I know she was, and who could blame her?" Tot added quickly, "I liked Ida, but she could be a real pain in the butt sometimes."

Ruby agreed. "I liked her too, but she was uppity, no two ways about it. Thank goodness Norma has Linda to help her get through it."

"And the new grandchild, that should be some comfort, not that mine would," said Tot.

They sat and stared at the table, this time thinking about poor Norma. After a moment Tot asked, "Well . . . what should we do now?"

Ruby said, "I guess we should probably go over to Elner's and make sure everything is all right, lock everything up, you know they won't be back until late."

"Yeah, I guess we should." Tot glanced up at the red plastic teapot-shaped kitchen clock, then went to the phone and called her daughter at the beauty shop. "Darlene, cancel all my appointments. I'm not coming in today. Poor Elner Shimfissle was just stung to death by wasps, I'm so upset, I couldn't do anybody's hair today if I tried."

Linda Gets the Call

10:33 AM

Linda Warren, a lovely blond woman of thirty-four, was in the boardroom, leading a meeting in St. Louis, when her secretary interrupted and told her she had an emergency phone call from her father. She ran down the hall and picked it up in her office.

"Daddy? What's wrong?"

"Honey, it's Aunt Elner. She fell off the ladder."

"Oh no, not again," said Linda, sitting down at her desk.

"Yes."

"Is she all right? Did she hurt herself?"

There was a silence. Macky did not know exactly how to tell her, and said, "Well . . . she's in pretty bad shape."

"Oh no. Has she broken something?"

"Ah . . . worse than that."

"What do you mean, worse than that?"

There was a long moment, then Linda said, "She's not dead, is she?"

"Yes," answered Macky flatly.

Linda felt all the blood drain from her head and heard herself ask, "What happened?"

"When Tot and Ruby found her, she was on the ground, unconscious, and they think she must have died in the ambulance on the way to the hospital."

"Oh my God. Why? From what?"

"They don't know exactly what caused it yet, but whatever it was, it was fast, she didn't suffer. The doctor said most likely she never knew what hit her."

"Where's Mother?"

"Here with me. We're at the Caraway Hospital in Kansas City."

"Is she OK?"

"She's OK, but she wants to know if there is any way you could get here. We have a lot of decisions to make, and your mother doesn't want to do anything without you. I know it's short notice, honey, but I really think your mother needs you to be here, if it's at all possible."

"Sure, Daddy, tell Mother to hang on and I'll get there just as soon as I can."

"Good, I know she'll be happy to know you're coming."

"I love you, Daddy."

"I love you too, honey."

Macky hung up and felt a wave of relief. The truth was, he needed Linda there as much as Norma did. Somehow he knew that when Linda got there everything would be all right. His little girl, that sweet helpless little angel who had depended on him for everything, had now grown up to become the one he could depend on. At times he looked at the successful and assured woman she had grown into and still saw that little girl there, then there were times like today when he realized she was more capable and smarter than either he or Norma. How the two of them had managed to produce her, he didn't know, but he was so proud of her he didn't know what to say.

As soon as Linda hung up, all the executive training she had received on how to deal with crisis situations kicked in, and in less than eight minutes she had arranged to have the au pair pick up her daughter, Apple, at school that afternoon and take her over to her best friend's house to spend the night. Her secretary on another line had her on a private corporate jet out of St. Louis, booked a limo to the St. Louis airport, and a pickup at the airport in Kansas City. Linda was out the door in the backseat of the car and on her way in less than fourteen minutes.

Linda had not been close with her grandmother Ida, who had moved away from Elmwood Springs when Linda was a baby to be closer to the Presbyterian church and her garden club meetings in Poplar Springs, and when your mother does not get along with your grandmother, it is hard to have a good relationship. Her grandmother told her she had been so disappointed in Norma: "I don't understand her, she could have gone to college, and made something of herself but she just threw her life away and became a plain old housewife." All Norma had said was, "Just be thankful she's your grandmother and not your mother." And so Aunt Elner had been the one she was close to growing up. As the limo rode through traffic, Linda began to think about her childhood and the many nights she'd spent up at Aunt Elner's house.

From the time she had been a baby until long after she was far too old for it, Aunt Elner had always put her to bed with a baby bottle full of chocolate milk. In the summers she and Aunt Elner would sleep out on her big screened-in back porch, and in the winters Aunt Elner would put her in the small bed across the room from her big bed, and they would lie there, watching the orange glow of Aunt Elner's electric heater, and talk until they fell asleep. When she had taken lessons at the Dixie Cahill School of Tap and Twirl, Aunt Elner had been at every dance recital, and she had attended every graduation, and the wedding of her one failed marriage. As she looked back on her life, it was the three of them who had always been there. Mother, Daddy, and Aunt Elner. When her daddy had not been able to convince Norma to let her train with AT&T instead of going to college, it was Aunt Elner who had talked Norma into letting Linda go. As a matter of fact, whenever there had been a problem between anybody, it had been Aunt Elner who had always been able to resolve it.

Over the years Linda had come to appreciate and to be somewhat in awe of Aunt Elner's ability to see both sides of any argument, see exactly how to negotiate a settlement, say the right thing to make both parties feel better. Long before they were teaching the win-win solution for problem solving techniques in business schools, Aunt Elner had already been doing it for years and without any training. Of course she was no fool. When she saw there was no way to solve a problem she knew it. When Linda was having problems with her marriage, after months of tears, talking, arguments, marriage counseling, break-ups and reconciliations, broken promises on his part, it was Aunt Elner who had finally given her the best advice, using only five little words: "Get rid of him, honey." Linda must have been ready to hear it, because that's exactly what she did, and considering her ex was now on his third marriage, it was the best advice she could have taken.

And when she had told her mother that she wanted to adopt a Chinese baby, Norma had tried to talk her out of it. "If you are not married, Linda, and suddenly show up with a Chinese baby, people will think you have had an affair with a Chinaman!" But thank heavens Aunt Elner had been on her side. "I've never even seen a Chinaman in person and I'm looking forward to it," she had said. Suddenly a wave of combined guilt, remorse, and grief swept over her. Why hadn't she found more time to go home and visit with Aunt Elner? Why hadn't she let her daughter, Apple, get to know her better? Now it was too late.

She suddenly remembered their last conversation. Aunt Elner had been so excited about some article she had read in *National Geographic* about a breed of mice that leaped in the moonlight. Some photographer had evidently hidden in the bushes and caught a picture of them leaping, and Aunt Elner thought that was the cutest thing she had ever seen and had called Linda long distance and pulled her out of a meeting to tell her all about it. "Linda, did you know that desert mice leap in the moonlight? Imagine those little mice leaping around in the moonlight and having fun when nobody was looking, I guess they call themselves dancing, isn't that something, you need to see this picture right away!" Linda had not been as patient as she should have been, and had lied to her on top of it, telling her she was running right out that minute and getting a copy of the *Geographic*. Then she lied when Aunt Elner called her back in a few hours wanting to know what she thought. "You were right, Aunt Elner, they are just adorable, the cutest things I've ever seen!"

Aunt Elner had been so pleased. "Well, I knew you'd want to see them, didn't it just make your day?"

"It sure did, Aunt Elner," she lied again. If she could only take it back.

Now Linda knew firsthand what she had always heard was true. There are always regrets when you lose a loved one. She would live the rest of her life with a thousand "Why didn't I's?" and "If only I had's." But now it was too late. Maybe after the funeral, when everything settled down, she and Apple would spend more time at home with Mother and Daddy. Life. You never know when a conversation may be the last one you will ever have. Linda vowed to never take life for granted. She had just learned the hard way—it can stop without warning.

Going Over to Elner's

10:39 AM

Ruby and Tot walked across the lawn to Elner's house, and Merle Wheeler, Verbena's husband, a large man with a potbelly who always wore a white shirt and suspenders, was sitting in his yard across the street picking weeds. He called out, "Have you heard anything about Elner yet?"

Ruby nodded and called back, "We just got the report a little while ago, she didn't make it."

Merle, an expert on the running and maintenance of L&N toy train sets, but a little slow elsewhere, said, "To the hospital? What happened?"

"No," said Ruby. "She didn't make it period, Merle. She's dead, stung to death by wasps. They said she was practically gone before she got there."

Merle stopped picking weeds and sat in his green and white plastic lawn chair, also not believing what he had just heard. He and Verbena had lived directly across the street from Elner for the past thirty years. They had talked back and forth every day, he in his yard, Elner on her porch swing. After he had his heart attack and had retired, he and Elner had both joined the Bulb of the Month Club and had spent a lot of time together tending to their flower beds, watching the many varieties of bulbs bloom. Their spring jonquils had just bloomed a few days ago, but with all the snails in her garden hers were already half gone. Elner, who had loved all living creatures, had had a particular fondness for snails. She would pick them up and show them to visitors. "Aren't they the cutest things?" she would say. "Look at those little faces." Consequently she never kept her flowers long.

Merle had tried sneaking over into her yard and sprinkling Suggs Slug and Snail Poison in her garden, but she had caught him and had come running out of the house. "Don't you be killing my snails, Merle Wheeler," she had said. Every year the birds got most of her fruit and the ants got the rest, but she didn't care. She said the only insects she felt OK about killing were mosquitoes, ticks, and fleas, and an occasional spider, if it bit her first. Then something dawned on Merle; after all the years of Elner loving insects, going out of her way to save them, it had been insects that had killed her. "So much for being nice," he thought. Tomorrow he would go over to her house and kill every damn last one of them, snails and all. Slowly he got up off of his chair and went inside to call Verbena down at the cleaners and let her know the latest bad news.

When Tot and Ruby got to Elner's back porch, Sonny was scratching on the kitchen screen door trying to get in and have his breakfast. Tot opened the door and said, "Poor old Sonny is an orphan now and he doesn't even know it." As they walked in the kitchen, the smell of coffee was still in the room. The coffeepot was turned on, and so was her oven. They turned off the pot and the oven and removed the pan of biscuits that were now black and hard as a rock, and threw them out. Her frying pan, with several pieces of burned bacon in it, was still sitting on the gas burner. There were a few dirty dishes from the night before in the sink, so Tot walked over and started washing them while Ruby went in the pantry and found the cat food and fed Sonny, who was sitting by his dish meowing.

After she fed the noisy cat, Ruby went into Elner's bedroom and found the bed unmade and the radio on, tuned in to Elner's favorite station. Ruby made the bed, and tidied up the bathroom. She picked up a few things off the floor and put them back in the drawer. She tried to straighten out all the things Elner had sitting on her bedside table, her hearing aid, an old photograph of her late husband, Will Shimfissle, standing by their old farmhouse, a glass paperweight with the Empire State Building inside, a sixth grade school picture of her friend Luther Griggs, and the small clear glass snail figurine Luther had bought her. Ruby wanted everything to look a little neater when Norma came back. She dusted off the top of the table and emptied a glass of water and closed her small Bible. When Ruby went back into the kitchen, Tot was still at the sink. She turned and said, "I wonder what they will do with Sonny?"

Ruby looked over at the orange striped cat, who at the moment was sitting by his dish, cleaning his whiskers, and said, "I don't know, but if nobody else wants him, I'll take him, I guess, Elner thought the world of that old ugly thing."

"She did," said Tot. "I'd take him if my cat wouldn't have a fit. You know, now that I think about it, it was Elner who gave me my first cat, after I had my breakdown, when I told her the doctor said I needed Prozac. She said, 'Tot, sometimes what you need is a kitten,' and you know, she was right."

"Oh yes, she's pretty smart about mental health matters," said Ruby. "Look at how she was able to turn Luther Griggs around."

"That's right. She had the patience of Job with that boy."

Ruby looked out the window at all of Elner's birdfeeders. "Somebody is going to have to keep feeding her birds, you know she would want that."

"Oh yeah, I'll do it, I guess."

"It's a big job. She feeds them three times a day."

"I know, but it's the least I can do for her, she loved her birds."

"She did. She loved her birds."

Tot looked around the room with all the pictures of insects and flowers taped up on the wall. "I wonder if Norma will keep the house or sell it or what?"

"I imagine they'll sell it."

Suddenly Tot burst into tears. "It's hard to believe she's not coming right back. Isn't life the strangest thing, one minute you're picking figs and the next minute you're dead. It's enough to make you not want to get up in the morning." She blotted her eyes with a tea towel. Growing up in a close-knit small town, she had been through this kind of thing many times before, but it was still sad to see it happen. When someone old dies, it is even sadder. First you notice that the paper doesn't come anymore, then gradually the lights are turned out, the gas turned off, the house gets locked up, and the yard is no longer kept up, then it goes on the market and new people come in and change everything.

Elner's phone rang, and they both looked at each other. "This could be Norma calling," Ruby said, and walked over and answered it. "Hello."

The voice on the other end said, "Elner?"

"No, this is Ruby, who's this?"

"It's Irene. What are you gals up to this morning?"

"Oh, Irene, hold on a minute, will you?" Ruby put her hand

over the receiver and whispered to Tot, "It's Irene Goodnight, do you want me to tell her or do you want to do it?" Tot was on the Elmwood Springs ladies bowling team with Irene, and said, "I'll do it," and took the phone from Ruby.

"Irene, it's Tot."

"Well, hey, what are you girls doing over there, having a party?"

"No, not really."

"Well, I won't bother you, but tell Elner to call me later, will you? I found some old *National Geographic* magazines she may want."

"Irene, I hate to be the bearer of bad news, but Elner's dead."

"What?"

"Elner is dead."

"You're kidding me, right?"

"No, honey, I'm as serious as a heart attack. She got hit by wasps, and fell out of her tree and killed herself."

"What . . . When?"

"Not more than an hour and a half ago."

Irene had been cleaning out her basement all morning and had not heard the siren go through town, or even been aware of Elner's fall, so this news was like a bolt out of the blue. "Well," she sputtered, "I'm just—I'm just . . . stunned."

"Oh, honey, we all are," said Tot. "After we finish straightening up the house, I'm going home and get in bed. I feel like I've been hit by a ten-ton truck."

Irene sat down on her bed and looked out the window toward Elner's house. "Well, I'm just stunned . . . Where is she?"

"In the hospital in Kansas City. Norma and Macky are over there with her."

"Oh. Poor Norma, you know she is going to take this hard."

"You know she is . . . I just hope they are giving her something for her nerves."

Irene agreed, "I hope so too. . . . well . . . what's going to happen now?"

"I don't have any of the details yet, but I'll keep you posted."

After she hung up, Tot walked over and sat back down. "She's all broken up, could hardly talk."

Ruby said, "Well, I guess we should start making a list of all the people we need to call and let them know, save Norma the trouble."

"You're right, you know she's going to be busy making all the arrangements, that will be one less thing she will have to worry about. I guess Dena and Gerry will come in from California, don't you think?"

"Oh, I'm sure, it will be nice to see them again, although . . . I wish it could be under better circumstances," said Ruby.

"Yes, I do too, I wonder when the funeral will be."

"In the next couple of days, I would imagine."

Tot looked at Ruby. "I'm so sick of going to funerals I don't know what to do."

Ruby, who was a little older than Tot, sighed. "When you get to be my age, all the different weddings, christenings, funerals, start to blend together. You get used to it after a while."

"Not me," said Tot. "I don't ever want to get used to it." She turned and looked out the kitchen window at the puffy white clouds in the blue sky, and spoke. "And it's such a pretty day too."

Irene Goodnight

11:20 AM

After Irene put the phone down, she felt sick. She looked over at the small bunch of yellow daffodils in a jelly jar Elner had brought over a few days ago. She felt a huge wave of sadness hit her as she realized that Easter was only a few weeks away and Elner would not be here this year, or ever again. Every Easter, for as long as she could remember, she had taken her kids, then later her grandkids, over to Elner's yard to hunt Easter eggs. Every year without fail, Elner had dyed over two hundred eggs and had hidden them all over her yard. She always held the Easter egg hunt for all the neighborhood children. Irene's own five-year-old twin granddaughters, little Bessie and Ada Goodnight, had found the golden egg one year. What were the parents and the children going to do this year with Elner gone? What was going to happen to the Sunset Club? What was she going to do without Elner? She had known her since she was a little girl, and remembered when Elner used to keep chickens in her backyard. Irene's mother used to send her over to Elner's house for some eggs, and she had always left with a sack of figs as well. One time Elner had said, "Tell your mother my hens have been laying double yolks lately, so be on the lookout," and sure enough there had been five in a dozen with double yolks. When Irene had been younger, she had only thought of Elner as the egg and fig lady, then as she grew older and spent more time with her, she came to know her as plain Miss Elner. And Miss Elner always had some funny story to tell, mostly about herself. She remembered the story that Miss Elner used to tell about what had happened in the snowstorm the first Christmas she had moved into town from the country. She had been waiting for Norma's husband to come pick her up and take her over to their house for Christmas dinner, and when a green car slowed down, she thought it was Macky and ran out and jumped in the front seat. She said a complete stranger had been driving around looking for Third Street, when all of a sudden a big fat woman jerked the door open and hopped in beside him. She said she scared that man so badly he almost wrecked the car. Irene and Elner had laughed so hard over that, tears had run down both their cheeks. Little silly stories, like the time when her husband, Will, had swallowed a mother-of-pearl button she had left on the bedside table, thinking it was an aspirin. She said she never did tell him. No matter how blue Irene had been, Elner could always make her laugh. It was going to be sad to go by the old house on First Avenue North and not see her out on her porch waving, and knowing she would never be there again. But Irene had discovered over the years that unfortunately that was the way life was, something was there for years, and in an instant, it was gone. One day Elner's out on the porch, the next day, it's just an empty swing, another empty chair, another empty house, waiting for the next people to come and start all over again. She wondered if the houses ever missed people when they left, or if furniture knew anything at all. Would the chair know it was a different person sitting there? Would the bed? She sighed. "Death—what was it all about?" She wished she knew.

The Elevator Ride

Elner was wondering when that elevator was ever going to stop and let her out. This was the craziest elevator she had ever been on in her life! Not only did it go up, the thing zigzagged, spun around, and went sideways. When it finally did stop, and the doors opened, she didn't recognize the place at all. Nothing looked familiar. "Lord, the crazy thing must have taken me clear over to some other building." This was certainly not the hospital where she had been, and it was a nice enough building, but she had no idea where she was. For all she knew, she could be clear across town, all the way over to the courthouse. "Well, I'm for sure lost now," she said to herself as she headed on down the hall, looking for someone to help her get back to the hospital. "Yoo hoo!" she called out. "Anybody here?" She had walked for quite a while when she suddenly saw a pretty blue-eyed blond lady rushing down the hall toward her, carrying a pair of black tap shoes and a white feather boa.

"Hey," said Elner. The lady smiled at her and said, "Hello, how are you?" but she went by her so fast, Elner didn't have a chance to ask where she was. A few seconds after the lady passed, Elner thought to herself that if she hadn't known better, she would have sworn the woman was Ginger Rogers! She knew exactly what Ginger Rogers looked like because she had always been Elner's favorite movie star, and Dixie Cahill, who had run the Dixie Cahill School of Tap and Twirl in Elmwood Springs, where Linda had taken dancing, had a big picture of the dancer up in her dance studio. But the more she thought about it, she realized that even though the woman was the spitting image of Ginger Rogers, it couldn't have been her. What in the world would Ginger Rogers be doing in Kansas City, Missouri? It didn't make any sense, but then she suddenly remembered, Ginger Rogers was originally from Missouri, so even if it wasn't her, it was for sure one of her relatives.

Elner kept walking and was admiring how clean and white the marble walls and the floors were. "Norma should see this," she thought. "This would be a building after her own heart." So clean you could eat off the floor, that's what Norma liked, but why anyone would want to eat off the floor was a mystery to Elner. A few minutes later, she began to see a little speck of something way down at the end of the hall, and as she got closer, she was relieved to see it was a person, sitting at a desk in front of a door. "Hey," she called.

"Hey, yourself," the person called back.

When Elner finally reached the end of the hall and got up close enough to actually see who the person behind the desk was, she could hardly believe her eyes. It was none other than her youngest sister: Norma's mother, Ida! There she sat as big as life, all dressed up, wearing her fox furs and her good strand of pearls, and earrings.

"Ida?" she said. "Is that really you?"

"It is indeed," said Ida, eyeing Elner's old brown plaid robe with disdain.

Elner was flabbergasted. "Well, heavens to Pete . . . What in the world are you doing here in Kansas City? We all thought you were dead. Good Lord, honey, we had a funeral for you and everything."

"I know," said Ida.

"But if you're here, who was that woman we buried?"

Ida instantly got that certain little look she got when she was displeased, which was most of the time. "Oh, it was me all right," Ida said. "And if you recall, the last thing I said to Norma was 'Norma, when I'm dead, for *God's sake,* do not let Tot Whooten do my hair.' I even gave her the number of my hairdresser to call, paid the woman for the appointment in advance, and what did Norma do? The first thing she did when I died was to let Tot Whooten do my hair!"

"Oh dear," thought Elner. At the time, she and Norma had figured Ida would never know about it, but they were clearly wrong.

"Well, Ida," Elner said, hoping to smooth things over a bit, "I thought it looked very nice."

"Elner, you know I never parted my hair on the left. And there I was, on view to the world, with my hair parted on the wrong side, not to mention all that rouge she put on me. I looked like a clown in the Shriners' parade!"

If Elner had entertained any doubts for a second that the woman before her was her sister, she didn't anymore. It was Ida all right.

"Now, Ida," she said, "try not to get yourself in a snit. Norma had no choice. Tot is a good friend. How can you tell somebody something like that and not hurt her feelings? She showed up at the funeral home with her supplies and everything. She thought she was doing you a favor. Norma didn't have the heart to tell her she couldn't do you."

Ida was not sympathetic. "I should think a dying wish trumps hurt feelings, any time of the day."

Elner sighed. "Well, I guess so, but you have to admit, you had a really nice turnout. You had over a hundred people, all your garden club friends came."

"All the more reason to want to look my best. I should have just gone over to the funeral parlor and handed Neva all my details in person, that's what I should have done."

"Well, anyhow, honey, I'm awfully glad to see you again," said Elner, trying to change the subject.

Ida managed a tight little smile, even though she was still upset over Tot ruining her hairdo. "I'm glad to see you too, Elner." Then she added, "I notice you've put on a few pounds since I saw you last."

"A few . . . but that comes with age, I guess."

"I suppose so. Gerta put on weight when she got older."

Elner looked around at the white marble hall and said, "Ida, I'm not clear about what's going on. If you're not dead, why didn't you just come on back home?"

"Oh, I am dead. This is my home now," she said, fingering her pearls.

"Where is this anyway?" asked Elner, looking around again. "And what am I doing here? I'm supposed to be in the hospital, you've got me all confused."

Ida looked at her, with that maddening little know-it-all look of hers. "Well, Elner, if I'm dead, and you can see me, what do you suppose that must mean?"

Now Elner was starting to get upset. "How should I know, Ida? I just fell off a ladder, I'm so addlebrained at this point, I thought I just saw Ginger Rogers go by . . . and now you're telling me that you're dead, when I can see you plain as day. I must have knocked my brain out of whack because none of this is making any sense to me."

"Think, Elner," Ida said. *"Me? Ginger Rogers?"*

Elner thought for a second; then it dawned on her. Ginger Rogers had been dead for years, so had Ida; not only that, she suddenly realized that she could hear every word Ida was saying without her hearing aid! There was definitely something odd and peculiar going on. Then it hit her.

"Wait a minute, Ida," Elner said. "Don't tell me I'm dead too?"

"Bingo!"

"I'm dead?"

"You certainly are, my dear, just as dead as you can be."

"Oh no! . . . Am I dead and buried?"

"No, not yet, you just died a few minutes ago."

"Well, for heaven's sake. You don't mean it?"

"I do. In fact, you just missed seeing Ernest Koonitz, he just came in yesterday."

"Ernest Koonitz? The one who used to play the tuba on the *Neighbor Dorothy Show*?"

"Yes."

Elner felt a little light-headed. "I need to sit down a minute and think this over." She went and sat in the red leather chair by the door.

Ida looked concerned all of a sudden and asked, "Are you terribly upset, dear?"

Elner looked at her and shook her head. "No, I don't think so, I would say surprised more than anything."

"That's to be expected, we are all surprised. You know it's going to happen but somehow you just don't believe it's going to happen to you."

"Oh, I never doubted it would happen," Elner said. "I just wish that I'd had a little more warning. I just hope I turned off my stove and coffeepot."

"Yes . . . well, we all have our regrets, don't we?" Ida said pointedly.

In a moment, after gaining her composure and coming to terms with what must be true, Elner looked at her sister. "Oh, poor Norma, first you and now me."

Ida nodded. "Into each life a little rain must fall, as they say."

"Yes, I guess so, but I hope it won't hit her too hard, and I am pretty old, so I guess it could not have been too unexpected, could it?"

"No . . . not like it was when I died, I was just fifty-nine. Now that was entirely unexpected, I was still in very good shape, if I do say so myself."

Elner sighed. "Now that I'm dead and gone, I just hope Sonny will be all right, Macky said he would take care of him if anything ever happened to me but I don't think cats miss you much anyway, as long as they get fed." Elner looked down at her hands and said, "You know, Ida, it's a funny thing, but I just don't feel a bit dead, do you?"

"No, not like I thought I would feel. One minute you're alive, the next you're dead, not much difference. It's a lot less painful than childbirth, I can tell you that."

"No, no pain at all. As a matter of fact I feel better than I have for years, my right knee had been giving me some trouble but I didn't tell Norma, or else she would have jerked me in for a knee replacement, but it feels just fine now," she said, lifting it up and down. "So what's going to happen next? Am I going to see everybody else?"

"I don't know all the details, I was just given the word to meet you and take you inside."

"That was mighty nice of you, Ida. Seeing a familiar face right off makes it easier, doesn't it?"

"It does," Ida agreed. "You'll never guess who met me when I died."

"Who?"

"Mrs. Herbert Chalkley."

"Who's that?"

"Just the past president of the Women's Club of America, that's all."

"Ahh . . . well that must have been nice for you."

Ida stood up and opened the top drawer of the desk and began looking for something as she spoke. "By the way, they called me so fast, what was it, a heart attack?"

Elner thought about it, then said, "I'm not sure, I might have gotten stung to death by a bunch of wasps, or maybe just the fall killed me, who knows, and I was hoping to die in my own bed, but you can't have everything, I guess."

Ida said, "I'll bet it was a heart attack. That's what killed Gerta and Daddy. Of course, my heart was just fine, but then, I was younger than you and your death was sudden . . . mine wasn't. The doctor said I had a rare blood disorder, although it had been quite common with the royal families of Germany."

"Oh Lord," thought Elner, "Here she goes again, dead twenty-two years and still putting on airs." She had been at least seventy and died from leukemia, but Ida always had to have something one step up from everybody else. She had been that way her whole life. Their daddy had been nothing but a plain old farmer, but to hear her tell it he had been a baron with personal ties to the Hapsburgs and with ancestral lands deeded to the family. After Ida married Herbert Jenkins, she only got worse. From time to time Elner had been forced to remind her where she had come from, but Elner figured that there was no point to saying anything to her now, not at this late date. If she hadn't changed by now, she was never going to change.

Ida rattled around in the drawer and finally found the key she was looking for.

"Here it is," she said. She stood up and went over and began unlocking the big double doors behind her. Finally she got it unlocked, and turned to Elner. "Come on, let's go." Elner got up and went over, ready to follow her, but then stopped in her tracks. "Hold on a minute, this is the good place, isn't it? I'm not headed to the bad place, am I?"

Ida said, "Of course not."

Elner was relieved to hear it. But then on second thought, she figured if Ida had made it, then everybody must have a pretty good chance. But she still had one more question.

"What's going to happen when I get inside?"

Ida turned and looked at her like Elner was crazy. "What do you think is going to happen, Elner? You're going to meet your Maker. That's where I'm taking you, silly, to meet your Maker."

"Oh," said Elner. "And wouldn't you know it, here I am in this old robe with the pockets falling off and not a stitch of lipstick on."

"Now you know how I felt," Ida sniffed.

"Yes . . . I see what you mean."

"Are you ready?"

"I guess I am, or I wouldn't be here, would I?"

"No, you wouldn't, and now that you're here, do you have many regrets?"

"Regrets?"

"Things you wished you had done, before it was too late?"

Elner thought for a second, then said, "Well, I never got to

Dollywood. . . . I would have liked to have done that, but I did get to Disney World, so I guess I can't complain too much. What about yourself?"

Ida sighed. "I wish I had spent some time in London, visited the palace gardens, maybe had high tea with the royals, but alas, it was not to be."

And with that Ida threw open the doors with a flourish, stepped back, and said, "TA DA!"

Verbena Wheeler
Spreads the News

11:25 AM

Down at the Blue Ribbon cleaners, after the call from her husband, Merle, Verbena was so upset that she started calling everyone she could think of to tell them Elner was dead. Her first call was to Cathy Calvert over at the newspaper office, but her line was busy. She knew that Elner's friend Luther Griggs would want to know as soon as possible, but there was no answer. She called Cathy again but her line was still busy. Frustrated, she sat there and thought of who else she should call, and picked up the phone to call Elner's favorite radio show. She knew they would want to know.

Over the years, Bud and Jay's early morning farm report on WDOT radio had slowly turned into Bud and Jay's drive time news, weather, and traffic report, geared to the early morning commuters who lived in the suburbs and drove to work in the larger cities. There were not many farms left in the fifty-mile radius, but Elner had remained a loyal listener to the show and was a regular call-in to the program. Bud and Jay always got a big kick out of her. For as long as they had been doing the Question of the Day contest, she'd always tried to come up with the answer, and sometimes her answers were the best thing on the show. When nobody got the right answer, they sent her a prize anyway. One of their sponsors was PETCO, and she got a lot of cat food for Sonny that way. Bud also did the eleven to twelve *Shop and Swap* show and took the call from Verbena during a commercial break.

A few minutes later he made the announcement on the air. "Well, folks, just got a mighty sad phone call from over in Elmwood Springs, and we are sorry to have to report that our good friend Elner Shimfissle has passed away this morning. She was a special lady and one of our favorite callers here at WDOT, and we will sure miss her . . . don't know when the funeral will be, but as soon as we do, we'll pass it on. OK, let's see what we have next. . . . Rowena Snite over in Centralia says she has a man's briefcase with the initials B.S. on it, she will swap for any back issues of . . . *Crafts Made Simple,* or a lady's watch. Now here's a word from the Valerie Girard Chiropractic Group."

꙳

At that moment, Luther Griggs, wearing a white T-shirt and a baseball hat, was driving on Interstate 90 in his eighteen-wheeler truck, headed to Seattle on a six-day run. He was having his breakfast, a Coke and a bag of salted peanuts, and when he heard the news come over the radio he immediately pulled over to the side of the road, shut the truck down, and sat in a daze. Luther was an unlikely friend for an eightysomething-year-old woman to have, but Miss Elner was about the closest person in the world to him. They had just spoken last night about whether or not he should go back with his old girlfriend who he thought was too skinny, but Elner had advised him to go back with her anyhow.

As he sat there and the impact of the news really hit him, his throat started to hurt and he felt sick to his stomach. He did not want to go to Seattle now, he wanted to turn around and hit the nearest truck stop, get himself some pot, drink a case of beer, and knock himself out, but he had promised Miss Elner he would quit that. He also had a load of produce in the back that would spoil. Besides, Miss Elner would have wanted him to go. She had co-signed the loan to get the truck so he could have a good-paying profession, and the thought of disappointing her even now made him start up and pull on out.

As Luther drove farther out of town, and reached the Kansas City turnoff, it was all he could do not to get off. What was he going to do now? The best friend he'd ever had was gone.

The friendship between Luther Griggs, a chunky six-foot-three trucker, and Elner Shimfissle had started in a most unusual way. He had been around eight years old that day, twenty-eight years ago, when he had walked by Elner's house and she had run out on her front porch and called to him sweetly.

"Yoo hoo . . . little boy . . . come here a minute."

He stopped and looked at her and remembered she was the same old woman who had given him that terrible fudge a few days before.

"Come here, honey," she said again.

"No, I ain't coming up there," he said. "You ain't my mother, I don't have to do nothing you say."

"I know you don't, but I want to give you something."

"I don't want no more of that candy, it wasn't no good," he said, making a face.

"It's not candy, it's a present, and if you don't come over here, you're not getting it."

"What is it?"

"I'm not telling you, but it's something you'll like, and you'll be sorry if you don't come here and get it."

He narrowed his eyes at her and wondered what the old lady was up to. He was highly suspicious of anybody who was nice to him. He had thrown rocks at her stupid cat, so maybe she was trying to get him to come close enough so she could hit him. But whatever it was she wanted, he was not taking any chances.

He called back, "You're a liar, you don't have nothing to give me."

"I do, too."

"What is it, then?"

"That's for me to know and for you to find out."

"Where'd you get it at?"

"The store."

"What store?"

"I'm not telling, but I bought it just for you, you don't want me to have to give it to somebody else, do you?"

"I don't care. I don't care what you do."

"Well . . . it's up to you, if you want your present, come over here and get it, and if you don't, don't, that's fine with me too," and with that Elner went back into the house and shut the door.

Luther walked over and sat on the curb in front of Merle and Verbena's house and tried to figure out what the old lady was up to. He did not go back over to her house that day, but a few days later Elner looked out the window and saw him skulking around across the street, kicking at the ground. She wondered how long it was going to take him to make up his mind. Finally about three days later, when she went out to pick up her paper, he was out in her yard there and said, "You still have that damn present you said you had?"

"I might, why?"

"I just wondered."

"I still have it, but if you are going to talk ugly, then I don't think I want to give it to you. Now if you ask me nicely, I'll give it to you."

She went back inside and waited. About ten minutes went by before she heard a little knock on the door, and it was all she could do to keep herself from laughing. She had shamelessly bribed an eight-year-old child, and she knew it, but what good is it being an adult if you can't outsmart children. Besides, she really did have a nice gift for him. A few weeks before, the minute she had given him that Ex-Lax candy, she had been sorry, and had prayed to God every day since to forgive her.

At the time, she had been so mad at him for hitting poor old Sonny in the head with a rock, and almost killing him, that she'd wanted to get back at the boy, but now she felt so horrible about what she had done, she wanted to try and make it up to him. After that day, when she gave him the big red kite she had bought him at the hobby shop, the two of them spent hours out in the fields behind her house flying it. When Macky asked what had made her pick a kite instead of something else, she said, "Well, Macky, the boy was always looking down, and I wanted something that would make him look up for a change." After Elner bought him the kite, Luther would come by and see her almost every afternoon. She was the first person who ever gave him a gift, the first person who treated him nice. His father was a lowlife mean drunk who could never hold down much of a job, and according to him, if he hadn't had to marry Luther's mother because she was pregnant with him, he might have become a famous race car driver like his idol, Junior Johnson. When Luther was seven, his mother, tired of being beaten up, had run off with some stranger she met at a bar, and had been killed in a car wreck six months later. No wonder Luther had been throwing rocks at everybody and everything.

And it did not get better. When he was thirteen, his father had gotten drunk and thrown him out into the yard in the middle of the night. Luther had gone over to Elner's house, and later, when his father, still drunk, had come banging on her door looking for him, she had run him off with a broom. The next morning, as he sat at her table in the kitchen, he had been so despondent, he'd said, "Don't nobody want me. I'm gonna go back over and get his gun, and shoot my brains out. The hell with it, I'm no damn good nohow. I don't have nothing, never will have nothing."

Elner let him talk on and on, and then said, "All right, Luther, if that's what you want, but don't say you don't have anything, because you do."

"What? I don't have a damn thing."

"That's where you're wrong, you have something nobody on this entire earth has except you."

"What? A daddy that's a no-good bastard from hell?"

"No, honey."

"What, then?"

"I'll show you," she said. She then opened up a drawer in the kitchen and pulled out a piece of paper and an ink pad. "Give me your hand," she said. She took his thumb and pressed it down on the pad, and then pressed his thumb on the piece of paper and held it up. "Look at that, your fingerprint is one of a kind. Never has been one like it before and there never will be another."

He looked at the paper. "So what?"

"So what? You are a one of a kind, put here for some purpose. Now me, I couldn't kill myself, I want to see what's going to happen to me next. Besides," she said, as she poured him more coffee, "you can't kill yourself today, you have to help me pull all my Christmas things out of the attic and decorate the house before you do." Luther stayed with her that Christmas, and on and off up until he graduated from high school.

And he might not have graduated if it had not been for her. He had been failing every subject but shop. One day she said, "I want you to bring me your grades and let me have a look at them. OK?"

Nobody had ever asked to see his grades before, and it had made him want to do better for her.

He never did make anything higher than a C minus average, but at least he went every day. He had made her a birdhouse in shop, and now that he thought back on it, it wasn't a very good birdhouse, but she had put it right in the front yard for everyone to see, and she had bragged on him.

In high school Luther had been two years behind Elner's great-niece Linda Warren. Besides being cute and having perfect skin and beautiful teeth, Linda was an all A student, head majorette, president of her senior class, and dated only football players. Not only was Luther a big nobody, he also had to have a tooth missing, and the worst case of acne of anybody in school, or at least it seemed so to him. On the high school pecking order scale, Linda and her crowd of clean-cut preppy-looking kids probably never would have even noticed him, but because Aunt Elner was a friend of his, whenever she passed him in the hall, she always smiled and said, "Hi, Luther," and all the other misfits and losers he hung out with would be impressed out of their minds. Just the fact that someone from the top echelon of high school royalty like herself spoke to him in the hall made high school at least bearable. He had even gotten a few dates with a couple of the halfway decent loser girls that weren't whacked out on dope, because they thought he was Linda's cousin. Secretly he even began to believe it himself, and when he'd heard Dwayne Whooten Jr. make some sexual comment about Linda, he had hit him in the face and broken his nose for it.

After his senior year he had joined the army, and Elner was the first person to see him in his uniform. When he came home after serving four years in the tank division, he went straight to her house where she had fixed him a "welcome home" breakfast. Miss Elner's house was the only real home he had ever known. He wondered what direction he might have gone had he not had her. "Don't get on that old dope, honey," she had said. "You don't want to grow up and be like your daddy, you need to be real careful, will you promise me that?" All he had needed was someone to check in with, to give him a clue how to be a human being. She had even taken him down to Dr. Weiser's and bought him a front tooth.

Across town, Mr. Barton Sperry Snow had heard the announcement over the radio at the exact time Luther Griggs did. He had been on his way to visit one of his company managers in Poplar Springs, to discuss revamping the entire district. When he heard the name Elner Shimfissle, he suddenly wondered if she was the same Elner Shimfissle he had met so many years ago. It had to be; it was the same town, Elmwood Springs, and after all, how many women in the world were named Elner Shimfissle? It was certainly not a name you would forget, and *she* was not someone you could easily forget.

At the time he met her, he had been working his way through business school and was doing a survey for Missouri Power and Light Company. Elner Shimfissle had been a big country type of a woman and, as he recalled, had a lot of chickens running around in her yard. She had been very friendly and had given him a piece of pound cake, and a sack of figs to take with him when he left. But the thing he remembered most about her was that she loved electricity and appreciated it more than anyone he had ever met before, or since. She told him one of the great regrets of her life was that she never got to meet Thomas Edison in person. "I just hate to think we were on the earth at the same time and I never got to shake his hand and thank him." She even had a picture of Thomas Edison she had cut out of a magazine on the wall in her kitchen and had been very upset that there was not a national holiday for Thomas Edison. "Why, he lit the entire world!" she said. "Just think, without old Tom Edison, we would all still be sitting in the dark, no lights, no radio, no electric garage door openers. I think, after the Lord, of course, I'd rank the Wizard of Menlo Park number two, that's how highly I think of old Tom." She told Mr. Snow that even though they did not have a national holiday, she personally celebrated his birthday every year by turning on all her electrical appliances at once and leaving them on all day.

What a character. He had spent only forty-five minutes with her thirty years ago, and hadn't seen her since, but somehow he felt sad that she had died. He had just turned fifty, so she must have lived to a nice old age, because she was an old woman when he met her. Mr. Snow had just been named vice president of the Missouri Power and Light Company and now looking back and remembering her so well, he wondered if somehow her enthusiasm for all things electrical had not made him decide to go to work for the company full-time. Come to think of it, it had been his idea to put a picture of Thomas Edison in the lobby. He couldn't say for sure, but maybe somewhere in the back of his mind she had influenced him more than he knew. All he did know was that if there was a heaven, he hoped the old lady would finally get to meet Thomas Edison in person. He knew old Tom would get a kick out of meeting her. Mr. Snow took out his BlackBerry and faxed his secretary. "Mrs. Elner Shimfissle of Elmwood Springs passed away today. Find out what funeral home. Send flowers. Sign 'An old friend.' "

Making Arrangements with Neva

11:38 AM

When Tot Whooten got back home from Elner's house, she picked up the phone and called the Rest Assured Funeral Home, and her friend Neva picked up.

"Neva? I just wanted to alert you that you're going to get a call from Norma Warren, probably later on today, we just got the word a little while ago, Elner Shimfissle just died at the hospital."

"Oh no! What happened?"

"Stung to death by wasps."

"Oh no . . . poor old thing."

"Yes, she hit a nest in her tree and fell clear off the ladder. She was out cold by the time Ruby and I went over. The nurse at the hospital said she never regained consciousness, probably didn't know what hit her."

"Oh no," said Neva again. "But I guess if you have to go, that's the best way . . . fast."

"I suppose so . . . if you have to go."

"Yes, well, thanks for the heads-up, Tot. I'll go ahead and get her file out, but as I recall I think it's pretty much ready to go, Norma did everything in advance."

"I'm sure she did, you have to admire her for that, she's always ahead of the game. I guess with everybody dropping like flies, I better get my own file in order. God knows what will happen to me if I leave my funeral details up to Darlene and Dwayne Junior."

After she hung up, Tot thought about just how much she was going to miss her neighbor. Elner had always seemed happy, always in a good mood, but she had never had children. Tot's children had been nothing but trouble from the beginning, even more so after they hit puberty. If there was a fool within fifty miles, they had either married it or had numerous offspring with it. Tot had begged her children to please stop breeding. "There's a serious genetic flaw on the Whooten side, not one of them has a lick of sense. Just because I married beneath my station is no reason you have to," she had said to her children on many occasions, but her warning had done no good. Darlene, at thirty-two, had five children and more ex-husbands than Elizabeth Taylor, and not a cent of alimony from a one of them. And God knows how many children Dwayne Jr. had roaming around out there. Six that she knew of, and with the women he had picked, it was no telling how those kids would turn out. Whenever he had said of his girlfriends "We think alike, Mama," she knew she was in big trouble. Her hopes of one of her kids bettering themselves by meeting someone a step above had been dashed time and time again. And now, her sixteen-year-old granddaughter, Faye Dawn, was already pregnant by some fifteen-year-old who wore a dog chain around his neck, black fingernail polish, a nose ring, and had no chin. "Why do birds of a feather have to flock together?" she wondered. "Water seeks its own level" was not a good thing in their case. She was already attending a bipolar prayer group, and Al-Anon meetings twice a week. "What next?" she wondered. What fresh hell was in store for her down the line?

Last year when Dwayne Jr. had asked her what he could get her for Christmas, she had requested "a vasectomy" and told him that she would even pay for it, but he had taken the money and bought himself an off-road vehicle instead. He was a lost cause. She was now working on Darlene to have her tubes tied, but that was going nowhere, because she said she was scared of anesthesia. When Linda Warren had adopted that little Chinese girl, Norma had come into the beauty shop wearing a sweat-shirt with the girl's picture on it, and under the picture it said "Someone Wonderful Calls Me Grandma." Tot figured she would wind up wearing one that said "A Lot of Potential Criminals and Misfits Call Me Grandma," and she was supporting almost every one of them. Tot got in her bed and pulled the covers over her head and cried about Elner, and herself as well, while she was at it.

A Surprise

11:59 AM

After Tot had gone home, Ruby stayed at Elner's house to answer the phone in case anyone called. While she waited, she decided to just go ahead and wash the sheets and towels and all the dirty clothes in Elner's dirty-clothes basket, so Norma wouldn't have to be bothered, and it was when she opened it and started pulling all the clothes out that she made a startling discovery.

Hidden at the very bottom of the clothes basket was a .38 revolver handgun, large enough to blow someone's head off. Ruby stood there with her arms full of clothes, staring at it and wondering why in the blazes Elner Shimfissle would be hiding a gun at the bottom of her clothes basket. Ruby assumed there was probably a perfectly good explanation for its being there, but on the other hand, she also was aware that even though you may think you know someone, you can never really be sure about people, it's always the quiet ones you have to watch out for. They can surprise you.

This unexpected and sudden discovery of a handgun in Elner Shimfissle's dirty-clothes basket presented a major dilemma for Ruby. What should she do? After running the thing around in her mind for a few minutes and considering the situation from every angle, she made a decision. "Oh well," she thought. A neighbor is a neighbor, and Ruby would have wanted Elner to do the same for her if the situation were reversed. So she reached down and picked the gun up, and wiped it off with one of Elner's nightgowns, in case there were incriminating prints. She then wrapped it up in a pillowcase, took it into the kitchen and looked under the sink for a paper bag, carried it back over to her house, and hid it in her cedar chest in the hall. Norma was going to be upset enough, without having to find a loaded .38 in her dead aunt's clothes basket.

When she walked back over to do the washing, she noticed Elner's birdbath and thought, "Somebody's going to have to keep that filled with water." And then she suddenly remembered something else. "Who's going to feed that blind raccoon his dish of ice cream and vanilla wafers every night?" Then she remembered something else. Every afternoon Elner had fixed an old black Labrador named Buster a cheese sandwich. "*Lord,*" Ruby thought, she would do the sandwich, but Merle was going to have to feed the raccoon. She was scared the thing might bite. Elner had not been scared of anything and had let those squirrels come into her kitchen and jump right up on her counter where she kept food. As her friend and as a health professional Ruby had warned her, "Elner, squirrels are nothing but big rats with furry tails and carry all kinds of diseases," but Elner never seemed to worry about germs. "Come to think of it," thought Ruby, "right up until this morning when she was killed by wasps, she had never been sick a day in her life."

The Cause of Death

10:55 AM

Norma, who was being tended to by several nurses, was now sitting up and talking but still having a hard time. She kept repeating over and over, "I knew it was going to happen someday, but I just can't believe it." The hospital chaplain on call, a Baptist with a bad haircut, in a brown polyester suit, stopped in and offered his card and his condolences. A short time later Macky walked back into the room, after having called their daughter, Linda.

Norma looked up. "Did you reach her?"

He nodded. "She's coming. She said she would get here as soon as she could."

"Was she upset?"

"Yes, of course, but she's worried about you and she said to tell you she loves you." Just then the doctor came back with a chart and sat down beside Norma and Macky and continued giving them all the information he had. He said that it seemed that as far as they could count, her aunt had received over seventeen wasp stings and must have gone into immediate cardiac arrest caused by anaphylactic shock, and then he added that the fall could have caused some brain trauma, but not enough to kill her, and so as of this moment, the official report read: "Cause of death: cardiac arrest due to severe anaphylactic shock."

"Did she suffer?" asked a tearful Norma.

"No, Mrs. Warren, I can guarantee you she most probably never knew what hit her."

Norma wailed, "Poor Aunt Elner, she always said she wanted to die at home, but I don't think she meant out in the yard, not like this and in that awful old robe. . . ." Macky put his arm around her as she blew her nose.

The doctor continued. "Now, Mrs. Warren, just so you know, you have the official cause of death, but if you are not satisfied, we can still do an autopsy."

Norma looked at Macky. "Do we need an autopsy? I don't know, should we? Just to be sure?"

Macky, who knew the details of what was involved, said, "Norma, it's up to you but I don't think so, it's not going to make any difference one way or another."

"Well, I want to do the right thing. Let's at least wait until Linda gets here." She looked at the doctor.

"Can we do that, Doctor, wait until our daughter gets here?"

"When would that be?"

"It should only be a couple of hours . . . maybe less, right, Macky?"

The doctor looked at the clock. "All right, Mrs. Warren, I suppose we can do that, and in the meantime, if you and Mr. Warren care to see her, I can take you back."

Norma quickly said, "No, I want to wait until Linda gets here."

The doctor nodded. "That's fine, whatever you decide, just tell the nurse if and when you want to go in."

Macky, who had said little, now said, "Doctor, I'd like to see her now, if that's OK?"

"Sure, Mr. Warren, I'll take you down if you want."

Macky looked at Norma. "Will you be all right?"

"Yes, you go on, Macky, I just can't right now."

The nurse said, "I'll stay right here with her, Mr. Warren."

The truth was, Macky did not really want to see Aunt Elner dead. He wanted to remember her as she was when she was alive, but the thought of that sweet woman lying somewhere in a room all by herself upset him even more. As they walked down the hall, the doctor said, "Your wife seems to be pretty shook up, they must have been pretty close."

Macky said, "Yes they were, very close."

As a male orderly passed by, the doctor called out, "Hey, Burnsie, you owe me ten bucks, I told you the Cards would take it in five," and acted as if it were just another day.

Macky wanted to grab him and choke the living daylights out of him, and out of everybody in the world, for that matter, but nothing he could do would bring her back. So he kept walking.

A Sad Business

Down at the funeral parlor, after the call from Tot, Neva stood up and walked into the back office and pulled out the "Decedent, Elner Shimfissle" file and then walked around the corner to where her husband, Arvis, was applying the finishing touches on the hairpiece for Ernest Koonitz, a recent arrival. She stuck her head in. "Hon, Tot just called. Elner Shimfissle is probably coming in late tonight or first thing in the morning, stung to death by wasps."

He looked up. "Huh. Two decedents within twenty-four hours. Not bad for April."

It was true, considering April was always their slow month, but Neva hated it when Arvis said things like that. Granted they were in the funeral business, but she had a heart. Lately it seemed all he cared about was numbers. If a plague hit town and took out a hundred people, he would probably dance a jig. She was aware that every passing meant money in their pocket; still, she hated to see the last of the old-timers leaving, but the Warrens were her regulars, and it was a job that needed to be done. They had handled all their decedents in the past, both Norma's and Macky's parents, various aunts and uncles, and an occasional cousin here and there. Neva knew she should not play favorites, but she couldn't help but have a soft spot for them. The entire family had been loyal to them throughout the years, and Neva always took special care with their decedents, treated them as she would one of her own.

Besides just plain liking them, she appreciated their business. Times had changed. Their business was no longer the only game in town; Costco out on the interstate was now selling coffins at a cut rate, and they had lost an awful lot of their customers when they moved into the building where the catfish restaurant used to be. A lot of people said that they did not feel comfortable viewing the body of their loved ones where they used to eat catfish and fries, and had switched over to the new mortuary in town. The new people did a nice job and they were fine, she supposed, for fast and impersonal services. She was not one to badmouth the competition, but theirs was a longtime local family-run full-service business and offered the follow-through that was so important. She and Arvis were there to serve their customers from the first pickup, on through internment. They prepared the body, arranged the viewing, ordered the flowers, provided free sign-in books, had a minister, a soprano, and an organist on twenty-four-hour call. They offered a His and Her two-for-one burial package and had a large selection of caskets and cremation urns at reasonable prices. They supplied a 10 percent discount on extra rooms at the local Days Inn for out-of-town relatives and friends, including a free continental breakfast on the day of the funeral and complimentary wine and cheese in the lobby that afternoon. They even arranged transportation to and from the cemetery and helped order and measure and place the headstones when they arrived. "What more could you want in a funeral package?" she wondered.

Other than not having your loved one die in the first place, of course. Short of that, they did everything that was possible to have done. In fact, their ad in the telephone book, which she had spent weeks creating, reflected her sentiments exactly.

THE REST ASSURED FUNERAL HOME
Come to us in your time of need.
And be rest assured of receiving
The very best in funeral care
Because we care about you.

The phone in the mortuary office rang again. This time it was Merle's wife, Verbena Wheeler, calling from the cleaners two blocks away.

"Neva, did you hear?"

"Yes, Tot just called. I just pulled her file."

"Isn't it horrible?"

"Terrible."

"She was the sweetest thing."

"She was."

"It's hard to believe, isn't it?"

"It is."

"Ruby said she probably never knew what hit her."

"That's what Tot told me. At least she didn't suffer."

"That's right."

"We can be thankful for that at least."

"Yes we can."

"Anyhow, I thought I'd go ahead and get my flower order in early and beat the rush."

"That's probably a good idea." Neva reached over for her floral order pad. "What do you want to send?"

"The usual, I guess."

Neva wrote down "One medium azalea plant in ceramic pot."

Verbena always sent a plant rather than flowers. She felt it could work at the viewing and again at the funeral, or be planted at the grave later on. She liked to give people options, like starch or no starch, or hangers or boxed.

"Same message?" asked Neva. " 'With our deepest sympathy, Merle and Verbena'?"

"Yes, might as well, I can never think of anything else to say other than that, can you?"

"No, that says it all."

"I know Norma is sure going to miss her."

"You know she will."

"No matter how old they are when they go, or what shape they're in, you always miss them. I remember how it was for me when we lost Momma Ditty, and then poor old Daddy Ditty in the same year."

"Yes."

"And then Aunt Dottie Ditty went the year after that, do you remember?"

"I do," Neva said.

"We lost all three Dittys in less than two years, and I don't think there is a day that goes by that I don't miss them."

"I'm sure."

"When is the viewing?"

"I don't know. Norma hasn't called us yet, I don't know when the body will be released. It could be as early as tonight or it could be tomorrow."

Verbena sighed. "Well, I'll see you over there . . . I just hate to have to get out that old funeral dress again, but that's life, isn't it?"

Neva hung up. She certainly remembered Verbena Wheeler's aunt Dottie Ditty. How could she not? Dottie Ditty had been their most difficult decedent, and she and Arvis were still living with the consequences to this day. Aunt Dottie Ditty had weighed in at 328 pounds at the time of death, and had presented a challenge right from the get-go. Aside from having to special order a casket large enough, during pickup Arvis had suffered a ruptured hernia, plus a slipped disk in his lower back that was still giving him trouble. Although the general public might not be aware of it, the funeral business has its share of injuries, just like any other line of work that requires heavy lifting.

Neva walked over and opened the Elner Shimfissle file and read that at one time the "Lily of the Valley" style casket had been ordered, but had been canceled in 1987 when Elner had changed her mind about burial and had suddenly switched to cremation. Neva cringed. Not because they'd lost a casket sale, but she hated having to deal with the uproar cremation caused, particularly among the older Baptists and Methodists. They became extremely upset, almost unruly, when they were told that there was no body to view. A few had even demanded that the money for the flowers they had sent be returned. She remembered now that at the time, Elner had said she hadn't switched to cremation to save money, she just loved the idea of disappearing in a flash of hot white light. She had said it seemed like a lot more fun than being embalmed.

Neva read on just to refresh her memory about the other details.

> Service: Methodist
> Rev. William Jenkins presiding
> Hymn to be sung: "Can't Wait to Get to Heaven"
> Interlude: "Just Over the Stars"

Since she was the soprano and also the organist on twenty-four-hour call, Neva figured she'd better go into the chapel and brush up on the numbers. They didn't get much call for the old gospel tunes anymore. People's taste in funeral music had changed drastically over the years. Just last month, there had been a request for "Fly Me to the Moon." Neva got up and walked across the hall through the slumber room to the chapel and sat down at the small organ. She flipped through her stack of sheet music until she found her copy of "Can't Wait to Get to Heaven," a hymn that had been written and made famous by Minnie Oatman and the Oatman Family Gospel Singers, whose picture appeared on the cover of the sheet music. Neva removed all her rings, wiggled her fingers, turned the organ on, hit the first three chords, and started singing softly in a thin little reedy voice.

> Can't wait to get to Heaven
> Oh I'll be so happy there
> When I walk down that ivory hall
> And run up those crystal stairs.
>
> Oh I'll know Him when I see Him
> I'd know Him anywhere.
> Then all my struggles will be lifted
> When I reach that kingdom in the air.
>
> Can't wait to shout hallelujah!
> No more earthly burdens will I bear
> 'Cause when I see the Heavenly throne,
> I know . . . Yes I know
> He'll be waiting for me there!

When she finished, Neva thought, "Nice lyrics, and very fitting." She guessed if anybody had a shot at getting to heaven, it would have to be Elner Shimfissle. The woman had been such a source of inspiration for the whole town, always had a smile on her face. Neva felt her eyes misting up, and reached for a Kleenex. You'd think that with all the years of experience in the funeral business, she would have become immune to feeling bereft, but she hadn't. Some passings were easier than others, of course, but as their ad stated, she cared deeply about all her customers, the living and the deceased.

Macky Goes to See Elner

11:15 AM

When they went through the double doors, the doctor turned Macky over to a young nurse to take him the rest of the way. As Macky walked through the hospital hall down to the room where they had Aunt Elner, he felt as if someone had kicked him in the stomach. Although he had tried to keep it together for Norma, when he had first heard the news from the doctor, he had been devastated. For the past forty years, rain or shine, he had gone over and had coffee with her before he went to work. And even when they had moved to Florida, she had come with them. The truth was, she was his best friend and had helped him through many a crisis, some things that Norma knew nothing about and, hopefully, would never know about.

One thing in particular had only been between the two of them. He had not meant for it to happen. Lois Tatum, a nice-looking girl with brown hair that she wore in a ponytail, had been a waitress at the Tip-Top café downtown, across the street from the hardware store. At the time, Linda had just gotten married, and Norma had been suffering terribly from empty nest syndrome. She had volunteered for a hundred different projects just to keep herself from, as she put it, "going stark raving mad." Norma had thrown herself into community service and had kept herself so busy with one committee meeting after another that he hardly ever saw her. So when Lois had always seemed happy to see him come in at lunchtime, and had always laughed at his jokes, Macky had been secretly flattered.

She was about fifteen years younger than he was, divorced with a little girl, and when she needed something fixed in the small duplex she rented, he had been happy to do it. He had helped out a lot of people in town; as far as he had been concerned they were just good friends. Then one afternoon she had come over to the hardware store and tearfully confessed, "Macky, I'm so in love with you, I don't know what to do." He had been caught completely off guard. In all the years he had been married he had never looked at another woman, never even entertained the idea. Maybe it had been the timing. After Linda had left home, although he had not talked about it, he too had felt lost, and with Norma being so busy, maybe he had been vulnerable. He didn't know the reason, but after Lois left, and he thought about it, he realized that he was attracted to her as well. Not that he ever did anything other than think about it. But he did think about it night and day until it had become an obsession, and the more he thought about it, the fantasy of being young again, running away somewhere with Lois, starting all over, began to appeal to him, until he could not get the idea out of his mind.

He didn't know if he was really in love with Lois, or just flattered, or whether he should take a chance or not. Elner had noticed that something was wrong and had asked. Elner had always been a good sounding board, and had talked him through a lot of problems before, but this was different. Norma was her niece, and he felt very conflicted about discussing something like this with her, but Aunt Elner knew him like a book, and there was no way he could hide it from her, and so finally he broke down and told her what was bothering him, admitted that he had been seriously considering asking Norma for a divorce. After he finished telling her everything, she had thought for a moment and then said, "Macky, this is very hard for me, you know I love both you and Norma like my own children and it would break my heart, but I want you both to be happy. I can't tell you what to do, honey, all I can do is hope before you make any decisions, that you will really take the time to think on down the line, because once you leave, if for some reason it shouldn't work out with this girl, you can never go back to what you had before. I'm not saying Norma wouldn't take you back, she might, but once you've done something like this, you chip away a good part of the trust, and when that's gone, you can never get it back."

She had not said *not* to go, or asked him to stay, but Macky went home that night, and had thought about it some more. Something she had said made him realize that as much as he was tempted, as much as he wondered what it would be like to start over, he was not willing to throw away all the years he and Norma had had together, upset Linda, and maybe risk ruining all of their lives. Lois's as well. When he told Elner of his decision, she had smiled and said, "I'm awful glad, Macky, I don't know what I would do without my buddy coming to see me every day," and they had never spoken of it again.

Norma had not known it at the time, but that was the reason he had sold the hardware store and had moved them all to Florida, to get away from Lois, not that he had stopped thinking about her, he hadn't. Even after she married someone else and had moved to another state, he still wondered about her, had a sad deep pain when he remembered her face, or a woman passed by wearing the same perfume, but as the song says, "Time Heals Everything." And time and distance had faded her memory to a point that when he did think of her, the old longings were not as painful and he hardly ever thought of her anymore.

Aunt Elner had not only saved his marriage, strangely enough, she had also been the one responsible for him and Norma getting married in the first place. They had only been eighteen and terribly in love, but Norma's mother, Ida, a holy terror, had declared that if Norma married Macky, it would have to be over her dead body. She had much higher aspirations for her only daughter than to marry a mere hardware store owner's son. Norma had been a week away from being sent off to college, when after a phone call from her older sister Elner, Ida had suddenly relented and consented to their marriage. They never did find out what Elner had said to Ida to get her to change her mind, but whatever it was, he couldn't begin to imagine what his life would have been without Norma or Linda and now his granddaughter, Apple. He also knew how hard life was going to be without Aunt Elner. He already missed her and knew his world was never going to be quite the same without her.

The young nurse the doctor had turned him over to led him down to the room at the end of the hall and quietly opened the door. When she turned on the light, he looked over and saw Aunt Elner lying there, still wearing the old brown robe Norma hated so. He walked over, sat in the chair beside her, and reached over and took her hand. Someone had smoothed her white hair back off her face, and she looked so peaceful, as if she had just fallen asleep.

The nurse said softly, "Stay as long as you like, Mr. Warren, I'll be right down the hall if you need me."

After she left, and he heard the door close, he put his head down on the side of the bed, still holding her hand, and sobbed like a baby. He looked over at her and wondered where she had gone. Where had that sweet woman gone?

Where She Had Gone

As soon as her sister Ida threw open the doors at the end of the hall, what Elner saw was so stunning, so dazzling, it almost took her breath away. Standing before her was a set of sparkling crystal stairs leading straight up into the sky, all the way up to the big round moon at the very top.

Elner turned to Ida with tears in her eyes. "Oh, Ida, it's prettier than I could have ever imagined."

"I thought you'd be impressed," said Ida.

It wasn't until after they had started their journey up the stairs that Elner noticed Ida was carrying a purse. She thought, "Only Ida would bring her purse with her to heaven," and she laughed out loud.

Ida asked, "What's so funny?"

Elner said, "Nothing, I was just thinking about something, that's all."

Norma had been the one who had put Ida's purse into the coffin with her, because she said her mother had said a woman was never fully dressed without her purse. She started to tell Ida that it had been Norma's idea but changed her mind; any mention of the coffin and Ida might bring up Tot Whooten again.

After they had been climbing up the stairs for a while, the sky suddenly began to grow a darker and darker, almost midnight blue; soon hundreds of tiny little stars started appearing and began twinkling all around them everywhere, above their heads, even under the stairs. It couldn't have pleased Elner more. She had always wondered what it would be like to walk around in the sky among the stars, and now she knew. A lot of fun.

As they went farther up the stairs, the big moon at the top seemed to grow larger and started turning a creamy yellow and gold color, and began glowing in the dark like a billion lightning bugs. It was a long climb but Elner was surprised at how easy it was, and remarked to Ida, "You'd think climbing all these stairs would wear me out, but I don't feel one bit winded." As they got closer to the moon it changed colors again and started turning from gold into a bright glossy white, and then just when they reached the top step, suddenly right before their eyes, the moon turned into a big, round shiny mother-of-pearl button.

"Ohh, interesting," said Elner. At that moment, as they stepped on the last step, an archway in the middle of the button opened up. When Ida and Elner stepped inside, the sun was bright and shining, and it was daytime again. Elner stood there for a moment and looked at what she figured must be heaven. It was not all white clouds and angels flying around as she had expected, but lovely. As a matter of fact, Elner thought it looked a lot like the big botanic garden in Kansas City, where Ida had taken her many times. The grass was deep green and lush, with highly colored flowers blooming everywhere.

Ida said, "Well?"

"Very nice," she said, and when she looked up she noticed that the sky was not one solid color, like it was at home. Here it was more iridescent. She held out her hand and the colors of the sky sparkled on her skin in pinks and blues and soft greens.

"This is just like walking inside a rainbow, isn't it, Ida? Hey, remember when that woman wrote in to the *Neighbor Dorothy* radio show and said how she and her family stood in a rainbow . . . Now I know just how she felt."

As they walked along, Elner thought of something else. "Hey, Ida, now am I going to get to know all of life's mysteries? Don't they say that when you are dead, that all will be revealed?"

"I really can't say, Elner, I'm just an escort. The rest you will have to find out on a need-to-know basis."

"I sure hope I find out life's mysteries. I've been just itching to know what they are. Can't you give me a little hint?"

"I'm sorry," said Ida, "but no."

"Well, if you can't tell me any mysteries or revelations, you can at least tell me what God looks like, can't you?"

Ida said nothing and kept walking.

Elner scurried to keep up with her. "Let me ask you this then—does he look like his picture? I'm not going to be scared, am I?"

Ida said nothing again but did shake her head no, to let Elner know she had nothing to be afraid of.

"Well, to tell you the truth, Ida, I'm a little worried. I've done a couple of things he might not be too happy about. One thing for sure, I should never have given little Luther Griggs that Ex-Lax and told him it was chocolate candy. I must have been out of my mind at the time. Can you plead temporary insanity? What do you think?"

"I think you are in for the surprise of your life."

"Ahhh," she said. "Am I going to be surprised a little, or a lot? Will it be a good surprise or a bad surprise?"

"All I can say, Elner, and then I will say no more, is I suspect that you are going to be very pleasantly surprised."

Elner was somewhat relieved. "Well, good," she said, and thought, "If he doesn't bring anything up, I'm certainly not going to say anything." But after they had walked a few more feet, she had still another inquiry.

"Can I ask him questions or am I just supposed to stand at attention and listen?"

No answer.

"Should I curtsy, kneel down, or what?" Elner wanted to do the right thing, but Ida was still not forthcoming and no help whatsoever.

"Well, at least tell me one thing. Do you think he's going to be mad at me?"

Ida, true to her word, would say no more, and it irritated Elner no end. "She knows," she thought, "she's just not telling me. Typical."

As they strolled along the path, Elner suddenly thought of something. "Hey, Ida, whatever happened to the Knott family Bible? The last time I saw it, Gerta had it, but then after you died nobody could find it."

"I buried it."

"Where?"

"I don't remember."

"Why did you bury it?"

"I thought it was for the best."

"Why?"

"Because, Elner, there is personal family information in there that doesn't need to get out in public, that's why. You don't want just anybody knowing your business, do you? And why do you care?"

"Because I would like to know how old I am, or was. I must be close to ninety right now, don't you think?"

"Oh, Elner," she scoffed. "I don't pay any attention to those things, and what difference does age make anyway. You're as old as you feel, I always said."

Elner knew Ida was holding back information. Ida knew exactly where she had buried that Bible and how old they both were. "Plus," thought Elner, "Ida was no more fifty-nine when she died than the man in the moon, and any person who would still lie about her age even after she's dead is pretty vain, if you ask me."

As they continued on, Ida thought back on the day their other sister, Gerta, had died. It had been a cold gray freezing day and she was wearing a big fur coat and had been able to stick the rather large Bible under her arm and get out the door with it. She knew, of course, she could not burn a Holy Bible, or throw it in the river or rip out the offending pages or anything blasphemous like that, so she hid it until spring, then wrapped it in cotton, put it in a large airtight Tupperware container, and buried it in her rose garden. She had no regrets or guilt about it. She had always lied about her age, and she saw no reason to stop now. Besides, shaving a few years off here and there was not really lying, it was a matter of survival.

Had the Jenkins family known that the girl their son Herbert wanted to marry was at least eight years older than he, they might have frowned upon the marriage. She had barely managed to snag a good husband as it was. Herbert's father had owned several banks around the state and was quite prominent. Herbert had not been much, but he had been her last chance to move up in the world, and she had made the most out of it. In fact, she had squeezed every last drop out of every advantage that she had, being the wife of the president of a bank. Even though it was only a small branch bank in the small town of Elmwood Springs, she had been as puffed up as a powder pigeon over it. However, keeping up appearances, plus hiding her true age, had been exhausting. She had almost been caught once, when some mean jealous person had shown Herbert her high school annual. She had lied, of course, and said it was not her: it was another Ida Mae Shimfissle, a distant cousin that had moved away years ago. And Herbert, a trusting man, had believed it.

And then after all that, Norma had married the Warren boy, who had no promising future at all, except to work in his father's hardware store. It had broken her heart. Even when Norma told her how happy she was with Macky, she never understood her own daughter. "Happy? Cows are happy, Norma, and look what happens to them."

Verbena Tells Cathy

Verbena must have called the newspaper office a hundred times, but the line continued to be busy. By this time she was so frustrated not being able to reach Cathy and tell her the news, she was red in the face. She could not stand it a moment longer, so she put the BE BACK IN FIVE MINUTES sign on the door of the cleaners and walked across the street. When she opened the door to the *Elmwood Springs Courier* office, she heard Cathy still talking to someone on the phone. She went into the back office and Cathy looked up, put her hand over the receiver, and said, "I'll be off in just a minute," and gestured for Verbena to have a seat. She was just finishing up her weekly interview with the school board president, gathering the latest updates concerning the ongoing fight about whether or not to include the theory of Intelligent Design along with Darwin's theory of evolution. When she saw Verbena, Cathy figured she was here to talk about that and knew she was in for an hour of Verbena arguing to include creationism. But Verbena surprised her when she reached across her desk and wrote on a piece of paper in big black letters "Elner's dead!" and put it in front of Cathy and banged on it with her finger. Cathy glanced down and said,

"What? Are you serious?" Verbena nodded. "Pete," Cathy said, "Elner Shimfissle just died, let me call you back," and hung up. "What happened?"

"We don't know, but Ruby got the call from the hospital a few minutes ago, I tried to call you as soon as I heard but the line was busy. You need to get call waiting."

"I know I do. Well this is just terrible news."

"Isn't it? I'm just heartbroken over it, and Merle is beside himself, life just won't be the same without Elner, will it?"

"No."

"I have to get back, but I thought you would want to know as soon as possible."

"Yes, thank you for telling me, Verbena."

After Verbena left, Cathy reached over and took the phone off the hook. She didn't feel like talking. Elner Shimfissle was dead. It was hard to believe, she had been so sure that Elner of all people would survive a few stings and a little fall off a ladder. She shook her head and thought how strange it was that she of all people, who wrote about life and death every day, was still mystified by the whole thing. "Here today, gone tomorrow, here's your hat, what's your hurry, don't let the door hit you in the back when you leave." A person lives for years, touches so many people, and then at the end winds up just a small picture and a few paragraphs in the paper, the paper gets thrown away, and it's all over.

Cathy had written hundreds of obits before and had just finished doing Ernest Koonitz's yesterday, but Elner's was going to be a hard one to write. Although hers was only a small town newspaper, when it came to writing obituaries, Cathy always took her time and tried to write something interesting, offer a little variety and do more than just facts. After all, other than a birth announcement or a wedding, this was one of the few times most law-abiding citizens got to see their names in the newspaper. Also it was important for the family to read something a little special, something they could keep and be proud of, and she wanted to do a particularly good job on Elner's obit. She opened the drawer, pulled out a piece of paper, and glanced over her list of suggested phrases.

Died
Died suddenly
Died peacefully
Passed away
Left this world for another
Met his/her Lord on
Was taken to heaven
Was delivered safe in the arms of his/her Lord and Savior,
Departed this life
Made his/her transition from this earth
Is happy at the side of his/her Maker

After finishing, she put it in the drawer. Somehow, writing this one, she didn't feel like trying to show off her literary skills. This one she would write from her heart.

Mrs. Elner Jane Shimfissle, longtime resident of Elmwood Springs, died yesterday at the Caraway Hospital in Kansas City. A fun-loving person who knew no strangers, she enjoyed gospel music, visiting with neighbors, feeding the birds, and was a friend to all living things. She delighted in making fig preserves and decorating and hiding Easter eggs in her backyard for neighborhood children. She was preceded in death by her husband, Will Shimfissle, sisters,

Mrs. Ida Jenkins and Mrs. Gerta Nordstrom. She is survived by her niece, Mrs. Norma Warren of Elmwood Springs, great-niece, Mrs. Dena Nordstrom O'Malley of Palo Alto, California, great-niece, Linda Warren, and five-year-old grandniece, Apple Warren, now residing in St. Louis, and her beloved cat, Sonny. She will be greatly missed by all who knew her. The family requests that all donations be made to the Humane Society.

After she completed the first draft, she put the obit in the basket on her desk. She would add all the funeral details later. She then got up and went into her photo file and found the two pictures of Elner. One she had taken sixteen years ago, of Elner holding an orange cat, the one with the six toes. She had been so proud that day. The cat had just turned twenty-five and she had given it a birthday party. Cathy sat there for a moment, looking at Elner's smiling face, then took out her checkbook and wrote a check to the Humane Society in memory of Elner, it was the least she could do. After she finished writing the check, she sat back and wondered where her life might have taken her if it had not been for Elner. She certainly would not have been able to go to college. She had a college scholarship but her family had not had the money to pay for room and board, once she got there. She had been heartbroken at the time and had told Mrs. Shimfissle. The next day, when she walked by the house, Mrs. Shimfissle called out to her, "Hey, Cathy, come here a minute." When Cathy walked up, she had handed her a blue envelope with her name on it. When she opened it, to her surprise she saw that it contained ten one-hundred-dollar bills.

"I can't take this, Mrs. Shimfissle."

"Don't be silly, it's just a little egg money, besides it will make me happy to think I'm helping somebody get a good education. We need more smart people in the world."

Cathy had paid the money back, of course, but she had always hoped to be able to return the favor in some other way, do something really nice for Elner, but now it was too late—she was gone.

A Heavenly Walk

As Ida and Elner walked along, it was very quiet, not a soul around, just the sound of birds.

When Elner asked her where they were going, Ida said, "You'll see soon enough."

Elner looked up and saw two zebras, with red stripes that looked like candy canes and with silver tinsel manes and tails, and a herd of tiny little bright yellow hippopotamuses no bigger than twelve inches high, pass right in front of them.

"That's different," Elner said. "You don't see that every day."

"You do here," said Ida.

After they had walked a little while longer, Elner asked, "Are we there yet?"

Ida ignored her.

"How much farther do we have to go?"

"Just hold your horses, Elner, we'll get there when we get there."

"All right. I just wondered . . . that's all."

They continued on for a few more minutes, and as they turned a corner and Elner looked around, she suddenly realized they were walking down a street that looked exactly like First

Avenue North; as she went farther and recognized the Good-night house, she knew for sure it was First Avenue North. She was back on her own street all right, but something was odd. There were streetcar tracks running down the middle of the avenue and there had not been streetcars in Elmwood Springs for years; not only that, the large row of elm trees that used to line both sides of the street, that had been chopped down in the fifties, were suddenly right back where they used to be. When they walked past Ruby's house, it had not changed much, but when they walked past her own house, she noticed that the fig tree in the side yard was only three feet tall. Elner said, "Ida, I don't know what we're doing here, but we're not in the right time period, I can tell you that. We must have flipped back fifty years."

"At least," said Ida, looking up at the trees and continuing on down the street. Although she couldn't figure out why she was back home again, Elner did not mind being back in time. It was really very, very pleasant, and so so quiet. All the new housing developments were gone, and the cornfields that used to be behind all the houses were back again. Then Elner saw several big fat squirrels running up and down the trees, only these squirrels were bright orange with white polka dots. "Look, Ida, wouldn't Sonny just love to catch one of them." Then something dawned on her. "Wait a minute, Ida, if we're back fifty years ago, poor old Sonny isn't even born yet, is he? And why are we flipped back? Am I going to get younger too?"

"Just wait, you'll see," she said.

Ida walked her all the way down to the end of the avenue, but instead of the little Shop & Go market the Vietnamese couple ran now, the old Smith house was there where it used to be, looking exactly as it had so many years ago, with the green and white awnings, and the big radio tower with the red light at the top still stood in the backyard. Ida stopped right in front of the house and announced, "Here we are!"

Elner was surprised. "Is this where we're going? Neighbor Dorothy's old house?"

"It is indeed. Come on," she said.

"Oh, for heaven's sake," Elner said, and happily followed her up the sidewalk. Elner was very pleased about this development. She would love to see the old house again. For years Dorothy Smith had broadcast Elner's favorite radio show from that very house. In fact, the *Neighbor Dorothy Show* had been broadcast from Dorothy's living room. Elner had listened to that show every day for all of the thirty-eight years it had been on the air. Dorothy had given out recipes and household hints and had even given away unwanted pets on the show. When Elner heard Dorothy describing a little orange kitten that needed a home, she had made her husband, Will, drive her into town and get it. She had even named it Sonny, in honor of the show's theme song, "On the Sunny Side of the Street." Standing there, Elner could still remember the song and the announcer's voice that had introduced Neighbor Dorothy every morning. *"And now, from that little white house just around the corner from wherever you are, here she is, the lady with the smile in her voice, your neighbor and mine . . . Neighbor Dorothy."*

Ida led Elner up the stairs to the front porch, and everything looked just the same, with the swing on one end of the porch and another swing on the other, and on the window to the right of the door, painted in small black and gold letters, was WDOT RADIO NO. 66 ON YOUR DIAL. Ida opened the front screen door and stepped back and indicated for Elner to step in, then said, "See you later, have fun" and turned to leave. "Wait," said Elner. "Where are you going? Am I going to see you again?"

Ida waved over her shoulder at her as she headed back down the stairs.

"Just go on in, Elner," she said as she disappeared around the corner.

Elner was a little nervous at being left alone. She wasn't sure what to expect next, this had been such a crazy trip, but the minute she opened the door and poked her head inside the house, it still had the same old familiar smell she remembered; Neighbor Dorothy's house always smelled as if there were something sweet baking in the oven, and usually there was. When she stepped inside the front hall, she got the surprise of her life. Princess Mary Margaret, Dorothy's old cocker spaniel, came running to greet her, and over in the corner, there sat her old friend, Neighbor Dorothy! She had died almost forty-eight years before, but here she was, looking exactly like herself, sitting in her favorite floral chair with that same sweet open round face smiling at Elner, as big as you please, with the same old twinkle in her eye.

"Hello there, Elner," she said. "I've been waiting for you!"

If Elner hadn't believed it was her, she would have recognized that voice anywhere.

"Well, it is you!"

"Yes, it's me!" said Dorothy, clapping her hands in delight. "Surprised?"

"Just as surprised as I can be."

After they had hugged, Elner said, "Oh my heavens. Ida never told me a thing, I had no idea I'd be seeing you again. Let me just sit down and look at you." She went over to the chair across from Dorothy's and just stared at her, shaking her head in amazement.

"Well . . . if you are not a sight for sore eyes, I don't know who is. For land's sake, how are you?"

"Oh, just wonderful, Elner, and how are you?"

Elner shook her head and laughed. "Honey, to tell you the truth, at this point I have no idea. Evidently I'm dead, but I haven't the slightest idea what is going on. All Ida told me was that I was going to meet my Maker. Am I in the right place?"

Dorothy smiled. "You are indeed, and you don't know how happy I am to see you, Elner."

"Me too, it's been too long, and you look great."

"Thank you, Elner. So do you."

"Oh well," she laughed. "I've gained a few pounds since I last saw you, but I feel fine . . . except I just fell out of my fig tree, that's why I'm in this old robe, I hadn't even gotten dressed for the day yet."

"I know," said Dorothy sympathetically. "You took a bad fall."

"I did, didn't I? But I don't think I broke anything. Nothing hurts so far."

"Good, we don't want any broken bones."

Elner sat back in her chair, crossed her feet, and looked around the room and noticed Dorothy's two yellow canary birds, Dumpling and Moe, were as fat as ever and still chirping away in their cage, and the milk-glass chandelier still hung over the dining room table, with the floral swag curtains. "The place looks just the same. I always loved your house, Dorothy."

"I know you did."

"And I loved your show too, everybody missed you so much when you went off the air. There's never been a better show than yours. Now they have Bud and Jay on in the morning, and they're pretty good, but they don't give out recipes like you used to."

"No, those were the good old days. . . ."

Elner looked around and said, "I smell something good, you don't just happen to have a cake in the oven, do you?"

"I do," said Dorothy. "A caramel cake, and as soon as it is done, you and I are going to have some."

"Oh boy, caramel cake, my favorite."

"I know, I remembered."

"So," said Elner, very happy at the thought of the upcoming cake, "am I in some sort of a holding pattern, resting up, having a little snack, before I go on to my final destination?"

Dorothy smiled and said, "No, honey, this is it."

"It is?" said a surprised Elner. "Now I'm all confused. . . . Are you the one I'm supposed to see? You're not the Maker, are you?"

Dorothy laughed. "Yes, one of them, at least, there are actually two of us, but I wanted a chance to say hello to you first, before we went in for our meeting. You were always one of my favorite people. I always got the biggest kick out of you, always asking those crazy questions."

"Well, thank you," she said. "You were always one of mine, but . . . I always thought you were just a regular person, it never occurred to me that you were anything other than just my friend, now I'm just mortified . . . I never dreamed you were . . . well, who you are. Will that count against me?"

Dorothy shook her head. "No, and you have no need to be mortified over anything."

"I don't?"

"No, the Dorothy Smith that you knew was the real Dorothy Smith, I'm just speaking to you in her likeness, sort of a look-alike. We always like to use a familiar form, one you would feel comfortable with: we certainly don't want to scare anybody. You're not scared, are you?"

"No, just a little confused. You say you *look* like her, but you're not really Neighbor Dorothy?"

"That's right, but in a way I am. There's a little part of us in everybody."

Elner tried her best to figure it out. "Oh dear, I think I'm still confused, who's 'us'? Ida told me I was going to meet my Maker, and if you're not you, then who's that dog over there? Is that Princess Mary Margaret, or just an imposter pretending to be her?"

Dorothy laughed. "I promise you, it's not all that complicated. Just wait, you'll see, the whole thing is really very simple. Come on with me, honey, I have someone I want you to meet."

Calling Dena,
Palo Alto, California

12:16 PM (10:16 AM Pacific time)

After having spent some time seeing Aunt Elner, Macky came back into the waiting room and sat with Norma. The nurse who had stayed with her had asked if there was anything else she could do, anyone she could call for them, when Norma said, "Oh, Macky, you need to go call Dena. Tell her we'll let her know as soon as we can about when the funeral . . ." Then Norma burst into tears again when she heard the word *funeral*. The nurse put her arm around Norma's shoulders and tried to comfort her. "I'm sorry," said Norma. "It's just so hard to believe. . . . Go on, Macky, call Dena. I'll be all right."

"I'll have to call collect."

"Just tell the operator it's an emergency."

Macky reluctantly got up and went down the hall again. He hated making this call, the one to Linda had been hard enough. If it had been up to him, he would have waited until they got back home, but he supposed that Norma knew best in these matters. Women seemed to know the rules and regulations about weddings and funerals, but he was not going to make it an emergency phone call. The poor woman was dead; there was

· 124 ·

no emergency about that as far as he could see. He would just make it a regular collect call. Dena Nordstrom O'Malley was Norma's second cousin, Aunt Elner's great-niece. Although she knew Aunt Elner had been old, she like everybody else was totally surprised when Macky told her. News like that was always the last thing in the world she expected to hear. When she put the phone down, she stood for a moment and considered calling her husband, but decided to wait and tell him in person when he came home for lunch. There was no rush; it had just happened and they didn't even know yet when the funeral would be. She walked over and sat down in the chair by the big bay window and gazed out at the yard, and felt the tears welling up in her eyes and running down her face. The last time she had seen Aunt Elner had been at Linda's wedding.

Ever since her husband, Gerry, had become head of the psychiatric department at Stanford University Medical Center, and she had started teaching journalism, their lives had been so busy they had not had a chance to get back and visit with Aunt Elner in person. The last time she had talked to her on the phone was just last week. Aunt Elner, who never understood the two-hour time difference between Missouri and California, had called at five AM, all excited. And when Dena picked up, she had said, "Dena, did you know that a watermelon seed can produce a watermelon two hundred thousand times its own weight? Isn't that something?"

"Oh yes," said Dena, half asleep.

"And here's what I want to know. How does that little black seed know to make the outside of the watermelon green and the inside of the rind white and the rest of it red? Can you figure it? How does it know how to do that?"

"I don't know, Aunt Elner."

"I guess it's just one of those mysteries of life, isn't it?"

Dena had hung up and gone back to bed.

Now, remembering their last conversation, it suddenly hit her just how much she would miss talking to Elner. They had talked at least once a week for the past fifteen years. As Dena sat there and thought more about it, she also realized just how much of her present life and happiness she owed to having known Elner. Dena and her mother had left Elmwood Springs when she was still a baby, and she hadn't gone back until she was a grown woman, and even then she had not intended to ever go back there. At the time she had been one of the new up-and-coming female network television news reporters. She had only gone back because she had been sick, and needed a place to recuperate. To her, Elner was just a country woman, certainly not very smart, not in the ways that Dena judged people as being smart.

Before Dena had become ill, her first priority had always been her career, getting ahead, chasing after success and money. It had never even occurred to her that anything else was impor-tant, and so a woman who lived in the most humble of circum-stances and seemed content to do so was an enigma to her. Having lived ten years in New York City, Dena couldn't believe the woman never locked her doors, didn't even own a key to her own house, and Elner was the first person she had ever met who actually seemed content, and she didn't understand it. Dena thought that she must be a little simpleminded and her almost childlike fascination with nature was just a lack of sophistica-tion. "God, who could get so excited at finding a four-leaf clover?"

Before she had left New York, Dena had certainly never paid the slightest attention to nature, had never seen a sunset or sun-rise unless it had been an accident. She had rarely even noticed the moon or the stars or even the seasons changing, other than switching to heavier clothes. And most of all she was at a loss to understand why anybody would go out of their way to see the same sunrise every morning, and the same old sunset every night. As far as she was concerned, if you've seen one, you've seen them all. But Aunt Elner had explained, "Oh, honey, it's never the same, every morning it's an entirely different sunrise, and every night an entirely different sunset, and it will never ever happen in quite the same way again." And Elner had turned to her and said, "My question to you is, how in the world could you stand to miss even one? It's better than any picture show and it's free too."

It had taken Dena a while, but after joining Elner every evening, sitting with her and watching the sun go down over the fields in the back of her house, she had come to see what Elner had been talking about. Aunt Elner had taught her to look for the tiny green flash that happened just as the sun dipped down into the horizon. The first night she came over and sat out back with her, Aunt Elner had said, "You know, Dena, there's a secret to watching a sunset, most people think that once the sun goes down, that's the end of it. They stop watching too soon, because the really pretty part is just beginning." Aunt Elner had been right, of course, and every night after that they sat in the yard and watched until the last rays faded and until after the sky had turned dark blue and the first star had appeared.

Aunt Elner said, "I just couldn't go to bed if I hadn't made a wish on the first star, could you?" Dena had always wondered what Aunt Elner wished for, but when she asked, Aunt Elner had just smiled. "If I tell, it won't come true, but it's a good one, I can tell you that much." Since those days, Dena had come a long way. Aunt Elner had been the one who had first opened her eyes, made her see the things that had always been right in front of her, all the things she had never stopped long enough to look at. Later, she came to realize just how smart Aunt Elner really was, and now she hardly ever missed a sunset. All of a sudden another wave of sadness hit her as she realized what a lonely old world this was going to be without Aunt Elner.

Meeting the Husband

Dorothy and Elner walked down the hall, past the old cedar chest, and when they reached the last door on the right Dorothy knocked lightly. "Raymond? May we come in?"

A man's voice answered, "Sure, come on."

Elner rearranged her robe. "Dorothy, do I look all right to be meeting somebody? I wish I didn't have on this old thing."

"You look just fine," Dorothy said, and opened the door. Inside the room, Elner could see a nice-looking older man with shiny silver hair sitting at a large desk. He looked exactly like Dorothy's husband, Doc Smith, who had been the pharmacist at the old Rexall drugstore in Elmwood Springs! As Dorothy escorted her into the room, she said, "Raymond, look who's here," and he immediately stood up and came around the desk, with a big friendly smile on his face, and he shook Elner's hand with great enthusiasm.

"Well, hello there, Mrs. Shimfissle, so glad to see you! Dorothy told me you were coming up today. Please, have a seat, make yourself comfortable, and forgive the mess." He indicated the room, packed with maps, papers, and files scattered everywhere. "I try to keep the place neat, but as you can see I'm not doing a very good job." As he was busy removing several books and papers from a chair so she could sit down, Dorothy commented to Elner, "How he manages to find anything in here is a mystery to me, but he does."

"Oh, that's all right," said Elner, "you should see my house." As she walked over to the chair, Elner was secretly pleased when she noticed several dirty coffee cups on the floor, and dust on the bookcases; just as she had always suspected, cleanliness, or neatness, for that matter, was not necessarily next to godliness. She thought, "Norma is going to be in for a big surprise when she sees this." She looked around the room and saw a wall full of pictures of thousands of little babies, and she was also happy to see that over in a corner, a big fat black and white cat was sleeping on the window seat, and he was the spitting image of Bottle Top, the cat that used to sleep in the window of the Cat's Paw shoe repair shop in downtown Elmwood Springs.

Dorothy sat down in the other chair across from the desk, and said to Raymond, "Honey, Elner has a few questions she wants to ask, so I thought it would be best if she talked to both of us."

Raymond sat back in his chair and removed his glasses. "Of course, happy to answer any questions you have, Mrs. Shimfissle."

It was at that moment when Elner noticed the small gold plaque on the edge of his desk that read SUPREME BEING, and she was unsure how she should address him. She sure didn't want to make any mistakes at this late date, and asked, "Should I refer to you as Supreme Being?"

Raymond looked at her, somewhat puzzled. "Pardon me, dear?"

She pointed to the sign. "Your plaque?"

Raymond reached over, picked it up, turned it around, and read it and then laughed. "Oh that, no, that's just a little something some people like to see, makes them feel better." He opened his desk drawer and pulled out a handful of plaques and showed them to her "Look . . . see . . . I have a GOD THE FATHER . . . BUDDHA. Here's a MUHAMMAD. I even have an ELVIS PRESLEY in here somewhere, but you just call me Raymond." He put the plaques in the drawer and smiled at her. "All right now, Mrs. Shimfissle, what's your question? And by the way, I like your robe."

"You do?" she said, looking down at it. "I've had this old thing for years, it's about to fall apart on me."

"Yes, but I'll bet it's comfortable."

"It is," she said. Elner was relieved and amazed at how relaxed she was. Who would have thought meeting your Maker would be this pleasant?

She sat back, happy that they were starting off with the "mysteries of life" part first, and said, "Well, Raymond, I know you probably get asked this all the time, but like everybody that comes up here, I guess, I've just been itching to know the answer to this one for years."

"Yes?" said Raymond.

"Which came first, the chicken or the egg?"

Raymond looked surprised at first, then he laughed. "I'm sorry to laugh, Mrs. Shimfissle, but that's usually not the first question most people ask, but the correct answer is the egg."

Now Elner was surprised. "The egg? Are you sure?"

"Oh sure." He nodded. "You can't put the cart before the horse, so it stands to reason, you have to have an egg for the chicken to come out of."

Elner was clearly disappointed, and said, "Well, darn it all. I sure figured wrong on that one, now I'm glad I didn't call Bud and Jay. Live and learn, I guess." She looked over at Dorothy. "Do I get to ask another one, or was that it?"

"You get to ask as many questions as you want, doesn't she, Raymond?"

"You bet. That's what we're here for . . . fire away."

"Oh, good," she said. "I guess my second question would be, what is life all about?"

Raymond nodded thoughtfully and repeated, "What is life all about . . . hmmm, let's see." Then he leaned over the desk, clasped his hands together, looked her straight in the eye, and said, "Darned if I know, Mrs. Shimfissle."

"Oh, Raymond!" Dorothy said. "Be serious." She turned to Elner. "He loves to do that."

Raymond laughed. "All right, I was just kidding. Seriously though, to put it as frankly and simply as I can . . . life is a gift."

Dorothy smiled at Elner. "That's right, a gift from us to you, with love."

"A gift?" said Elner, thinking it over for a moment. "Well, that was awfully nice of you, and I thank you for it. Of course, I can't speak for anybody else, but I just loved being a human being, enjoyed almost every minute of it, really, from beginning to end."

Raymond said, "We know you did, Mrs. Shimfissle, more than most people, I might add, and we're so glad, that's all we ever wanted, for you to enjoy it, isn't that right, Dorothy?"

"Absolutely." She smiled.

Elner shook her head in amazement at what she had just been told, and she said, "It's kind of funny, really, all these years, everybody has been so busy trying to figure what life was all about, and all the while, it was just something for us to enjoy."

"That's right," said Raymond. "You see, Mrs. Shimfissle—"

"Oh, please call me Elner."

"Thank you. You see, Elner, life is not nearly as complicated as people think."

"No," said Dorothy cheerfully. "It's kind of simple, really."

Raymond turned around to the wall behind him and pulled down a large picture of a carnival scene that lit up with hundreds of colored lights going around in circles, and played carnival music, then said, "You see, Elner, life is like one big roller-coaster ride, with all kinds of bumps and twists and turns, and ups and downs along the way."

"Ahh," said Elner, "so all we have to do is just sit back and enjoy it."

Raymond said, "Exactly. But the problem is . . . most people think they are steering, and get so busy trying to control it that they miss all the fun parts."

Elner turned to Dorothy. "I wish Norma could hear this, she's holding on to that roller coaster for dear life. She'd be better off just relaxing a little."

"That's exactly right," said Raymond, rolling his carnival picture up. "So . . . Elner," he asked, "is that answer too far off from what you thought?"

"No, not really. . . . I always had a feeling it was something like that, but of course you can never be sure, I was dead wrong about the chicken and the egg, so it's good to know that I was at least on the right track. You want us to be happy."

"You bet," he said. "We sure wouldn't have gone to so much trouble just so people could be miserable all the time, would we, Dorothy?"

"No," Dorothy said. "Coming up with everything was a lot of hard work. Of course, Raymond did most of the big heavy things, planets, mountains, oceans, elephants. I did ponds, freshwater lakes, and smaller animals. I did dogs and cats . . . aren't they fun?"

"Oh, yes," said Elner. "Old Sonny keeps me entertained night and day, and I always said if anybody is depressed all they need to do is get a kitten. When Tot Whooten had her breakdown, I got her a kitten, and within a week she snapped out of it."

Dorothy agreed, "Yes, I was very pleased with how kittens turned out, if I do say so myself, and Raymond did oxygen, water, all the major minerals: iron, steel, copper, what else, hon?"

"Silver, gold." Then Raymond looked at Dorothy and said proudly, "But she came up with flowers, music, art. . . . I would never have thought of it."

"Listen," said Dorothy, waving it off, "I'm still amazed at all you came up with. The sun and the moon, I think he's a genius, myself."

Raymond seemed embarrassed. "Now, Dorothy . . ."

"Well, you are. Isn't he, Elner?"

"I agree with her, Raymond. The sun and the moon? Just those two alone would make you a genius in my book. Which one of you came up with the idea for people?"

"We both did!" they said in unison, then looked at each other and laughed.

Then Dorothy repeated, "We both did. He did the chemical makeup, cells, DNA, and all that, but it was pretty much a joint effort and it was not easy."

Raymond agreed, "No, getting every little thing to turn out right, the knees, elbows, not to mention the eyes, the fingers, the opposable thumb."

At the mention of the word *thumb* Elner said, "Oh, here's another question I have . . . how did you ever come up with so many different fingerprints?"

Raymond said, "Excellent question! Here, let me show you."

He took out a piece of paper and quickly drew a perfect picture of a thumb and held it up. "You see, Elner, by superimposing upon certain recurring patterns variations derived from . . ."

Dorothy stopped him. "Honey, she's not going to understand all that biochemistry stuff."

Elner laughed. "She's right, it's too deep for me, but it's sure something to be proud of yourself for."

"Oh, all right," he said, putting his pencil down. "So," said Raymond, smiling. "Tell me, Elner, what did you enjoy the most about being a human being?"

"Well, let me see, I enjoyed nature, birds, fowl of any kind, really, and I loved insects."

Raymond's eyes lit up. "Me too! What was your favorite?"

"Oh, let's see . . . potato bugs, grasshoppers, moths, june bugs, ants, snails . . . Wait a minute, is a snail an insect?"

"No, it's a mollusk," said Raymond.

"Well, whatever they are, I always liked them, and dragonflies, lightning bugs, caterpillars, bees." She looked at Raymond. "No offense, but I'm afraid I don't care too much for wasps anymore."

"No," said Dorothy. "And who can blame you?"

Elner continued, "And I loved a good gospel song, and all the holidays, Christmas, Thanksgiving . . . Easter especially, I enjoyed being a little girl, being a grown woman with my own home, loved being married, and coffee, bacon, I particularly loved bacon, me and my neighbor Merle even joined the Bacon of the Month Club, of course I didn't tell Norma." When she realized what she had said, Elner winced. "Uh-oh, is that considered a lie . . . me not telling her?"

He thought about it, then said, "I would say it falls into the 'What she doesn't know won't hurt her' category, wouldn't you, Dorothy?"

"I agree."

"Whew! I'm glad about that," said a relieved Elner. "I have a lot of those where Norma is concerned." And then she continued. "I loved homemade peach ice cream . . . black walnut was my second favorite, but you don't see that so much anymore, and turnip greens, mashed potatoes, black-eyed peas, fried okra, cornbread, and biscuits." Elner looked over at Dorothy. "And pie and cake of course!"

"That's a lot of things," said Raymond appreciatively.

"And liver and onions . . . most people don't like liver and onions, but I did. And rice puddings . . . Oh, I could just go on and on, if you want me to," she said.

"No, that's all right, Elner, like we said, this is your time for asking questions."

"Oh, OK then, here's something else I always wanted to know: What good is a flea?"

Dorothy put her hand over her mouth and tried not to laugh.

Raymond leaned back in his chair, put his thumbs in his vest, and cleared his throat. "Well, you see, Elner, monkeys—all primates in general—have a rather complicated set of social rituals and grooming behaviors, and the picking of fleas is an important element for bonding."

Dorothy looked askance at her husband. "Raymond?"

He sighed. "Oh, all right, I don't know what they're good for. I'm sure I had something in mind but I just forgot."

"I told you she was smart, Raymond," said Dorothy.

"Well, don't feel bad about those old fleas for one minute," Elner said to Raymond. "Like I said, I thoroughly enjoyed your sunsets, sunrises, the stars and the moon, and the rain, I loved a good summer rainstorm, and the fall . . . all the seasons, really, they were all just wonderful."

"Thank you, Elner, I'm glad you enjoyed them. We tried to come up with a lot of nice things to balance it out, because regretfully, in life bad things do happen."

"And we just hate it when they do," said Dorothy sadly.

Elner said, "Well, now that you mentioned it, people do wonder about why they happen."

Raymond looked very sympathetic and said, "I know they do, and I don't blame them, but in order for them to have free will, I had to set up concrete laws of cause and effect, or else it wouldn't have worked." He shrugged. "I had no choice, what else could I do?"

"Well, Raymond," Elner said thoughtfully, "I know it's always easy to second-guess anything, but you might want to rethink the free will thing. I know that was Luther Griggs's problem, if he could do anything he wanted, he usually got himself in a lot of trouble."

Raymond nodded. "I understand, and believe me, Elner, we thought long and hard about free will, but we didn't want to force people to do things."

Dorothy added, "You can't force people to love you, or each other, for that matter."

Raymond agreed. "No, but we did give them everything we thought they would need to help: logic, reason, compassion, a great sense of humor, but . . . whether or not they use it is up to them. And after that, all you can do is love them, and hope for the best." He then looked over at Dorothy. "I think it was the hardest thing we had to do, let them make their own mistakes. . . ."

"Oh, by far," Dorothy said.

Then Raymond said to Elner, "But I suppose everybody feels that way, you know they have to leave the nest . . . but you just hate to see them go."

"I see your point," said Elmer. "When Linda left home, Norma went to bed for six months with a rag on her head. . . ."

Suddenly a bell went off in the kitchen, and Dorothy jumped up.

"Oh, good!" she said. "The cake's done, let me run and take it out of the oven, I'll be right back."

Elner perked up at the thought of cake.

Norma's Lady Minister

After Irene Goodnight had a good cry over Elner, she pulled herself together and called Neva and ordered her flowers and then wondered what she could do to help Norma. She would be so upset, she was going to need all the help and support she could get. Irene would start fixing some food, to take over to their house. Maybe some baked chicken, a green bean casserole, macaroni and cheese, and a Bundt cake. No onions or bell peppers. Nothing too spicy. When you are upset, you need bland and simple cream-based food. Before she went to the kitchen to start preparing, she decided to call Reverend Susie Hill, Norma's lady minister over at the Unity Church, and alert her.

She dialed her home number.

"Hello?"

"Susie, it's Irene Goodnight."

"Well, hello, how are you?"

"Just fine, but I'm afraid I'm calling with some bad news. Elner Shimfissle just died, so I wanted to let you know."

"Oh no!" said a surprised Susie. "What happened?"

"Wasps got her, knocked her clean out of her tree. Norma

and Macky are up in Kansas City at the Caraway Hospital right now, so you might want to call or something."

"Oh, of course . . . yes . . . thank you for letting me know."

Susie put the phone down, and felt terrible. Not only was Norma a member of her congregation, she was also a good friend. When she had first moved to town, she had met Norma at Weight Watchers and had liked her immediately. Norma was such a lovely woman, a classy woman, really, always so beautifully and tastefully dressed. Susie had been so pleased when Norma had started coming to her church; even though she was Norma's minister, it was Norma she confided in, and asked for her help and advice about many things. Norma had helped her decorate her small town home, and had sent her husband, Macky, over to fix her pipes in the bathroom. But right now she knew poor Norma must be devastated. Norma had worried so much about Elner and had even brought her to church with her several times, and she had been a delight, so full of life, so full of fun, even at her age. That first day at church Mrs. Shimfissle had hugged her and said, "I'm just tickled to death, I lived to see a real lady minister in the flesh, and you're so cute too." Susie was newly ordained and had not had much experience with death as of yet, but it was now her duty as Norma's minister and friend to try to comfort Norma in her time of loss.

Susie had worked long and hard to get to where she was finally able to help other people; she had struggled through a long agonizing period of ten and a half years, losing around a hundred and ten pounds, going from a size eighteen down to a size eight. And it had not been easy. She had tried every diet, from Pritikin to Atkins, from low fat to high fat and back again, but she had never been able to keep it off for more than a few months. Her last stop had been Overeaters Anonymous, and along with Weight Watchers, and praying every day, it had worked so far. Her sponsor in Overeaters Anonymous had told her to stay away from trans fats, walk every day, and pray like a son of a bitch, which she did, but it had still been a daily battle.

She had become a Christian Scientist for a while, had studied Buddhism, Hinduism, the Kabala, Catholicism, Scientology, read the Book of Miracles; studied and searched and prayed to just about anybody and everybody at one time or another, but somewhere along the line, something had happened. In September of 1998 while attending a "Silent Retreat" week at Unity Village outside of Kansas City, she had received a calling to become a Unity minister, and the little Unity Church in Elmwood Springs was her first congregation. So far they had over fifty members. Few people who saw the five-foot-four minister would have believed by looking at her that there was a huge, fat woman sitting inside her, who at the slightest sign of stress was ready to run to the nearest International House of Pancakes. She had to be careful. Death was a stress-producing situation, and the thought of having to deal with seeing Norma's poor old Aunt Elner dead in her coffin made her want to eat an entire coconut cake. But she would have a glass of water and a protein bar instead, then she would get dressed, suit up, and show up for Norma.

Telling Lies

As Linda Warren ran through the private hangar at the airport, and boarded the plane, one thought kept running over and over in her head. *Aunt Elner is dead.* She knew that's what her daddy had said, but still she couldn't quite believe it. As the plane took off headed for Kansas City, another wave of guilt hit her as she remembered what she and her father had done to Aunt Elner. Lying about the mice was not the first time she had lied to Aunt Elner, and the first time had been even a worse deception.

Over the years Aunt Elner had had a series of orange tabby cats named Sonny, and seventeen years ago, when her mother and Aunt Elner had gone to visit Aunt Elner's niece Mary Grace, Linda had volunteered to stay in her house and take care of Sonny number six while she was away. But on the second day, the cat disappeared. Linda had been frantic and had called her daddy in hysterics, and for the next four days she and Macky had looked everywhere, but had not found him, nor had he come home. On the sixth day, when they realized he was gone for good, they were now *both* frantic because they knew how upset Aunt Elner would be when she came home and he was not there. They started calling all the humane societies and pet stores within a hundred miles, looking for an orange cat to replace Sonny.

Finally a woman from the Poplar Springs Humane Society called them back and said they had a male orange tabby cat over there named Marmalade that a woman had to get rid of because he was clawing up all her furniture. She and her daddy had jumped into the car and rushed over to see him, and thank heavens, although he was younger, and a few pounds heavier, Marmalade was the spitting image of Sonny. They grabbed him and rushed back to Elmwood Springs and hoped for the best. When Aunt Elner came home and saw him, all she had said was that Sonny certainly looked well fed, and thanked her. They had not told Norma a thing, because she would never have been able to keep a secret, and they had held their breath for the next two days, and both had breathed a sigh of relief when Aunt Elner called and said, "Linda, old Sonny sure must have missed me, because he is being so sweet, all he wants to do night and day is sit in my lap."

Things went smoothly, until six months later when they had another close call. One morning Aunt Elner had called Macky and said, "Macky, Sonny is going to have to be fixed again, the first time must not have taken, because he's spraying all over the house." When Macky had picked him up and taken him to Dr. Shaw, Abby, the vet's wife and assistant, had been puzzled.

"I have it on my records that he was already neutered, eleven years ago."

"That was another Sonny," Macky said, "but don't tell her."

Abby and Dr. Shaw had gone along with it, thank goodness. And Aunt Elner never knew that Sonny number six was really Sonny number seven, and because of their lie, Aunt Elner thought she had a twenty-five-year-old tomcat and had bragged on him to everyone. "Look what good shape he's in," she had said. "Why, in cat years he must be way over a hundred and fifty years old!" Of course, Linda and her father had felt terrible every time she said it, and were both horrified when she had her picture in the paper holding what she thought was a twenty-five-year-old cat, but there was nothing they could do.

Linda made her mind up right then and there and as soon as the plane landed, even though she did not particularly like cats, she took out her cell phone and called her daughter. "Hi, sweet-heart, Momma will be home as soon as I can, and I'm bringing you a kitty when I come." Apple had been delighted and couldn't wait until she got back. She had been asking her mother for a cat for a long time, and Aunt Elner would have been pleased to know that Sonny was going to live with her and Apple. It was the least she could do. As she jumped into the car waiting for her at the airport, and sat back, she had another thought: "How old is that cat?"

Chatting with Raymond

As soon as Dorothy left the room to take the cake out of the oven, Raymond waited for a second, then asked, "Do you mind if I smoke?"

"No, not at all," said Elner, "go right ahead."

He grinned as he pulled out his pipe and a can of Prince Albert tobacco from the back of the drawer, and said, "This is one of those 'What Dorothy doesn't know won't hurt her' things. OK?"

"OK," she said. "My lips are sealed."

After he lit his pipe, he sat back and said, "Elner, I know you're supposed to be asking the questions, but would you mind if I asked you a few things?"

"Sure, as long as they are not too hard."

"You know," he said, blowing out a long puff of smoke, "we really admired the way you handled your life, even during the Depression, never a complaint. I'm curious, what would you say was your philosophy of life?"

Elner laughed. "Philosophy? Oh, Raymond, I'm not smart enough to have a philosophy, I guess I just tried to do my best and get along with other people, that's all."

He nodded at her and said, "Well, that's enough, I can't ask for more than that." He then leaned in and said, "Confidentially, Elner, just between you and me, and feel free to be perfectly candid, what do you think about people?"

"Me?"

"Yes," he said, looking at her intently. "I'd really like your opinion."

"Well, Raymond, personally, I always liked them. They just tickled me to death with all their funny little ways."

"Like what?"

"Oh, I don't know, I guess the way they all have their little routines, get themselves dressed up in some of those crazy rigs they put on, get their hair all fixed and get so puffed up, I don't know why, but I always thought they were kind of funny. I've been sitting on my porch for years, watching them go by, running here, running there, and watching people has been better than a picture show, and I'm not saying this just because you made them, but really, with only a few exceptions, I never met one I didn't like, but now, Raymond," Elner said, looking over at him, "what do you think about people? It's your opinion that really counts, not mine."

He was a little taken aback. "Me? Oh, well," he said. "Hmmm . . . let's see . . ." He sat there for a while seriously contemplating the question, took a few drags off his pipe, and then said, "The God's honest truth, Elner? And being as objective as I can be . . . under the circumstances."

"Of course."

He smiled. "I'm just crazy about them, each and every one."

"Ahhh . . . and what is it about them you like?" she asked.

"Oh, everything," he said with a faraway look in his eye. "How hard they try, how they just keep going no matter what . . . and brave? Why, those crazy fools will run into burning buildings or jump into rivers, just to save a complete stranger! Did you know that?"

"Oh, yes, I've read about it."

He continued, "And smart? Imagine, they figured out how to get all the way to the moon! And I'm constantly amazed at all the hundreds of little things they do for one another, even when they think no one is watching. . . . Of course, they still have a long way to go, but oh boy, when they all finally evolve into who they are supposed to be, it's going to be just great!"

Elner asked, "How much longer do you figure we have to go? You don't think we are going to blow ourselves up before we get there, do you?"

"No. I don't."

"Well, I hope you're right."

"Oh, I am, no doubt about it."

"That's good news. So let me ask you this, then. Of all the humans that ever lived, who was your favorite so far?"

"Let's see, not counting the ones coming in the future." He said as he nodded over to the wall with the pictures of little babies on it, "Hard to say, they are all special . . . teachers . . . visiting nurses . . . firemen—excuse me, firepersons now—but I was particularly fond of the U.S. women's soccer team, weren't they something? But really, Elner, I have no favorites, they are all different and unique in some—"

Suddenly Raymond's cell phone rang and played Elner's favorite hymn, "Can't Wait to Get to Heaven." He put on his glasses and looked at the readout, and said, "Pardon me just a second, I need to get this," and picked up.

"Hello," he said, and then Raymond looked over at Elner and smiled and winked at her. "Yes, she sure is. She's sitting right here with me as we speak. . . . Well, come on, then." He hung up and smiled at her. "That was an admirer of yours who wants to stop by in a minute and meet you. . . . Now, where were we? Do you have another question?"

"Oh, well, it's not that I'm not having a good time visiting with you, but I was wondering when we were going to get to the judgment part? I'm kind of anxious to get that over with."

"The *what* part?" asked Raymond.

"Judgment? Don't I have to account for my sins or something before I move on?"

He laughed. "Oh good Lord, no, you're not here to be judged."

"I'm not?"

"No. You're human, for heaven's sake; everybody makes mistakes, even me, and besides, mistakes happen for a reason. Hopefully you can learn from them."

Elner asked tentatively, "Then, you're not mad at me over the Ex-Lax candy thing?"

Raymond laughed again. "Nooo, I thought it was pretty funny myself, but that's a perfect example. If you hadn't done it, then felt bad about it later, you never would have gotten to know Luther Griggs."

"I did feel bad about it. Imagine me, trying to get revenge on an eight-year-old boy for throwing rocks at my cat."

"Yes, but if you hadn't been sorry, and then made a decision to be nice to that boy when you did, he would have led a much different life. You don't know what you saved him from. I do!"

"But how do you know if you're making the right decision?"

"Easy!" he said. "Just like two and two always add up to four, kindness and forgiveness is always right, hate and revenge is always wrong. It's a fail-proof system; if you just stick to that one simple rule, why, you couldn't make a mistake if you tried." He sat back and crossed his arms. "Pretty neat, huh?"

"Wow!" she said. "I like it. It sure takes all the guesswork out of living, doesn't it?"

"Doesn't it?"

There was a light rap on the door and Raymond looked at her. "Uh-oh, get ready, here comes your admirer," and called out, "Come on in, the door's open."

Elner could not imagine who it could be, but when she turned around and saw the man with the white hair walk in, she recognized him instantly.

"Elner Shimfissle," said a smiling Raymond, "say hello to Thomas Alva Edison." Elner could hardly believe it; there stood the Wizard of Menlo Park himself, looking exactly like his picture, hanging on her living room wall.

"Sorry to interrupt, Raymond," Thomas said, "but I just had to stop by and shake this lady's hand."

Elner started to get up, but he stopped her. "Oh, don't get up, Mrs. Shimfissle. Just wanted to say a quick hello, and thank you for all your good wishes and support over the years."

"Oh, my heavens," said a flustered Elner. "Well, it's just a thrill to meet you. I've always wanted to shake your hand and thank you for everything you did."

"Oh, it was nothing."

"Nothing!" she said. "Why, honey, you lit the entire world, if it hadn't been for you, we'd all still be sitting in the dark."

"Sit down for a minute, Tom," said Raymond, thoroughly enjoying watching the two of them. Tom sat in the chair next to her and said, "Well, thank you so much, Mrs. Shimfissle."

"Call me Elner. I always told people that, next to the Maker here, of course," she said, nodding over at Raymond, "you rank pretty high up there in my book."

Tom laughed. "Thank you again, but it was Raymond who came up with the ideas, he just let me think of them."

Raymond, knocking his pipe on the ashtray, said, "Don't sell yourself short, Tom. You put in a lot of hard work."

"Maybe, but I had a lot of fun too. Elner, I also wanted to thank you for thinking of me on my birthday every year, I really appreciate that."

Elner waved it off. "Shoot, after all you did for the human race, it was the least I could do. My niece Norma said it was a waste of electricity, running my appliances all day, but I always say electricity is the best bargain there is. Why, for just a few cents a day, I had lights and heat and I got to listen to the radio, I never missed one of Neighbor Dorothy's shows, you have no idea what a comfort it is to have company coming into your very own house over the radio or the TV. . . . Just imagine how much company you have given to all the shut-ins and so forth, people don't have to be all alone anymore."

Tom nodded. "I hadn't thought about that aspect."

"Well, think about it, and pat yourself on the back, and I'll tell you something else, Tom. May I call you Tom?"

"Oh, please."

"I wish your idea for running cars on batteries had caught on back then. Macky said gasoline prices were going through the roof."

He shrugged. "I tried, but old Henry Ford came up with the Model A and beat me to it. What can you do? The early bird gets the worm."

"Yes, but if it makes you feel any better, I think they are going to have to go right back to your idea anyway." She suddenly thought of something. "Hey, did you know they made a lot of movies about you?"

"Oh, yes?"

"Yes, good ones too. I saw two of them at the Elmwood

Theater, Mickey Rooney was in one, then Spencer Tracy played you as a grown man. I liked both of them, really."

"So, Elner," asked Tom, "how do you like it here? Are you enjoying yourself so far?"

"Oh, am I! Even more, now that I know I'm not in any trouble. I was just getting ready to tell Raymond, this is the grandest place I've ever been, it's even better than I thought it would be."

Tom said, "And isn't it great to get your hearing back?"

"Yes, it is, and not only that, I'm getting some homemade caramel cake in a little while."

"Well," said Tom, getting up, "I'd better run on, let you finish your talk with Raymond, but I look forward to visiting with you again sometime soon, I hope."

"Anytime. I'd be glad to see you."

As soon as he left, Elner turned to Raymond still somewhat in awe. "Imagine, me getting to visit with Thomas Edison, and I just can't get over how sweet and humble he is. Why, if I was as smart as him, I'm afraid it would go to my head, and you, Raymond, look at you. With what all you have accomplished, and you seem just like a regular person . . . and my hat's off to you because I'll tell you, if I had created everything there was to create . . . why . . . there would be no living with me."

Raymond laughed. "Elner, you are a riot."

She laughed. "Am I? Well, it's true, though, and Dorothy is just as down to earth as she can be—oh, here's a question I always wondered about. What's it like being God? Is it any fun? Or is it all work and no play?"

He took a long draw off his pipe. "Well . . . it's just like being anything else, I suppose, a lot of fun, but also a lot of responsibility, a lot of heartbreak."

"I can see how it would be, considering the way the world is going."

"Yes, having to sit up here watching them make the same old mistakes generation after generation."

"What would you say was the biggest mistake?"

"Without a doubt, it's that revenge thing, you know . . . you hit me, so I hit you back. I swear, it's almost like the whole world is stuck in the second grade. I'll be so glad when they finally get out of this phase and move on."

"I see your point, and how long will that be?"

"Not too much longer," he said, emptying the last of the tobacco into the ashtray and putting it back into the drawer. "You know how sometimes it takes a long time for an idea to finally catch on?"

"Like the Hula Hoop?"

He chuckled. "Well, yes, but I was thinking more like, let's say, the Internet. You know how once that caught on, the idea suddenly spread around the world like wildfire?"

"Oh, yes, everybody seems to be online now."

"Yes, that's a perfect example of an idea whose time has come, and just like the Internet, living in peace with one another is also an idea whose time has come."

"Really?"

"You bet! More and more people are beginning to understand, it's not just a religious thing, it's just common plain sense, particularly right now, when they have the means to blow themselves up. They don't have too much of a choice."

"No, they don't."

"And that's what the majority of people want now anyway. I see the big picture and I can tell you, there are many more good people on earth than you know, you just seldom hear about them."

"No, you don't, not on television anyway."

"And don't forget, Elner, I can also see way down the line to the next generations coming in; and I know what's about to happen." He looked up at the wall of new babies and suddenly seemed as excited as a young boy. "And guess what else?"

"What?"

"When it happens, there won't be a bit of difference between earth and here. People won't have to wait to get to heaven to be happy. Isn't that fantastic?"

At that moment Dorothy came back into the room, wiping her hands on her apron, and said cheerfully, "Well, I'm stealing her away, we are going to have our cake now. Do you want to join us?"

Raymond said, "No, you two go on and enjoy yourselves. I'm sure you have a lot more girl talk to catch up with. See you later."

Elner stood up to leave, and as she headed out the door, she turned and said, "Oh, I forgot to ask one thing. What about prayer . . . does that work?"

"Of course!" he said. "We want you to have anything you want, and if what you are praying for is not bad for you in the long run, we do our best."

Elner nodded. "You can't ask for more than that," she said. "Well, so long, Raymond. I enjoyed our little chat."

"Me too," he called back.

Mrs. Franks, an Old Friend

12:01 PM

Mrs. Louise Franks had been a neighbor of Elner's when Elner had still lived out on the farm, and they had spent a lot of time visiting back and forth with each other over the years, cooking recipes they had heard on the *Neighbor Dorothy* radio show. After Elner's husband, Will Shimfissle, had died, and before Elner moved to town, they had seen each other almost every day. Louise still ran a ten-acre farm and today had had a busy morning tending to all the usual chores. It was around noontime when she ran into the small convenience store at the gas station to pick up a pack of marshmallows for her daughter, Polly, who was allowed one bag of marshmallows a week. And while she was there, she'd grabbed a six-pack of caffeine-free Diet Coke and a bottle of Windex as well. As the clerk scanned the Diet Cokes, he said, "Were you listening to Bud and Jay this morning, Mrs. Franks?"

"No, I missed it today. Why?"

"They said that Mrs. Shimfissle died."

Mrs. Franks was stunned, she had just talked to Elner on the phone yesterday about the Easter egg hunt.

"What?"

· 154 ·

"Yeah, Bud said she died this morning in the hospital in Kansas City. Didn't you know her pretty well?"

Mrs. Franks suddenly felt herself getting dizzy and sweaty. "Yes, I did."

The clerk saw the stricken look on her face and said, "I'm sorry, I figured you might have heard by now."

"No. I hadn't heard." Then Mrs. Franks turned around and walked out the door.

The clerk called after her, "Hey . . . you left your things here.

"Well, I guess she didn't want them," he mumbled to himself.

Mrs. Franks drove out of the parking lot in a daze and about a block later pulled over and parked.

She sat there thinking about what the clerk had asked so matter-of-factly. "Didn't you know her pretty well?"

Pretty well? Even the words "She was the best friend I ever had" would have been inadequate. No one would, or could, ever know what Elner had done for Mrs. Franks and her daughter. Then her thoughts and concerns went immediately to her daughter, Polly, who was now at day care waiting for Mrs. Franks to come pick her up. How would she ever be able to explain to Polly that Mrs. Shimfissle had died? Polly loved Mrs. Shimfissle; she had been the only other person in the world whom she would spend the night with without crying and screaming for her mother. Every year, Mrs. Franks had dressed her daughter up in her new outfit and driven her to town for Elner's big Easter egg hunt. Other than Christmas and having her picture made with Santa Claus, Easter was Polly's favorite day of the year. She loved playing with the other children, and no matter what eggs she found in the yard, Elner always made a big fuss over it, gave her the biggest prize. One year her prize was a jeweled silver cowgirl belt with two cap guns that she still loved to play with to this day.

Poor Polly, even though she was now forty-two years old, she was severely retarded and had the mind of a six-year-old; she would never be able to understand why Mrs. Shimfissle would not be there anymore, or where she had gone. "I won't tell her today," she thought. "I'll just give her a bag of marshmallows and let her be happy, for just a little while longer." She was halfway home when she realized she had left her groceries on the counter and had to turn around and go back and still could hardly believe it. Elner Shimfissle dead. Elner, the bravest and purest soul she had ever known. Gone. "Where is she now?" she wondered.

As Louise drove along, she thought that if there was such a thing as heaven, then surely Elner had to be there right now.

What a Surprise, Huh?

As they walked down the hall, Dorothy said, "We could have our cake in the dining room or out on the front porch. Which would you prefer?"

Elner said, "Let's have it on the porch."

"Oh, good, it's such a pretty day, I was hoping you would say that." As Elner followed Dorothy, she suddenly heard a noise coming from the living room where Dorothy used to broadcast her show, and realized the noise was someone playing "You Are My Sunshine" on the tuba. "That sounds like Ernest Koonitz," she said.

Dorothy said, "It is. Why don't you go say hello to him while I get the cake. I know he'd love to see you."

Elner walked by and poked her head into the room, and there he was, bad hairpiece and all, wearing that same black and white checked suit he always wore, with the red bow tie. "Hello, Ernest! It's Elner Shimfissle."

He looked up and seemed thrilled to see her. "Hello! When did you get here?" He walked over and shook her hand through the tuba.

"Just a little while ago. I got stung by wasps and fell out of a tree, so please excuse the robe. How about yourself?"

"I was on my way to the dentist's office when I just dropped out in the parking lot with a heart attack. It was good timing too, I was just about to fork over a fortune for new dentures."

"Ahh . . . well . . . how are you, Ernest?"

"Oh, I'm just fine now. I had been sick, but I've never felt better in my whole life. This is the first time I've been able to play in years. Isn't this just the best place? . . . I'm meeting with John Philip Sousa, the great bandmaster himself, in just a few minutes, he's agreed to come over and give me some lessons. Isn't that great?"

"Yes, it is. I guess it's never too late to learn, even after you're dead."

He looked around. "And isn't it good to see the old house again. When they tore it down, I thought it was gone forever. I thought when I died I was going to be gone forever too, but here I am. What a surprise, huh?"

"A pleasant surprise, and weren't those crystal stairs just beautiful?"

He looked at her blankly. "What crystal stairs?"

Elner realized he must not have come that way, and asked, "How did you get up here?"

"I came up in a brand-new Cadillac convertible with heated seats!"

"Ahh, well . . ."

"Have you seen everybody yet?"

"No, not yet, just Ida so far, but I think I'm still in the checking-in part. If I pass that, then I think I'll get to go on and see everybody else, and I can't wait to see my husband, Will, again."

Elner heard the front door slam, and said, "Well, I better go. I just wanted to say hey . . . and good luck with your lesson."

"Thanks. I'll see you later. Have fun."

"Oh, I will," she said. As Elner headed on out to the front porch, she chuckled to herself. Ernest had never struck her as being a particularly enthusiastic person before, but he seemed just tickled to death to be dead. Who would have ever believed it?

A Comforting Message

About an hour later, Macky was sitting with Norma, holding her hand trying to think of things to say to help, but after a while he was more or less at a loss for words and was very happy to see Norma's Unity minister, Susie Hill, coming down the hall. When Norma looked up and saw her she burst into tears.

"Oh, Susie, she's gone. I've lost Aunt Elner."

The two women hugged. "I came as soon as I heard."

Norma said, "I'm so glad you're here, but how did you know, we haven't called anybody at home yet?"

"Irene Goodnight called me and told me."

"She did?" said a teary-eyed Norma. "How did she find out?"

"I think somebody from the hospital called Ruby."

"I guess I should go and try to call people and let them know."

Susie said, "It's already been done, everybody knows and they all send you their love. Ruby and Tot said to tell you that they were taking care of Elner's house, and for you not to worry about a thing."

"Oh, I forgot about the house. I'm sure it was standing wide open. She never locked her doors." Norma choked up again. "All this time I was worried about her being robbed and murdered in her bed, I never dreamed it would be wasps!" She wailed and fell apart again.

"I know, it's a terrible loss, Norma, and I know you are going to miss her," said Susie, "but at least we know she's gone to a better place."

"Oh, Susie, do you think so?" said Norma hopefully.

"Yes, I am sure that right now she is happy and at peace."

Macky took this time to excuse himself and phone work and let them know he would not be coming back in for a few days. Although he certainly didn't believe it, if it helped Norma to think that Aunt Elner was in heaven, fine. Let her. He had stopped believing in any of that pie-in-the-sky stuff years ago. He had been in the army and had seen men blown up, right beside him. He had seen far too much to have much faith in anything, other than the here and now. It would be nice to think that Elner was in some sort of heaven, but unfortunately, he knew better.

Eating Cake

A little while later, when Dorothy and Elner were outside on the front porch having their coffee and cake, Elner sat looking out, amazed at the sight before her. While she had been inside talking to Ernest, the sky had turned an exquisite shade of aqua, a color Elner had never seen before in her life, and the entire front yard was filled with flocks of beautiful pink flamingos. Large blue swans with bright yellow eyes swam around in a pond that wound all around the house, while hundreds of tiny multicolored birds flew overhead. Elner said, "Don't you just love birds?"

"I do."

Elner said, "By the way, I was surprised to hear that Ernest came up in a Cadillac."

"We like to make the trip as pleasant as possible. Your sister came up on the *Queen Elizabeth,* in a first-class cabin."

"Of course," said Elner, laughing. "I'll bet Macky will come up in that motorboat he just loves to fish in."

"Maybe so," she said, pouring Elner more coffee. "Raymond and I say whatever you want, you get, and everybody is different, some people like sailboats, some prefer private jets.

We had a couple come in last week on a Harley-Davidson motorcycle."

"Why did I get to come up in that elevator that went every which a way?"

"We know you loved to ride the Loop de Loop at the fair."

Elner laughed. "That's true. I tell you, Dorothy, you and Raymond certainly go out of your way to make dying a real nice experience."

"We try."

"Shoot, if more people knew how pleasant it was up here, they would be dropping like flies."

Dorothy laughed. "Well, we don't want people to come up before they are ready, but it's certainly nothing to be afraid of."

"No. It certainly isn't."

Then Dorothy pointed over to where bright deep purple wisteria and snow white baby roses were cascading over the side fence. "Look. It's so pretty this time of year, isn't it?"

"It is, especially here, I feel like I'm sitting in a picture inside a magazine," said Elner as she started on her second piece of cake. After she took the first bite, she looked over and remarked, "Dorothy, I swear I haven't had good homemade cake like this since you died. I don't know how you get it to turn out so light and fluffy, mine are never near this good."

"Do you still have the recipe I gave out over the radio?"

"Yes, it's in your cookbook, and I follow it to a T, but it never turns out like yours."

"Next time, try preheating the oven to three seventy-five, it could be your oven is not as hot as it should be, that happens sometimes."

"I will, and thanks for the tip." Elner looked over at her. "And by the way, I just loved meeting Raymond, he seems like a really nice person."

"Oh, he is," said Dorothy, pouring herself another cup of coffee. "He is the sweetest thing and he cares so much."

"That's the impression I got."

"It just breaks his heart when people don't get along."

"I can imagine it would."

"Raymond thinks it's all the radicals and fanatics that cause most of the trouble. He says they take themselves far too seriously, get themselves and everybody else all worked up in a frenzy."

"He could be right, Dorothy. Come to think of it, your average fanatic doesn't seem to have much of a sense of humor, does he?"

"No," she said, "not a laugh in the bunch, I'm afraid. And you can't be happy and in a rage at the same time."

"No, you sure can't."

"But I am beginning to suspect that it could be something else as well."

Dorothy glanced over at the front door to make sure Raymond wasn't coming out, and whispered, "I wonder if Raymond made a slight mistake with the hormone mix; gave the men a little too much testosterone? Think about it, Elner . . . it's the men who start most of the wars. Not us."

"That's a good point," Elner said, taking another bite of her cake.

Dorothy sighed. "But bless his heart, he did the best he could, and thank heavens, he let me help, because everything he had done—the oceans, the trees, everything—was a muddy gray."

"You don't mean it?"

Dorothy nodded. "I do, he's as color-blind as they come; to this day, I have to pick out his socks or else he winds up with one blue one and one brown one."

"I'm glad you caught it in time," said Elner. "It sure would have been a dull old place if we hadn't had any color."

"Thank you, but you know, Elner," she said thoughtfully, "speaking of color, I wonder if I didn't make a mistake."

"How so, honey?"

"With people? I wonder if I shouldn't have made them all one color? I had no idea it would cause so much trouble, and I just feel terrible about it."

"Oh, I wouldn't worry too much about that, Dorothy, things are changing in that department. My niece Linda just adopted a Chinese baby and she's a real pretty color, everybody says so."

"Well, I'd like to think it's getting better, and I must say, even with all the problems, Raymond is very optimistic about the future."

"I know he is, and after talking to him, I feel a whole lot better," said Elner. "And I felt pretty good before."

Just then Raymond came out onto the porch and pointed to his watch. "Ladies, I hate to break this up, but Elner has to get on back."

Dorothy looked at her watch. "Oh, dear. I was having such a good time, I've kept you far too long."

Elner was totally surprised. "Am I not staying?"

"No," said Raymond, "as much as we would love to keep you, unfortunately, we have to send you back home."

"You mean, I'm not going to get to see Will?"

"No, honey, not this time," said Dorothy.

Elner slowly put her coffee cup down on the table. "Well . . . I'm very disappointed, of course. I sure wanted to see Will. But mine is not to question, I guess. Anyhow, it was sure nice being with you again, Dorothy, and visiting with you, Raymond."

"Wonderful to see you too, dear," he said.

Dorothy wrapped a piece of cake in a napkin. "Here, honey, take this with you."

Elner said, "Are you sure you don't want it for later?"

"No, you take it, I have half a cake left in the kitchen that we'll probably never finish."

"All right, then," she said, standing up and putting the cake into her pocket. "You know I'll enjoy it." She looked at both of them. "Is there anything I can do for you? Any messages you want me to take back?"

Raymond thought for a second, then said, "You could tell them that things are not really as bad as they seem, more people are getting educated every day, more women are voting, new technology is coming, new medical discoveries—"

"Wait a minute, hold it, Raymond," said Elner, looking around for a pencil. "Shouldn't I be writing all this down?"

"No, that's all right," he said. "Just tell them we love them, we're pulling for them, and to hang in there, because good things are just around the corner. Anything else, Dorothy?"

Dorothy said, "You might want to remind them that life is what they make it, to smile, and the world is sunny, and it's up to them."

"All right," said Elner, trying to remember it all. "Good things are coming, and life is what you make it, anything else?"

Dorothy looked over at Raymond, and he shook his head. "No, I think that's basically it." Suddenly Elner felt her robe filling up with warm air and expanding all around her; then she slowly began to rise up off the floor and gently float off the porch, on out into the yard like a big hot air balloon. As she rose higher in the air, she looked down to see Raymond and Dorothy standing in the yard surrounded by pink flamingos, and blue swans, who were all smiling and waving good-bye to her. "Good-bye, Elner!" they said. "Well, bye-bye . . . thanks for the cake," she called back, as she floated higher and higher right over the top of the Elmwood Springs water tank and on over toward Kansas City.

Saying a Final Good-bye

2:46 PM

When Norma looked up and saw her daughter, Linda, walking down the hall, she burst into tears all over again. After they had pulled themselves together a bit, they discussed the matter of the autopsy and agreed not to have it done. As Linda said, if it couldn't bring her back, then what was the point? The harsh reality of death was so damned final, so irreversible. They would just let her go in peace and not prolong the inevitable. They would follow Aunt Elner's wishes and go ahead and arrange for the remains to be picked up for cremation. Norma burst into tears again. When she heard the word *remains,* she couldn't bear to think of someone who had been so alive just this morning as just "remains." Reverend Susie Hill said, "I know it's hard, Norma, but I think it's what she would have wanted." Macky and Linda agreed. After a while, Macky got up and told the young nurse who was waiting that they were ready to go and see their aunt and say good-bye. Norma asked Susie if she would like to come, but Susie said, "No, this is family, I think it's best that just the three of you go, I'll be right here in the hall waiting."

The three of them walked down to Elner's room, and the

young nurse opened the door, and they all stepped into the room, and quietly walked over to the side of the bed. Macky put his arm around Norma and held Linda's hand and they stood there together looking down at Aunt Elner. The young nurse stood back from the bed as the family had their last moment with the woman before she was to be taken downstairs. Seeing her was not as frightening as Linda had thought it would be. Just as her daddy had said, Aunt Elner looked as if she had just gone to sleep. Norma leaned on Macky as tears welled up in her eyes. Elner looked so sweet and peaceful, it was hard for her to realize she was actually dead. They did not speak and the room was so quiet all they could hear was their own breathing. They were standing there in dead silence, each mentally telling her good-bye in their own way, when Elner said, "I know you're mad at me, Norma, but I wouldn't have fallen if those wasps hadn't gone after me."

Macky literally jumped back a foot from the bed. "Jesus Christ!"

Upon seeing Elner open her eyes, the young nurse at the foot of the bed let out a bloodcurdling scream and ran out of the room, shrieking at the top of her lungs. Linda screamed at the same time, threw her purse up in the air, and ran out right behind the nurse. Macky's feet were glued to the floor and he could not get them to move or he would have gone out the door with them. But for once in her life Norma, who was far too stunned to faint, said, "Aunt Elner? What in the world do you call yourself doing, pretending you're dead? Do you have any idea what you have put us through? We called Linda and everything!" Elner looked over and was about to answer, but before she had a chance, a woman's hysterical voice came blaring out over the hospital intercom.

"Stat! Stat! Room 212, Stat!"

And the next moment, sounding like a herd of wild buffalo, doctors and nurses came thundering down the hall at breakneck speed and stampeded through the door, pushing machines and three or four IV stands before them, knocking Macky and Norma back against the wall. When the young doctor from the emergency room came running into the room, he turned as white as a sheet when he saw Elner sitting up on her elbows in bed and talking, and he began frantically barking orders. As the room filled up with more staff and machines, Macky and Norma were shoved outside into the hall, and it wasn't until then that Norma realized what had just happened, and fainted again.

Back in the room, Elner was now surrounded by screaming and yelling doctors and nurses, and being hooked up to several machines all at once, and lifted out of bed, rushed down the hall on a gurney. As Elner, traveling at least forty miles an hour, sped by Linda, who was leaning against the wall still in a state of shock, she called out, "Hey, that's my niece! Hey, Linda!" By this time the young nurse who had been the first to run out of the room had made it all the way down six flights of stairs, and she ran screaming past Nurse Boots Carroll, almost knocking her down, through the lobby, out the double glass doors, and was now past the parking lot headed down the block, still running as fast as she could. Within five minutes the entire hospital was alive and buzzing with the news. Dead woman talking! As Elner whizzed by Reverend Susie Hill standing down at the end of the hall, she called out, "Hey, Susie, what are you doing here?" "That's my niece's lady preacher," she said to a nurse, who was running alongside her. After they had run all the way down to the end of the hall with her, turned the corner, and rolled her into a waiting elevator, Elner asked, "Where am I going now?"

A male nurse barked at her, "Just relax, Mrs. Shimfissle, calm down."

Elner said to herself, "I am calm, you're the one who's huffing and puffing."

Once the elevator doors opened again, they ran down another hall and then right through the open door of the intensive care unit. Once inside they quickly sat her up, removed her robe, and started hooking her up to different machines a mile a minute. As they were doing this, Elner was not happy about it, and said, "You know what, I need to get on home. Norma and them are here to get me, and I don't think I fed Sonny yet." But the doctor and the nurses completely ignored her and acted like she wasn't even there. They just kept talking about her vital signs, looking at screens, and shouting out numbers. Elner figured she must be all right, though, because in between the numbers, they kept answering "Stable" and "Normal" to the doctor's questions. Elner made a vow right then and there that if she ever got out of there, she would never come back to a hospital, because once they get you, you can't get away. "Does this hurt?" the doctor asked as he pushed all over her body. But he did not wait for an answer, and said, "Let's get her downstairs. I need an MRI right away." And off she went again . . . being pushed down another hall, and pushed onto another elevator.

When they got downstairs, they rolled Elner into a large room that had what looked to Elner like a big washing machine.

As they lifted her from one gurney to another one, she asked, "Am I going in that thing?"

"Just for a little while," said a nice new nurse she had not seen before.

"Is it going to hurt?"

"No, you won't feel a thing, Mrs. Shimfissle."

"What's it for?"

"We just want to look and make sure you don't have any broken bones or anything. It won't take long. Are you claustrophobic?"

"I don't think so . . . never had been."

"I can give you headphones, if you like. Is there any special kind of music you prefer?"

"That might be nice. Do you have any good gospel music? I like Minnie Oatman."

The nurse shook her head. "No, I don't think so. I could try to get a radio station."

"Oh, do you get Bud and Jay?"

"Who? I can try, do you know the station?"

"No, that's all right, they are probably off the air by now, I don't need to listen to anything."

"All right, Mrs. Shimfissle, I'm going to be right in the next room," the nurse said. "And I'll come back as soon as we are finished, OK?"

As she started heading into the machine, Elner realized she had no idea what time it was. The last time she had looked at a clock, it was eight in the morning, and now Linda was here all the way from St. Louis. "Where had the day gone?" she wondered.

Nurse Calls Ruby Back

2:59 PM

Boots Carroll was at her station at the hospital doing her paperwork when the order came down from upstairs to change Mrs. Shimfissle's condition from deceased to stable. "What?" she said, as she read the change. She immediately went upstairs, marched down the hall with paper in hand, and found the floor nurse who had called her in the first place. "What in the Sam Hill is going on with Mrs. Shimfissle's report?"

Her original source looked very distressed and whispered to her, "Dr. Henson made a mistake, she's back in OR and sitting up and talking."

"Are you sure?"

"Yes, I'm sure. . . . They just rolled her by here two minutes ago, and she sat up and waved at me."

"Good God! Heads are going to roll on this one. Does her family know yet?"

"Oh, yes. They were in the room when the old woman started talking. The niece fainted dead away." She pointed down the hall, and Boots could see a group of people standing around talking.

"I'll go down and see them in a minute, but I need to make a phone call first."

Boots picked up the phone, but could not reach Ruby at home. She then called the nurses' exchange and they gave her Ruby's emergency cell number.

Ruby was at Elner's, busy going through her refrigerator, wondering what might go bad and what she should throw out. She figured Norma would not be able to deal with it for a few days. She was trying to read the expiration date on a carton of milk when her cell phone rang.

"Hello?"

"Ruby, it's Boots. Listen, I was given the wrong information about Mrs. Shimfissle, she was not a DOA like I told you."

"What?"

"They just took her back up to OR. Apparently she's recovered and is doing just fine, at least that's the latest report. I don't know what's going on here, but I called you the minute I heard."

Ruby was flabbergasted. "What do you mean, she's not dead? I was just fixing to throw out her milk!"

"I am so sorry, Ruby, somebody made a mistake. I'm so mad at that bunch upstairs, I could spit nails. I'm telling you, if you knew half the things that go on here now, it would just curl your hair."

Ruby said, "Oh, dear. Well, let me get on the horn and pass this along . . . good Lord, we were practically planning her funeral."

After she hung up, Boots felt terrible; she had broken the rule of patient confidentiality, but they had been so sure upstairs. She and Ruby had been in nursing school together, so it was not as if she had told a civilian, but if they ever found out she had released the condition of a patient to a nonfamily member, she would lose her job, and at her age they were looking for a reason to get rid of her as it was. The one good thing was she knew that Ruby would protect her. There was always that unspoken nurse to nurse loyalty she could depend on. And it was true. Ruby would have protected her source with her life. But right now Ruby didn't even have time to stop and be happy that Elner was alive. She would have to do that later. Right now she had to get busy and stop this thing at the pass, before the news of Elner's death went any further than it had. She immediately called Tot down at the beauty shop. Not more than thirty minutes before, Tot had had to get up out of bed and drag herself down to the beauty shop, because Darlene could not find the formula for Beverly Cortwright's hair color.

Luckily, Tot answered the phone. "Beauty shop."

"Tot, it's Ruby, I just heard back from the hospital and Elner's not dead after all."

"What?"

"They made a mistake, so call whoever you told and tell them, pronto. I've got to go," she said, and hung up.

"Good God Almighty," Tot said to herself. "A mistake?" And here she was with a beauty parlor full of upset and crying women, thinking Elner Shimfissle was dead.

Tot walked around the room and turned off all the dryers, told everyone to take the cotton out of their ears, and made Darlene turn the water off and stop washing the dye out of Beverly Cortwright's hair. When she had everyone's attention, she announced, "Everybody, I just got a call from Ruby Robinson, and as it turns out, Elner Shimfissle is not dead after all. They gave out the wrong report at the hospital."

Everyone gasped and as a shock wave went around the room, Marie Larkin dropped her *Modern Style Cuts* onto the floor, and Lucille Wimble spilled coffee down the front of her dress. They had all spent the past hour crying and talking about how much they were going to miss Elner. Some were even going so far as to plan what they would wear to her funeral, and what kind of casserole they would make to take over to Norma's. What a shock! Lucille was beside herself. "I've never heard of anything so crazy in all my life!" she said, blotting her dress with a paper towel. "What would possess them to do such a thing, tell everybody she was dead and get people all hysterical, I had started my grieving process and everything and now they say it was all for nothing?"

Vicki Johnson agreed. "I don't know whether to laugh or cry."

"Well, I'm just stunned," said a teary, red-eyed Beverly with brown dye running down one side of her face. "I don't know what to think or feel."

"Me either," said Darlene, reaching into her pocket for the other half of her candy bar.

Tot said, "Well, I don't feel much of anything right now, I just took two Xanax an hour ago or so, but I'll probably have a fit once the pills wear off."

Elner's niece in California was on the Internet looking up the best flights from San Francisco to Kansas City. She didn't know when Elner's funeral was going to be, but she wanted to see what flights were available. When the phone rang, she picked it up, and it was another collect call from Macky and he sounded quite upset.

"Dena, I don't have time to go into detail, but I wanted to let you know, Aunt Elner is not dead like they thought, there was some kind of mistake."

"What?"

"Not dead. I'm sorry I called you the first time, but I was just telling you what they told us."

"Not dead?"

"No, apparently they gave us the wrong information, anyhow she's in intensive care right now, I'll try and keep you posted just as soon as I know something. . . . I have to run, Norma's having a fit, talk to you later."

Dena was still standing with the phone in her hand when her husband walked in the door.

When she saw him, she dropped the phone and ran to him and threw her arms around him. "Oh, Gerry, Aunt Elner's alive! Isn't that wonderful?"

Gerry, who had no idea what she was talking about, smiled and hugged her back. "Yes, honey, it is wonderful."

After she locked everything up at Elner's house, Ruby scurried across the lawn to her house and saw Merle across the street and called out to him. "Merle! Elner's not dead, call Verbena and let her know."

Merle stood there, not quite sure he had heard. "What?"

"She pulled through, pass it on!" Ruby yelled as she ran in her front door.

Merle hurried into the house as fast as he could and immediately called his wife down at the cleaners.

When she picked up, he was almost breathless. "Guess what?" he said. "Ruby just got a call from the hospital and Elner's not dead after all."

"What?"

"She didn't die."

"Merle," Verbena said, making a face, "don't be telling me crazy stuff like this, I've got two customers standing here wanting their dry cleaning."

"Verbena, I swear, I'm telling you the truth," he said, holding his right hand up in the air. "She's alive."

"Are you joking?"

"No. They said she was talking and everything."

Verbena looked over the counter at her customers and exclaimed, "Elner didn't die! Thank the Lord. I've just been all torn up about it all morning. Well, God bless her. She pulled through."

As soon as the customers, who had no idea who Elner was, left the cleaners, Verbena was so happy about her friend and neighbor being alive that she jumped up and down in place and shouted hallelujah. It wasn't until the third jump that she remembered what she had done. Oh dear, now she wished she hadn't called the radio station and told Bud that Elner was dead.

⟨⟩

Across town, Neva picked up the phone down at the mortuary.

"Neva, it's Tot . . . false alarm."

"What?"

"Tell Arvis I'm so sorry, but as it turns out, Elner Shimfissle is not dead after all." And then she hung up. Neva was somewhat confused; still not quite believing what she had just heard, she stood up and walked to the back, stuck her head in the door, and relayed the message anyway.

"Arvis, Tot Whooten just called and said to tell you she was sorry but as it turns out Elner Shimfissle is not dead after all."

He looked up. "What?"

Neva thought about what she had just said. "Wait a minute.

That doesn't sound right, does it? I don't know if Tot meant she was sorry Elner wasn't dead . . . or sorry she told you she was dead, but anyhow, that's what she said."

Arvis said, "Good God, is Tot hitting the bottle?"

"I don't know, but I've got to figure out what to do with all those flower orders."

"She must have flipped out again, calling and telling everybody that Elner Shimfissle was dead. Call Verbena and make sure Tot's not drunk or crazy before you do anything about the flowers."

Neva called Verbena, but the line was busy. She was on the phone with the radio station.

⌒

Bud, the other half of the *Bud and Jay Show*, had not gone home yet and was still at work when he received the second phone call from Verbena. "Bud," she said somewhat sheepishly, "this is Verbena Wheeler over in Elmwood Springs. Listen, uh, cancel what I told you earlier about Elner Shimfissle. It was a mistake, she's not dead after all."

"What?"

"Yes, Bud, she's somehow defied the odds and lived. Praise the Lord."

After Bud hung up, he vowed that was the last time he *ever* reported anything on the show that had not been verified. Now he knew just how CNN and FOX News felt when they jumped the gun on a story. He quickly jotted down a note to give Bill Dollar of the *Dollar Bill and Pattie* afternoon show that was currently on the air. He wanted to get it announced as soon as possible. In a few minutes, after Pattie finished doing the commercial, Bill, just having read the note handed to him, said to his cohost, "Well, Pattie, it looks as if we've had a little miscomputation somewhere down the line. According to Bud, Mrs. Elner Shimfissle of Elmwood Springs has not passed away, as earlier reported this morning on the *Shop and Swap* show, and evidently is very much alive. Sorry about that, folks . . . What was it that Mark Twain said, 'The news of my death has been greatly exaggerated.' Well, it seems like that's the case here." Pattie was laughing and called out to Bud, who was standing in the control room. "Hey, Bud, you kinda jumped the gun on Mrs. Shimfissle, didn't you? I'm sure if she was listening it was news to her. Well, anyhow . . . welcome back to the living, Mrs. Shimfissle!"

By the time the last report was broadcast over the air, Luther Griggs was already out of state and long out of the WDOT listening area, but was still thinking about what an impact Miss Elner had had on his life. True, he had spent six months in the state prison because he had trashed his daddy's and his daddy's new wife's trailer while they had been in Nashville attending a Clint Black concert. He had taken only what was rightfully his: hunting boots, a gun, four Kennedy silver dollars, and a television set that his daddy had kept when he had thrown Luther out the last time. But nevertheless, they called it breaking and entering, and when he had been in jail, Elner had sent him some fig preserves with a note.

"Honey, don't get yourself all tattooed up, that's all I ask."

Luther had wanted the flaming sword with "Jesus Saves" on his shoulder, but didn't get it. He was the only person his age, man or woman, who did not have at least a nose ring or something, but he had not wanted to disappoint Elner. He was sorry about not being able to be there for the funeral. At one time she had picked him to be one of her pallbearers, before she'd changed her mind and decided to have herself cremated instead.

He had been disappointed at the time, because he had entertained so many fantasies about himself walking into the church,
having people whisper, "There's Luther Griggs. She thought the
world of him, you know. He was like a son to her." And things
like that. He thought that maybe after the funeral was over, he
would stand around with the family, maybe right beside Linda,
and shake people's hands. After that he would probably be in-
vited over to the house for food and drinks. He wasn't sure
what all went on at funerals, but he figured as an "official pall-
bearer" he certainly would have to be included in everything.
He had felt important just thinking about it, but now the only
thing that was important was the fact that she was dead, and he
felt all alone in the world again. He now wished he had a picture of her. When he had worked as an exterminator's helper
one summer, he had seen inside a lot of nice houses and noticed
that people had photographs of their families sitting around
everywhere. He sure did not want any pictures of his family, but
now he thought that it would be nice to have one of Miss Elner
in a frame. He could keep it on his dresser.

He planned it all out in his mind as he drove. When he got
back he would ask Mrs. Warren if she had a picture of Miss
Elner that he could borrow, and then he'd take it out to the Wal-
Mart and have them make a copy. He then wished he had a picture of them together. Maybe there was some way the people
out at Wal-Mart could take a picture of him and make one up
of the two of them. Make it look like they were together at the
time. He had seen a lot of nice frames out at Tuesday Morning
right next to the plastic flowers.

A Happier Time

3:38 PM

As Elner lay there being scanned from tip to top, she was bored, and wished she had taken the nurse up on that headphone thing. Just to pass the time, she closed her eyes and let her thoughts slip back to another place, long ago. She thought about the old farm; she could almost see her husband, Will, again, way off in the distance, plowing the fields with his mule, waving at her. She smiled to herself as she recalled the best time of day, when Will finished his work and would come banging into the house calling out for her, "Hey, woman. Where's that good-looking wife of mine?" After he had his bath, they would have a big supper: some kind of meat, fresh vegetables, and a good dessert, and spend the rest of the evening just being together, listening to the radio or reading. Usually in bed by eight-thirty or nine.

Will had originally come from Kentucky. When they first met, he was working his way across the country, trying to get to California, and her daddy had hired him for a few weeks to help out on the farm. Six years earlier, their mother had died, leaving Elner, the eldest girl, to take over the cooking and cleaning and the raising of her two younger sisters. During Will's stay, Elner had prepared all his meals, but he had not said much except "mighty fine victuals" and "thank you, ma'am."

When his two weeks were up, Elner, her father, and her sisters had all been sitting out on the porch when Will walked up and stood in the yard, took his hat off, and said, "Mr. Knott, before I leave, I'd like your permission to speak to your daughter." Henry Knott, a big six-foot-three man, had said, "Sure, son. Go ahead and speak your piece."

Although he was a quiet boy, Elner liked him, and so she was happy he was interested in one of her sisters. She assumed he was probably sweet on Gerta, she was slender and had red hair, or maybe Ida, a dazzling brunette with green eyes who was only sixteen but already had plenty of boys buzzing around. Elner was a tall big-boned girl who had taken after her father's side of the family and had never had a beau, and with her two pretty sisters around certainly never planned on having one. However, that afternoon, little Will Shimfissle, not more than five-foot-five inches tall and one hundred fifteen pounds soaking wet, hat in hand had walked over and stopped directly in front of her. "Elner Jane," he'd said, clearing his throat, "as soon as I can earn enough money to get a place of my own, I intend to come back and ask you to be my wife. What I need to know before I go is, do I stand a chance?"

This unexpected event had taken Elner so by surprise, she had immediately burst into tears, jumped up, and run into the house. Will was totally taken aback and had looked over to Mr. Knott for help. "Sir, was that a yes or a no?" Her father was as baffled as Will and answered, "Well, son, it could mean either one, you never can tell about women, let me go find out." He got up and went inside and knocked on the bedroom door. "Elner, that boy's out there waiting for an answer, you need to tell him something, I don't think he's going to leave till you do."

Then he heard Elner cry even louder. He opened the door and went in and sat on the bed beside her. She looked up at him tearfully. "It was just such a surprise, I don't know what to say."

He took her hand and patted it. "Well, I guess it comes down to this, you have to decide. Do you want that little bitty thing for a husband or not?"

She looked up with tears running down her face. "I think I do, Daddy," she said, and burst into tears again.

"You do?" Now he was surprised. He had not seen this coming at all. He hated the thought of losing Elner but said, "Well, honey, he's not big enough to make much of a husband, but he's a hard worker, I'll say that for him, so if you want him, go on out there and tell him."

"I can't. You tell him."

He said, "Well, daughter, it would mean a lot more coming from you, but all right." He stood up and walked out onto the porch, shook his head in amazement, and said, "I don't understand it, boy, but you got yourself a yes." Both the girls screamed, jumped up, and ran inside to find Elner, giggling and excited. Will beamed from ear to ear and walked up and shook Mr. Knott's hand. "Thank you, sir, thank you," he said. "You tell her I'll be back as soon as I can."

"I will." Then Mr. Knott put his hand on Will's shoulder, pulled him aside so the others couldn't hear, and said quietly, "You know you got the best of the lot, don't you, son?"

Will looked him straight in the eye and answered, "Yes sir, I do."

True to his word, Will came back a year and a half later and bought twenty-five acres about ten miles from her daddy's farm. Elner had never expected to marry, had never dreamed she would be the first sister to get married. But later Will told her he had her picked out from the start. "I knew it the first time I laid eyes on you that you were the one for me. Yes sir." He said, "You are my big strong beautiful woman." They made an odd couple, tall and stocky Elner and little skinny Will, but they had been happy together, and she couldn't wait to see him again.

⌇

Meanwhile, back in Elmwood Springs, poor Verbena Wheeler had been so embarrassed to have to call the radio station back, and now she wished she hadn't walked over and told Cathy at the newspaper office about Elner, but she had. She picked up her Bible and flipped through it looking for help. After finally finding the perfect quote, she dialed Cathy.

"Cathy? Verbena. I want to read you something from Luke 8:52 to 55."

"Oh, Lord," thought Cathy, "not again." But said, "All right."

"Are you listening?"

"Yes. Go ahead."

"But he said, 'Do not weep; for she is not dead but sleeping.' And they laughed at him, knowing that she was dead. But he took her by the hand and called out, 'Child, get up!' Her spirit returned, and she got up at once."

Cathy tried to be patient and waited for her to explain why she had to read it to her, but Verbena was silent.

"Yes, and . . . ?"

"I think you should know that we have a similar situation going on right this very minute. *Elner Shimfissle just got up!*"

She Did What?

3:39 PM

Franklin Pixton, the head of Caraway Hospital administration, was a tall, natty, preppy-looking man of fifty-two. He dressed in a neat suit, striped shirt, and bow tie, and wore horn-rimmed glasses. He was a typical upper-level executive whose main job was to hobnob with the old rich and the new rich and raise money for the hospital, a job he did well. He and his wife belonged to the right clubs, his children attended the right schools, they lived in the right redbrick English Tudor home. He was not about to let some small matter like a patient mistakenly being declared dead put his hospital at risk. After he received the phone call, he told the nurse that he wanted to see all involved personnel in his office in one hour, and gave instructions that they were not to discuss the matter with anyone.

He then hung up and immediately dialed the hospital lawyer, Winston Sprague, a specialist in risk management matters.

"We have a situation," Pixton said.

"What?"

"Patient pronounced dead. Several hours later she started talking."

"Oh shit," said Sprague.

· 186 ·

"Graphic, but correct."

"Who was informed?"

"Just the immediate family, as far as I know."

"OK," said the lawyer, "do not . . . accept responsibility, admit any blame or fault. You can apologize that it happened, yes, but make it vague . . . nothing specific. Do not think or say the word *malpractice*. Give me thirty minutes to get there. I'll meet you downstairs." The young lawyer, who was nicknamed "Preppy Number Two," grabbed his briefcase with the usual waiver inside, threw on his jacket, slicked his hair down in the back, and took a deep breath. He had to go over there and win one for the Gipper. The Gipper in this case was his boss, Preppy Number One. Franklin Pixton. Winston Sprague was most interested in getting into the country club, and Pixton was his ticket in. Sprague was also going to make a million dollars by the time he was thirty, and he didn't care who or what he stepped over to get it. His motto: "Screw the little people." He had lied before, and he would lie again. Ethics were for suckers. He'd gotten over thinking there was right and wrong years ago. As far as he was concerned, there was only winning or losing. But, other than having total disdain for the entire human race and thinking everybody in the world was stupid, he was just your average snide, cynical, smart-ass.

A half hour later the red-haired lawyer walked out of one elevator and Franklin came out of the other one. They walked over to the desk and Franklin inquired, "Where is the next of kin?" The girl pointed to room 607.

Norma was now in a private room, sitting up on the bed, drinking a glass of orange juice, after having fainted again, and was being observed by an emergency room doctor to make sure she was going to be all right.

"Oh, Mrs. Warren," Franklin oozed, "I'm Franklin Pixton, and this is my associate Winston Sprague. We were just called and told of the situation . . . and I came down as soon as I heard. First of all, how are you?"

Norma said, "Well, I'm still so rattled I can hardly think straight. First they told me she was dead and then we find out she's not, one minute I'm heartbroken and then the next I'm overjoyed she's alive, and now I just feel like somebody has thrown me up against a wall."

"I can understand." Franklin nodded.

"My poor daughter's so upset, I'm just surprised my husband didn't have a heart attack. Look at this, my hair is coming out." She showed them a few strands of hair that had indeed fallen out, then turned to the doctor. "Can shock cause your hair to fall out, Doctor? Oh, God, don't tell me that now I'm going to have to wear a wig."

"Mrs. Warren, is there anything, anything at all, we can do? All of us here feel so terrible about this. Naturally all of your aunt's hospital expenses will be voided."

"Oh, that's very sweet of you, Mr. . . . ."

"Pixton."

"Mr. Pixton, but you don't have to do that, we're just so thankful she's alive, surprised but thankful."

"No, Mrs. Warren. I insist, we really want to make it up to you and your family for any . . . uh . . ." He glanced over at Sprague for the correct word.

The lawyer said, "Inconvenience."

"That's right, any inconvenience you might have experienced," he said as the lawyer handed him the paper he had just pulled out of his briefcase.

"But in the meantime, if you could just sign this for us."

"What is it?" asked Norma. "I already signed a lot of things earlier."

"Just a small formality, making sure that down the line you are protected if anything . . . ah . . . if you need something . . . and that we are protected. We feel it's best to take care of it now, so we can get it processed as soon as possible."

"Protected from what?"

Sprague jumped in. "It's really more to assure you that no expenses will be incurred while your aunt is here under our care."

"Oh, I see," said Norma. "I appreciate that, but really, you shouldn't have to pay our bills, it's not your fault this happened."

If anything was music to somebody's ears, to Sprague and Pixton, Norma's last statement, "It's not your fault," was an entire concerto by Beethoven.

Norma continued, "If anything, we should apologize to you. I feel so bad about that little nurse. I think she was scared half out of her wits. I hope she's all right. They say she hasn't come back yet."

"I'm sure she's fine, Mrs. Warren."

"I hope so. I'm sorry I got so upset and fainted twice, but you have to understand, you may be used to this happening all the time, but I'm not."

They both nodded sympathetically. "No need to apologize to us, Mrs. Warren. The only thing you can do for us is to sign the paper so we can get everything in motion."

Norma still seemed reluctant. "Maybe I should ask my husband. I don't think he would want you to pay for anything. It's probably going to be a big bill."

The lawyer jumped in. "Don't you worry about it, we have insurance that covers this kind of thing."

Franklin added: "Very common, happens all the time . . ."

The lawyer Sprague nodded. "Very common."

"Well, all right," said Norma. "I still think I shouldn't, but if you insist."

"Oh, we do, it's the least we can do."

"The least we can do," echoed the lawyer.

As Norma signed the paper, it was all they could do not to jump up in the air and give each other a high five, but they remained cool. She had not read the clause stating that she waived her right to hold the hospital responsible.

Mr. Pixton pulled out his card and wrote a number on it. "Here is my office number and my home number, and promise me, if you or your family need anything, anything at all, you call me."

"And here's mine," said the lawyer. "I'm available twenty-four hours a day." After they left the room, Norma turned to the doctor and said, "Wasn't that nice of them, to do that?"

The doctor wanted to say something, but didn't.

As both men stood waiting for their elevator, Franklin said quietly, "We just dodged a big fat bullet."

Later, back at his office, Winston Sprague felt not even the slightest twinge of guilt. He had an obligation to protect the hospital before that slimy shyster, slip and sue, ambulance-chasing lawyer Gus Shimmer found out and showed up and got ahold of the Warren woman. Somebody inside the hospital had been supplying him with information about every potential malpractice event that took place, and it had cost the hospital millions. Good thing the Warren woman had been so stupid and had not read what she'd signed. She had a legitimate case; it was clearly their fault. But how much should one mistake cost? Was it worth the millions of dollars they would have to pay? It's not like they were trying to kill their patients.

Franklin Pixton went straight back to his office as well. Now that the legal matter was handled with Mrs. Warren, he needed to get to the bottom of the situation ASAP. He pushed his intercom. "Brenda, I want the names of all staff on duty this morning."

One staff member, the young nurse who an hour earlier had run out of Elner's room screaming at the top of her lungs, had just been picked up by her mother at a 7-Eleven about two miles from the hospital. As they drove home her mother asked her again.

"Are you sure you don't want me to take you back to work?"

"I told you, I'm never going back there. I quit."

"You can't just quit."

"Yes, I can too."

"Are you going to let all your nurse's training go to waste over this one little incident?"

"When dead people sit up and start talking, you bet I am."

"What will you do?"

"I'm doing nails, like I wanted to in the first place."

The mother sighed. "Well, it's your life, I guess."

After the MRI

4:30 PM

A bit later that afternoon, after Elner's MRI and CAT scan, they wheeled her up to intensive care and plugged her back up to all the machines again. By this time Norma was back in the waiting room with the rest of them, wondering what was going on. Macky was getting very impatient. He finally walked over to the desk and asked the girl where Elner was, and why they weren't coming out and telling them anything. The girl made a phone call and then said, "She's back up in intensive care, that's all the information I have."

"Where is intensive care?"

"That's on seven, but you have to wait."

Macky did not wait. He walked over to the others and said, "Come on, this is ridiculous, we are going to see her right now." Susie stayed behind in case the doctor came out. When they reached the seventh floor Macky said to Norma and Linda, "Wait here and let me go in first, then I'll come back and get you." Macky passed by several rooms before he found her room, and just as he was about to go in, a male nurse was just walking out. When he saw Macky standing there, he asked somewhat indignantly, "Just where do you think you're going?"

"I'm going in to see my aunt," said Macky.

"Oh no, you're not!" the nurse said, closing the door behind him. "Can't you read? The sign says no visitors."

"Oh, I can read, but I'm going to see my aunt."

"Oh no, you're not!" he said again, putting his hands on his hips and almost stomping his foot.

Macky looked at him and said calmly, "Now, buddy, if you want to try and stop me, that's your business, but make no mistake, I am going in."

The nurse sized up the man standing in front of him. He was older and not as tall as he was, but there was something about the look in Macky's eye that caused the nurse to suddenly step aside and let him go in. He sensed that this man was not someone he wanted to tangle with.

Macky walked into the room and went over to the bed; when Elner looked up and saw who it was, she was glad to see him. "Hey, Macky!" she said, trying to reach for his hand.

"Hey, yourself," he said, looking at her with a smile. "How you doing, old gal?"

She laughed. "I'm all hooked up."

"I can see that," he said.

"This is a fine mess, isn't it? How did Linda get here so fast? What time is it anyway? I'm all turned around, I hope I didn't make you miss work."

"Don't worry about it. How do you feel?"

"Oh, fine, except these wasp bites are starting to itch. Are Norma and Linda still here?"

"They're right outside, waiting to see you."

"Macky," she said, looking up at him. "I sure am sorry I fell out of that tree. Is Norma real mad?"

"Nooo, not at all, she's just glad you are OK. Do you need anything?"

"I need somebody to go over and give Sonny his breakfast and feed my birds; make sure my oven is off."

"All that's been taken care of. Ruby and Tot already did it."

"They did? That's a relief. By the way, where am I?"

"You're at the Caraway Hospital in Kansas City."

"That's what I figured, but how did I get here?"

"The ambulance picked you up and brought you."

"An ambulance? I don't remember being in an ambulance."

"You were knocked out."

"I was?"

"Out cold."

"Did they have the siren going?"

"Sure did."

"Well, shoot, I had a ride in an ambulance and I missed the whole thing."

"Are you up to seeing Norma and Linda? They're having a fit to see you."

"Oh, sure . . . And Macky, find out what they did with my robe, will you?"

When Norma and Linda walked into the room, they went over and kissed her, and Aunt Elner said to Linda, "I'm sorry you had to make the trip for nothing."

"Don't be silly, I'm just so glad you are all right, we thought you were dead."

"I thought I was too," she said. "When I woke up alive, I was as surprised as anybody."

"Well, I doubt that," said Norma.

It was around five-thirty by the time the doctor finally had all the results of the tests and came to find Norma and Macky. When they came out into the hall, he explained that so far all they had found were the wasp stings and a few bruises, but everything else looked good. Then Macky asked him, "What the hell happened earlier? Was she in some sort of a coma and just snapped out of it?"

"I really can't say what happened."

"Why did you think she was dead?"

"Mr. Warren, all our indications said that she was dead."

"Well, maybe you should check your indications then, because something was off."

The doctor shook his head. "Mr. Warren, we just don't know what went wrong yet, but I promise you, we'll get to the bottom of it, and as soon as we know, I'll let you know."

Norma saw that the doctor seemed genuinely upset and looked absolutely exhausted, and she said, "We're just happy she's all right now, and her hip's not broken."

"No, no broken bones, but we do need to keep her for a few days and do a few more tests just to make sure she's OK."

Norma said, "Whatever you think, Doctor."

As the doctor walked away, Norma said, "I hope he doesn't get into any trouble."

A few minutes later, when Dr. Henson came into Franklin Pixton's office, he was visibly shaken.

Franklin asked, "What is her present condition?"

"Stable, vital signs all normal, MRI, CAT scan both normal."

"What happened?"

"She flatlined. . . . I tried everything."

Franklin held up his hand to stop him, and pushed the intercom. "Order another complete check on all the OR machines immediately." He then sat back. "All right, Bob, go on."

"She came in on a Code Three and by the time I got to her, she was gone. But we did everything. . . . What can I say?"

"You know there will be an inquiry. I'm going to have to drug test you."

"Yes, I know."

"Are you OK?"

The doctor nodded. "Yes, I'm just tired, but that's no excuse. I take full responsibility, but I just don't understand how I could have been so wrong. I've gone over and over—"

"Where is she now?"

"We're keeping her in intensive, and I've called in a neurologist to do a cognitive exam first thing in the morning."

After the doctor left his office, Franklin was surprised that something like this had not happened sooner. The doctors working down in ER were exhausted, surviving week after week on two to three hours' sleep, working under pressure, having to make life-and-death decisions. It was almost inhuman to expect a person to go through that. Franklin understood about being tired. Everybody was tired. He himself had been exhausted for years. It seemed that all he did was careen from one catastrophe to another. If it wasn't one damn thing, it was another: appease this one, meet with this or that group, who were bellyaching about something, threatening to walk out on strike. The entire hospital was always on the verge of some disaster.

In the past ten years, operating expenses had shot through the roof. With all the criminals and dope fiends in and out of the hospital, they were now forced to spend a fortune on security

guards, then last year they had to fire seven security guards for
stealing painkillers. The linen supply company had upped their
prices, the garbage pickup service they used went on strike, their
computer system had to be completely updated when some
hackers got into the system and gained access to all their patients' reports.

Caraway Hospital was an institution originally set up to
help people, but now everything seemed intent on making it almost impossible. The insurance companies, the unions, the
shyster lawyers; if they could manage to get a patient in and out
of the hospital these days without getting sued or robbed, it was
an accomplishment. Their emergency room was jammed with
people who were now using it as their own personal clinic. Forget the hospital getting paid for their services; most patients did
not have insurance, and for the ones who did, it took months
and years to get full payment, and all the while his payroll had
to be met. The people who could afford to pay wound up pay-
ing a small fortune for what most everybody else got for free. Of
course, there were people who really could not pay. He understood that, but it was the others, the ones looking for any excuse to sue, the ones who believed they shouldn't have to pay,
that medical care was owed to them. Never mind that they were
costing the system millions and forcing him to lay perfectly
good workers off, leaving others underpaid and overworked.

He was vehemently opposed to the somewhat gleeful practice of the public and the government soaking the rich. Most of
the rich people he knew, including himself, worked very hard
for their money and were responsible for almost all the hospital's larger donations. It was the generosity of the rich that kept
it going. He did not think the rich owed everybody else a free
ride; and yet, that very thing was happening at Caraway. Everybody wanted a free ride, including a lot of his staff, and if the

hospital was to survive, things had to change soon or he did not hold out much hope. He worried about both the rich and the poor, about what would happen to them when the hospital was forced to close its doors for good.

Brenda buzzed him. "Your wife on three." He closed his eyes for five seconds. He knew she was calling about the Have a Heart Charity Ball tonight. He picked up and listened to her problems about the centerpieces not being the right color.

"Yes, dear," he said. "Yes, dear, I agree, that's terrible."

At that very moment a phone call was made on the q.t. from the hospital cafeteria to the lawyer Gus Shimmer.

"Gus?"

"Yeah."

"It's me."

"What do you have for me?"

"Patient. Mrs. Shimfissle, closest relative, Mrs. Norma Warren."

"Yeah?"

"Mistakenly pronounced dead, left for five hours."

"You're kidding?"

"No, I saw the file."

"Have they signed anything yet?"

"Yes . . . the two happiness boys got to her right away."

"That's OK. This could be big. Really big. Telling you somebody's dead is one hell of a misdiagnosis."

"I thought so."

"If it goes, you're in for twenty percent this time. OK?"

"Plus my usual finder's fee."

"Of course," he said, thinking but not saying, "You greedy little bastard."

But when the two-hundred-and-eighty-pound lawyer hung up, he was ecstatic. This could be a really good case. He was not worried that the family had already signed the usual no-responsibility waivers. There was not a waiver, an irrevocable trust fund, a prenuptial agreement, a contract, verbal or written, that he could not get somebody out of, or around. Caraway Hospital was his big fat personal gold mine, just waiting to be mined over and over again. He calculated that after he paid off the nurse and maybe threw a little dough at the clients, by the time he got through, he would make plenty. Of course his wife, Selma, hated it whenever he took on another lawsuit against a hospital. She said, "Gus, you keep suing these hospitals for every little thing. God forbid if I should ever wind up in the emergency room, and they find out who I'm married to, they will be afraid to touch me."

A Doctor's Dilemma

At around five that afternoon, Reverend Susie Hill, who was still a little shaken up from the ordeal of having seen a woman she thought was dead fly by her and wave at her, left the hospital, and Norma, Macky, and Linda stayed with Elner until visiting hours were over. They decided Linda would go home with Norma and Macky that night, and they would all try to get a good night's sleep and come back in the morning. If Aunt Elner was still doing as well as she was tonight, Macky would drive Linda to the airport so she could get back to work tomorrow.

Downstairs, Dr. Bob Henson had just handed his urine sample over to the guy working in the lab, and walked out the door. He had started out in medicine the same way most had: young, full of ambition, fueled with the desire to help mankind, to save lives, make a difference. Now he was thirty-two, a little jaded, but mostly exhausted and pretty fed up with the stupidity of the mostly flotsam and jetsam array of humans that came in and out of the emergency room, day and night. The sheer futility of spending hours digging bullets out of young men, sewing up

knife wounds, dealing with drug overdoses, drunks, insane people, beaten-up prostitutes, suicide attempts, treating the same
ones over and over again for the same thing, had made him
quick-tempered and irritable. Having to constantly deal with
the screaming mothers of dead sons shot down in the streets
over some gang rivalry, having to tell nice middle-class parents
that their children were dead because they had been driving
doped up or drunk, or had been hit by someone who was. In
only two years of ER his opinion of the human race had plum-
meted.

He was beginning to believe that a lot of people were just
taking up space, wasting the time of doctors, draining the hospital's resources, using up time and energy and money that
could be used elsewhere. When he confided his feelings to a fellow ER physician, the guy had said, "Jesus, Bob, what an attitude, you better get some help." But he hadn't. He hadn't had
time; with his life at the hospital, where he spent long hours either in ER or in his grubby, messy little office, doing endless paperwork, or trying to grab a few minutes of sleep on the lumpy
futon, he barely had time to brush his teeth.

And home was no better. He had married a girl a few years
older than he was who had been intent on getting pregnant as
soon as possible. He had wanted to wait but she had been determined, and now, thanks to all the new fertility methods, he had
two small children, one three, the other two, and now according to the sonogram she'd had last week there were twins on the
way. Home was already a too-small house, with two screaming
kids under the age of three, and a wife who was also so tired
and busy she hardly had time for herself, much less for him. Between work and home he couldn't remember when he had had
more than thirty minutes of uninterrupted sleep, much less a
good meal. He ate on the run, drank coffee and Mountain Dew,

and ate energy bars to keep himself going. Was it any wonder he'd made a mistake? Maybe if he hadn't been so tired he might have paid more attention, not been quite so quick to give up. But doctors are not allowed to make bad judgment calls, make mistakes. He had hoped it had not been his mistake.

He sat waiting after the incident while they had brought in technicians to check and recheck the machines, but when the two men came out and reported that they were in perfect working order, he felt his life and career going down the tube. Why had it happened? Granted, he was exhausted, but he had been tired before. Could it have been the fact that the patient was so old? Could he have somehow unconsciously, for the slightest second, thought that her death was not as important as a younger patient's? There was always a somewhat higher sense of urgency if the patient was young, a little more of an effort. But why? Who was he to judge how important a life was, and yet he may have done that and almost killed a patient because of it. Just the slightest turn of events, the fact that he had agreed to wait a few hours for the Warrens' daughter to arrive, had saved her life. If they hadn't waited, Mrs. Shimfissle might have wound up shoved into a drawer down in the morgue, or worse yet, somebody could have started an autopsy. Even if he didn't lose his job, he could never forgive himself. As far as he was concerned his career was over, no matter what the machines said. He should have tried harder, worked on her longer, not given up so soon. All the years of sacrifice, all the years of study, working, all for nothing.

After he had changed from his scrubs and before he left for the night, Dr. Henson walked down to Elner's room.

"Hey, Mrs. Shimfissle. How are you doing?"

"Just fine, thank you, and how are you?"

It was clear she did not know who he was, and he explained, "Mrs. Shimfissle, I'm the doctor who was in charge of ER when you came in this morning."

"Oh, I didn't recognize you without your shower hat."

"May I sit down?"

"Sure."

He struggled to find the right words. "Mrs. Shimfissle, I just think you should know that I'm the one who pronounced you dead, and I want you to know that I am so sorry."

"Well, don't be sorry on my account," Elner said. "It scared my niece and them a little, but I'm certainly none the worse for wear."

"No, you don't understand, it was my fault. You could have died because of me."

She looked at him. "But I didn't. Look, I'm fit as a fiddle and guess what, I don't need my hearing aid anymore. When I woke up, I could hear as plain as day. What do you think about that?"

"That's great, but I wanted you to know that I'm thinking about leaving medicine."

"Why?"

"Because . . . I almost killed you," he said, fighting back the tears.

"Oh now, listen here, you didn't have a thing to do with it. Besides, everything that happens, happens for a reason. So don't you be talking about leaving medicine, that's just silly."

"I may be forced to, Mrs. Shimfissle, your niece is probably going to sue me and the hospital, and at this point I wouldn't blame her."

Elner looked at him, surprised. "Norma? Why, Norma Warren is the sweetest girl in the world, she's not going to sue anybody, for heaven's sake, you just get that out of your mind right now."

After the doctor left, the nurse came into Elner's room to give her a pill. "You get some good sleep now, Mrs. Shimfissle," she said. "I'll be right outside if you need anything . . . just push your call button."

"All right. Hey, where is my call button, anyway? In case I do want to call somebody."

"It's right here on the side of your bed, just push this little white button and your room number lights up down at the nurses' station."

"Well, good night." After the nurse left, Elner picked up her call button and looked at it. She liked the idea of having a call button. It pleased her no end. She thought it was almost like having one of those beeper things they advertised on television, on that "Help, help, I've fallen and I can't get up" commercial. Then an old song popped into her head and she lay there singing, "When I'm calling you ooh ooh oh ooo, Will you answer too oh oh ohooo," and then she drifted off to sleep. She was tired. It had been a big day, and she had been looked at, poked at, and stuck with needles up until an hour ago.

Driving back home that night, Macky said, "When I was in the room with her before, I could have sworn she was dead, and then when we went in and she started talking, it scared the hell out of me."

Linda said, "Scared me so bad, I almost wet my pants."

"This has certainly been a day, hasn't it?" said Norma. "Do you believe what all we have been through in the last twelve hours? I fainted twice, and that poor little nurse, I've never heard anybody scream like that in my life."

Linda suddenly started laughing. "You should have seen Susie Hill's face when she saw Aunt Elner roll by. Her eyes almost popped out of her head, she jumped back, and went whooooo!!" Then, more out of relief than anything else, all three of them started to laugh uncontrollably until tears rolled down their faces. By the time they reached the house, they were exhausted. Norma said, "I don't think I've cried and laughed so much in one day in all my life!"

As Norma drifted off to sleep that night, she thought at least one good thing had come out of such a disaster. When the orderly had handed her a white plastic bag containing Aunt Elner's personal effects, Norma had quietly walked over and thrown it in the large garbage bag by the door.

She had finally been able to get rid of that hideous brown plaid robe once and for all!

The Quiz

Dr. Brian Lang had been called at home the night before and asked to examine a patient first thing in the morning. As he read over the chart they had e-mailed him, he was amazed at the fact that the patient had managed to survive a fall like that. Her CAT scan showed absolutely no signs of anything, all her vitals were good, but he was being brought in as a safety measure, to check on any short-term or long-term memory loss before they released her. He was an expert on brain injuries and had his own set of questions, which were set up to catch even the slightest damage they may have missed.

When he walked into her room early that Tuesday, he said, "Good morning, Mrs. Shimfissle, I'm Dr. Lang." She looked up and said, "Good morning," then added with caution, "You're not here to take me someplace for another test, are you?"

"Oh no, Mrs. Shimfissle," he said as he pulled a chair to the side of her bed. "I just want us to have a little chat right here, if that's all right with you."

"Sure, I'd love to chat with you as long as you're not going to stick me with something. Have a seat. I'd offer you something to drink, but I can't find my call button. They'll bring me anything I ask for."

"No, I'm fine," he said as he sat down and got out his papers.

"Look at this," she said, pushing the control on her bed and starting to sit straight up. "Isn't that something?"

"Yes, it is. Now, Mrs. Shimfissle, have you experienced any headaches in the past twenty-four hours?"

"No, not a one," she said, letting herself back down again. "It's a good thing I don't have a bed like this at home or I'd never get up."

"And how is your vision . . . any spots, fuzziness, or changes in vision?"

"Nope. Like I told my eye man, I can see fine, all the way to the moon and back."

He could see for himself that her eyes were bright and clear, that was good.

"Mrs. Shimfissle, can you tell me what today is?"

She looked at him strangely. "Well, honey, don't *you* know?"

"Oh yes I know, but these are just questions I need to . . ."

He stopped talking, because he could see she was not listening and was now preoccupied with something underneath her covers. "Oh, here it is," she said, pulling out her call button. "I was laying on it. What was it that you wanted to chat about?"

"Well, it's not a chat in the pure sense of the word, I'm really here to ask you a few questions."

She perked up. "Oh, is it a quiz?"

"Sort of, I suppose."

"Oh, good. Fire away. But don't make it too hard."

"No, I'll try not to. OK. Let's start over. What day is it today?"

She looked at him. "Ahh . . . this is a trick question, I'll bet. It's somebody's birthday? I know it's not Thomas Edison's, or George Washington's. . . . Oh, shoot, I don't know. I give up. What is today?"

"I'm just looking for the day of the week."

"Ohhh," she said. "That's easy. I thought you were looking for something harder than that, it's Tuesday."

"Could you tell me what month it is?"

"It's April the second; I would tell you what time it was, but I don't have my watch."

"I see. Your full name?"

"Elner Jane Shimfissle."

"Maiden name?"

"Same first name. Last name, Knott."

"Your mother's maiden name?"

"Nuckle, and she married a man named Knott, so her full name was Mrs. Nancy Nuckle Knott. You try saying that five times in a row."

"Mrs. Shimfissle, what is the first major event you can re-call?"

"Well, when I was three, a duck pecked me on my big toe. . . . Wait a minute. Are you talking about family or non-family events?"

"Historical events."

"Ahh, let's see. Pearl Harbor, December seventh, 1941. Thomas Edison, born February eleventh, 1847; died . . . October eighteenth, 1931. FDR died 1945. Then the opening of Disneyland, July seventeenth, 1955. Do you want more?"

"No, just the last important date you remember."

"September eleventh, 2001. That's one I would like to forget."

"Your birth date."

"July twenty-eighth."

"How old were you on your last birthday?"

"I don't know."

"Do you know the year you were born?"

"No, I sure don't. I'm sorry."

The doctor looked up. "You can't remember the year?"

"No, I was too little to remember the exact year, and my sister Ida buried the family Bible, so I have no idea."

He glanced down at his chart. "Your niece put down eighty-nine."

"Oh, that was just a guess, sometimes she puts me older, sometimes younger. It all depends on her mood. How old are you?"

"Thirty-four."

"I have a niece that's thirty-four. Are you married?"

"No, but Mrs. Shimfissle, I have a few more questions. . . ."

"She's not married either, and she has a Chinese daughter. Got her in China. What do you think about that?"

"That's just great. Now—"

"Her name is Linda. Linda Warren. She lives in St. Louis and has a good job too. With the telephone company, just like Mary Grace. You can't beat the telephone company for benefits."

"I'm sure," he said. "Can you recall what you were doing right before your fall?"

"Picking figs. Her daughter's name is Apple. Of course, Norma hated that name. She said, 'Why would you want to name your daughter after a computer?' But Linda said it was after the fruit not the computer. . . . What is this quiz for, anyway?"

"Just checking for any signs of short- or long-term memory loss."

"Ahh, well that makes sense. Trying to see if I still have my wits about me."

"That's right."

"Well . . . did I pass?"

He smiled and closed the chart. "Yes, you did. With flying colors, I might add."

"Hey, listen, are you going to be around in another few hours?"

He looked at his watch. "Yes. I should still be here. Why?"

"I want you to come back and see me, OK?"

"I'll try."

As he left, he had to laugh. The old lady was as sharp as a tack. Hell, he didn't remember half the dates she did. But then, how many people *would* remember Thomas Edison's birth date?

Where's Elner?

8:30 AM

Back in Elmwood Springs, the phone lines had been buzzing all morning with the news and latest reports about Elner. Out on the farm Elner's good friend Louise Franks had been up all night worried and wondering how she was going to tell Polly, her retarded daughter, about Elner. Polly didn't understand about death. How could she explain that Polly would never see Elner again? Louise burst into tears when Irene Goodnight called her and told her that Elner was alive. Tot and Ruby had been so busy answering questions and calling people that they totally forgot about feeding the cat, feeding the birds, or filling the birdbath, and Sonny the cat was not happy. He had just walked over to his dish and discovered that it was empty. This was a shock to him. His breakfast was always there at this time. He hunched down and stared at the dish for a while, then got up and wandered around the house. Then he came back to his dish and sat there thinking cat thoughts, wondering whether or not to take a nap or try to catch one of those birds that were flying all over the yard, also upset and wondering where their birdseed was. One old blue jay was squawking his head off, and three smaller birds sat in the birdbath looking for water to splash around in. Two squirrels sat in a tree nattering at each other. The old lady had always thrown a couple of biscuits out the back door for them by now. Something was not right. After a few minutes of debating the issue, Sonny opted to take a nap and went to his spot on the back of the sofa.

Meanwhile a red-eyed Luther Griggs was just pulling into a Flying J truck stop outside of Yuma, Arizona, and he had never felt so alone in his entire life. As he climbed into the back of the truck to get some shut-eye, he thought about what Elner had told him over and over. "Honey, you need to get married. I'm not going to live forever, and I want to think that you won't be left all by yourself. As much as you don't think it, you need to be with somebody. Women can handle it, but men don't do well alone." He had not wanted to get married, and as much as she'd said it, he never thought she would really die. But now that she had, he saw that she was right. He was so lonesome, and if Elner had liked Bobbie Jo Newberry, he figured she was the one. Miss Elner had always known what was right for him, so why fool around? And so before he drifted off, he made up his mind; when he got home, he'd go on over to the Dairy Queen where she worked and pop the question.

The Arrangements

By the time the Warrens arrived back at the hospital the next morning, Elner's room was filled with flowers. All the arrangements that had been ordered yesterday to be sent to the funeral home had been rerouted to her hospital room instead. Unfortunately, Neva down at the Rest Assured Funeral Home had not had time to change the cards, and most were still signed "With deepest sympathy" or "Our thoughts and our prayers are with you." And the flowers from Elner's friend Louise Franks said "Gone but not forgotten."

When the Warrens walked into her room, she was sitting up in bed and happy to see them. "Look at all my flowers!" she said. "It looks like a funeral parlor in here, doesn't it?" Then she laughed. "I never knew I was so popular till everybody thought I had croaked." She then pointed to a large arrangement of orange gladiolus. "That's from Bud and Jay, wasn't that nice, those others are from the Missouri Power and Light Company. Beverly Cortwright sent me those white roses, you know that set her back a pretty penny."

"Wow, Aunt Elner," said Linda, "I've never seen so many flowers in my life."

"I know! We had to put some in the bathroom. I feel kinda guilty people spent all this money on a false pretense. Merle and Verbena sent me an azalea that I can plant, but the rest of them are just money wasted." She turned to Norma and said, "Norma, promise me that next time you will tell everybody, no flowers. They shouldn't have to send them twice."

After a while Dr. Brian Lang, true to his promise, stopped back by and knocked lightly on the door. "Hello."

When Elner saw him, she waved. "Hey. Come on in, I want you to meet everybody. This is my head doctor . . . he examined my head."

He walked in and said, "Hello, I'm Dr. Lang."

Elner said, "This is my niece Linda I was telling you about, the one with the Chinese baby. This is my niece Norma, and her husband, Macky."

They all said hello and shook hands. Dr. Lang quickly glanced at Linda again, and then said, "Mrs. Warren, may I speak to you for a moment?"

"Oh, of course."

When they walked outside the door, he said, "Mrs. Warren, I just wanted to let you know, all her tests show that there was no brain damage, or long-term or short-term memory loss."

"Oh, well, that is a relief," said Norma. "She was out for a long time, and I was worried it might have done something."

"No, she's perfectly fine. Her conversation is slightly disjointed, but that is entirely consistent with someone her age, so I wouldn't be concerned about that."

Norma said, "Oh, I'm not, Doctor, her conversation was always slightly disjointed, long before this."

When they went back inside, Dr. Lang walked over to Elner.

"I have to take off now, but I wanted to say good-bye before I left."

"I'm so glad you did. I wanted you to meet Linda."

The doctor then looked at Linda. "So your aunt tells me you live in St. Louis, is that right?"

"Yes," she said.

"I see." Then he turned back to Elner. "Well, good luck, Mrs. Shimfissle. Don't be falling out of any more trees, OK?"

Elner laughed. "No, I won't. I have a feeling my fig picking days are over."

After the Warrens visited for a while, they concluded that Elner was doing well enough for Linda to go back home, and Macky and Linda left for the airport.

The second they walked out the door, Elner suddenly became very excited and said to Norma, "Lock the door, Norma. Hurry before the nurse comes back, I've just been wanting to get you alone, I've got something to tell you. Hurry up."

Norma walked over and locked the door and then came closer to the bed. "What is it?"

Elner said, "I know you're mad at me for falling off the ladder, but when you hear what I have to tell you, you'll be so glad I did, you'll thank me."

"What do you mean?"

"Well, you know the old saying 'I felt like I just died and went to heaven'?"

"Yes?"

"Well . . . I really did!"

"Did what?"

"*Died and went to heaven!* I wanted you to be the first to know. Aren't you happy? And oh, Norma," Elner said, with her eyes shining, "I just wish you could have been with me to see how wonderful it all is! I know how you worry about your health and dying, but now you won't have to be scared ever again, because people don't ever stop, we just go on and on forever. . . . Isn't that just the best news?"

Norma said, "Well, yes, honey, we all hope that's true, but—"

Elner interrupted her. "Oh, it is! And you'll never guess in a million years who I saw."

"Who?"

"Your mother!"

"*My mother?*"

"And guess what else? She knows Tot did her hair."

Now Norma was alarmed. "*What?*"

"Yes, but don't worry about it, I smoothed it over, and after that I had a nice visit with Neighbor Dorothy and Raymond. You remember Neighbor Dorothy?"

Norma, who at this point was totally confused by the conversation, said, "Of course I remember Neighbor Dorothy . . . but I don't understand what you are talking about. . . . Who's Raymond?"

"Dorothy's husband."

When Elner said that, Norma realized what was going on and said, "Oh, Aunt Elner, you must have been having some sort of dream, honey. Don't you remember, Neighbor Dorothy's husband was named Robert."

Elner said, "Well, I can't help that he looks like her first husband, but she's married to Raymond now, and it was no *dream,* Norma. Dorothy was as alive as you and I are right now. And I saw Ginger Rogers and Princess Mary Margaret, Dorothy's old cocker spaniel. There are dogs and cats up there too. Isn't that good news? And, oh, I had a nice visit with Ernest Koonitz, and Thomas Edison stopped in to say hello."

Norma sank down in the chair. "Oh dear God," thought Norma as an excited Elner continued, telling her in great detail everything that had happened from the moment she got onto the elevator until she floated up off the porch and over to the hospital and woke up back in her room. When Elner finished, she looked at Norma with a big smile and exclaimed, "So, what do you think about that? I was dead down here, but still going up there!"

Norma sat there in a daze, not really sure what to say, and just stared at Elner with a pained little expression for a moment. Then Norma asked, "Aunt Elner . . . are you *sure* you were really dead?"

"How should I know, honey? I'm not a medical expert, I'm just a person, all I know is what I saw, and who I talked to, and imagine, Tom Edison came to see me! He is the nicest man, so humble."

"Oh my God," Norma thought again. The doctor had been totally wrong. Aunt Elner's brain *had* been damaged. The poor thing really believed she had been to heaven and talked to dead people. Norma knew this was a serious situation with untold consequences and that she would have to tread lightly, so she reached over and took Elner's hand and asked sweetly, "Aunt Elner, have you told anybody else about your . . . visit?"

"No, not yet, I wanted you to be the first to know."

Norma forced a small smile. "And I'm so glad, but, sweetheart, I really think it would be best if you didn't mention this to anyone else, OK?"

Elner was taken aback. "Why?"

"Well, just promise me that this will be our little secret. All right? Will you do that for me?"

"But why? Shouldn't everybody know? I have a few messages I was supposed to deliver."

"Aunt Elner . . . Please, if you love me, just promise me that you won't tell anybody about seeing polka-dotted squirrels or Thomas Edison or any of the rest, OK?"

"But why? I don't understand."

Norma was firm. "Just trust me, Aunt Elner, I have my reasons."

Elner was disappointed. "All right, Norma, I promise but—"

At that moment the nurse knocked loudly on the door. "Mrs. Warren, you have a phone call at the desk."

Norma, still somewhat addled, went outside and picked up the phone. It was Louise Franks.

"How is Elner? Is she all right?"

Norma said, "Oh, Louise, she's doing just fine. They did a lot of tests and everything looks good, no broken bones, just a few bruises and wasp stings, but other than that she's OK."

A much relieved Louise said, "Well, thank the Lord. I've been worried to death."

"Well, don't worry, everything else seems to be fine," she lied again. "I'll tell her you called, Louise."

"Oh, please do, and tell her Polly and I are sending her all our love."

"I will."

"Do you think she'll be home for Easter?"

"I'm not sure, but I'll let you know."

Norma hung up, and thought, "Aunt Elner might be home for Easter, if she keeps her mouth shut and they don't cart her off to the loony bin first."

As Norma turned around she saw a familiar face smiling at her.

"Mrs. Warren?" he said. "I wonder if I might have a word with you."

She did not want to talk to him, but even under stress

Norma was polite. She knew who he was. She had seen his ad on television enough times. Gus Shimmer, the largest lawyer in town, as he liked to call himself. Macky said he was one of those ambulance chasers, but as much as she wanted to get back in the room with Aunt Elner, she sat down with him and let him run through his entire speech, while she kept an eye on the door to Elner's room.

After he finished she said, "I appreciate your concern, Mr. Shimmer, but we're just grateful she is alive, thank you for coming."

Shimmer, not to be put off, said, "Mrs. Warren, I don't think you quite realize what mental and emotional stress this mishap—or as I prefer to call it, this gross case of negligence and malpractice—has placed on you and your family."

"Listen, believe me, I do know, better than anybody. . . . It's going to take a week to write all those thank-you cards for the flowers alone, but really, I don't want to sue anybody. All I know is, that poor doctor certainly didn't do anything on purpose."

"Mrs. Warren," he said, "in a situation like this, purpose is neither here nor there, the fact is that it did happen and in their hospital. To pronounce a patient dead when she is still alive is certainly more than grounds for a lawsuit—a major lawsuit. And if you let me handle this, I can guarantee you that by the time we get through, you might very well own this entire hospital."

Norma looked at him, puzzled. "Why would I want to own a *hospital?*" she asked while still watching the door. "No, I just wouldn't feel right about it."

"How would you feel about twenty-five, or depending on the jury we can get, maybe as high as fifty million dollars? Would that make you feel any better?"

Suddenly Norma did not like the tone of his voice, and turned to him and said, "Mr. Shimmer, I'm not a fool. Who wouldn't like to have that kind of money? But to get it by ruining a doctor's life and costing these people so much. No, I just couldn't do it, not and sleep at night. I'm sorry but you are wasting your time." She stood up to leave.

Shimmer stood up and said, "Maybe I should talk to your husband and explain to him. He might make you understand a little more clearly."

"I do understand, and I am trying to tell you just as politely as I know how, I'm really not interested in suing anybody, and my husband isn't either."

Mr. Shimmer looked over at the door to Elner's room. "Then I suppose I will have to go straight to Mrs. Shimfissle. After all, she is the injured party here."

Norma felt her face flush. "Do what you think you have to, but I can tell you she is not suing anybody, except maybe you, for harassment of an old sick lady. She might even get a restraining order against you, and have you thrown out of the hospital, and I mean that in the nicest possible way."

After Shimmer waddled away in a huff, Norma was glad she had watched so many Perry Mason shows with Aunt Elner, because she had pulled out some legal terms she didn't even know she knew. She hoped she had not hurt Mr. Shimmer's feelings, but some people just force you to be rude. Then it dawned on her, for the first time in her life, she had finally put her foot down about *something*.

A Disturbing Call

9:48 AM

Upstairs in the executive offices, Franklin Pixton had just received a disturbing phone call and had called his lawyer again.

"Gus Shimmer was here. Somebody spotted him talking to Mrs. Warren. Should we be worried?"

Winston Sprague thought a moment, then said, "I guess it wouldn't hurt to get a deposition from the old lady, in case Shimmer tries to make trouble."

"What about Mrs. Warren?"

"Give me an hour, then think of something to get her out of the room for a while. It's better if she's not there."

An hour later Norma, still somewhat thrown for a loop, was trying to act as normal as possible, considering that Aunt Elner was convinced she had died and gone to heaven. Norma and the nurse were busy rearranging the flowers around the room when there was a knock on the door.

"Mrs. Warren?" said an attractive older woman in a gray dress.

"Yes?"

"I'm Brenda Hampton, Mr. Pixton's assistant, and he's wondering if you could come upstairs to the office."

"Oh. Well, I hate to leave my aunt, I just got here."

Unfortunately, Elner piped up. "You go on, Norma, I'm fine." Norma really did not want to go. She was still concerned about Aunt Elner telling someone about her trip, but she couldn't be rude, so she reluctantly went upstairs with the woman.

As soon as Winston Sprague saw Miss Hampton and Mrs. Warren get on the elevator, he and paralegal Kate Packer walked into Elner's room. "Good morning, Mrs. Shimfissle," he said. "How are we today?"

Elner said, "Just fine, thank you, and how are you?"

"Fine. Are they taking good care of you?"

"Oh, yes. I had a good breakfast, right here in bed."

Sprague turned to the nurse and indicated rather rudely that he wanted her out of the room.

After she left, he said, "Mrs. Shimfissle, we need to ask a few questions. It's just boring legal stuff, but we need to get it down on record."

Elner said, "Oh well, if it's legal, maybe we should wait for my niece, she handles all my paperwork."

"No, we really don't need her to be here, and this will only take a minute. Go ahead, Kate," said Sprague, snapping his fingers at her. "This is Miss Packer. She'll be asking the questions."

Miss Packer, an efficient-looking young woman in a blue business suit, came over and sat by the bed.

"Mrs. Shimfissle, do you swear that the facts you are about to state are the truth and nothing but the truth?"

"Oh, sure," said Elner, raising her right hand. Then she

looked at Miss Packer. "Aren't you going to make me swear on the Bible?"

"No, that's not necessary. State your full name, please."

Elner held out her arm. "Look for yourself, here's my name written out on my wristband, only they misspelled Shimfissle."

"Just skip to the questions, Kate," said Sprague, who was standing by the door making sure no one came in.

Miss Packer looked put out. She liked to do things by the book, but she did what he said.

"Could you please state the events of the morning of April first to the best of your recollection?"

"Yes, I can," said Elner. "I woke up, and as usual had my coffee with Macky. After that, I had just finished jotting down the question of the day on the Bud and Jay show. It was 'How tall is the Empire State Building?' So I thought I'd call my niece Dena in California and ask her, she used to live in New York, and she sent me a paperweight with the Empire State Building inside, so I figured she might know. It's not cheating, they say you can phone a friend. The trick is to be the first to call with the right answer, and I was just about to pick up the phone when that nice lady Mrs. Reid from up the street brought me a basket of cherry tomatoes, and I said, 'Oh, won't you come in and sit awhile?' And she said no, that she had to get on back home. Her husband had just had all his teeth pulled and wasn't feeling so well, so she needed to run to the store real fast and pick up some apple sauce, and I said, 'Well, thank you so much—' "

Miss Packer was busy taking down every word, but Sprague was impatient and started cracking his knuckles. "Uh, Mrs. Shimfissle . . . you can skip that part. We really need more about the accident."

Elner said, "Well, I'm getting to that part. So after Mrs. Reid

left, it occurred to me that she might like some fresh fig preserves, and I thought about calling Macky, but I hated to bother
him for a few—"

"Then what happened?" Sprague interrupted her again.

"Then I went out and got up the ladder and I was reaching
for a fig, when all of a sudden here comes a load of wasps right
at me. I remember thinking to myself 'Uh-oh,' and then the next
thing I knew, I looked up and saw people in green shower hats
leaning over me and talking a mile a minute."

"Do you recall what they were saying?" asked Miss Packer.

"No, because I didn't have my hearing aid on, I just knew
they were talking because their lips were moving. Then I wondered where Norma and Macky were, and if she was going to
take my ladder privileges away, and then I took a nap."

Miss Packer looked up. "Yes?"

"And then the next thing I knew, I woke up in a dark room.
I waited for somebody to come get me but they never did, so I
just lay there for a while."

"Did you push your call button for help?" asked Miss
Packer.

"No, at the time I didn't even know I had a call button. If I
had known I had one, I would have pushed it."

"How long did you wait?"

"I don't know. It was dark and I didn't have my watch on,
but it seemed like a long time, and after a while I started to wonder if they might have misplaced me or something so I got up
and went down the hall looking for somebody, but there was
nobody there."

Sprague interrupted again. "Mrs. Shimfissle, are you aware
that the nurses say they never left the nurses' station?"

She looked over at him. "Well, honey, I don't know what to
tell you, because when I came out, there was nobody there."

"Is it possible that you could have somehow slipped by them without them seeing you?" he asked.

"Anything's possible, I guess. But I'm a big heavyset woman, so I would be hard to miss, don't you think? Besides, I was calling out asking if anybody was there. If they didn't see me, they would have heard me."

"What specifically did you call out?" asked Miss Packer.

"I said, 'Yoo hoo, anybody here?' "

"How loudly did you say it?" asked Miss Packer.

"I didn't shout it at the top of my lungs. I didn't want to wake anybody up. But I said it loud enough for somebody to hear me if they had been there."

"Mrs. Shimfissle, is it possible that you were confused and just think you left your room?" asked Sprague, peeping out the crack of the door.

"All I can tell you is what I remember, and I'm under oath." Elner looked at Miss Packer.

"Are you a candy striper?"

"No, ma'am, I'm a paralegal."

"My late husband Will's cousin in Mount Sterling, Kentucky, was a candy striper, worked her way up the ranks until she was running the hospital gift shop. From bedpans to gift shop manager in less than two years, that's pretty good, isn't it?"

"Yes, it is," said Miss Packer.

"Then what happened?" Sprague shot an impatient look at the paralegal.

Miss Packer asked, "What happened next, Mrs. Shimfissle?"

Elner had been hoping Miss Packer wouldn't ask that. She was now in a real dilemma. She had to make a decision whether to lie under oath and break the law, or break her promise to Norma.

And so she decided to apply the "What they don't know won't hurt them rule," and left out the part about visiting with everybody and skipped on to the end and said, "Well, I remember just floating around in the air above the hospital."

Kate looked up from her pad, not quite sure what she had just heard. "Above the hospital?"

"Yes, and I just kind of hovered up there in the air for a few minutes, kind of like a hummingbird."

Kate looked over at Sprague, her eyes wide. "Should I write this down?"

"Keep going," he said, nodding, as Elner continued.

"Then I remember looking down and wondering who lost their shoe up on the roof."

"Could you describe it?" asked Kate.

"Just an ordinary roof, with a ledge around it, and the flat part was gray, with what looked like some sort of gravel and some black tarlike stuff in a few places."

"No, the shoe, Mrs. Shimfissle."

"Oh, it was just a plain old brown leather shoe, lying over in the corner by one of those square chimneys."

"Was it a man's shoe or a woman's shoe?" Kate asked.

"A man's, unless some woman has mighty big feet. Will's other niece, Mary Grace, wore a size nine narrow, they had to special order her shoes all the way from St. Louis. She could be standing in one room with her toes sticking out the other, that's how long they were."

"Anything else?" asked Kate.

"Humm, well, I didn't pay all that much attention, I was too busy wondering what I was doing floating around up in the air, but I do remember the shoe had some kind of spiky things sticking out of the bottom of it. Little nail-like things."

Miss Packer was now fascinated. "Like cleats? Like what you might find on a baseball shoe or a golf shoe?"

"Forget the shoe," Sprague said. "What happened next?"

Miss Packer repeated the question. "What happened next?"

"Right after that, I was back in my room, and Norma and them were standing right beside me, and I thought, 'Norma is going to be mad at me for getting up in that tree,' and I was right, she was. She's like her mother in that respect. She doesn't let go of a thing. Not that I'm saying she isn't right. I should have listened to her. Hey. I just thought of something you might want to write down, honey."

Kate looked up. "Yes?"

"I had a cat that lived to be twenty-five years old."

Later as they walked down the hall, Miss Packer, a rabid *Star Trek* fan, said, "Don't you wonder if she entered another astral plane, and went into another dimension?"

Winston Sprague looked at her as though she were insane. "All I wonder is, was she nuts before she came to the hospital, or after?"

Oh Dear...

11:30 AM

As she left the office, Norma was a little confused. Mr. Pixton was very nice, of course, but she wondered why he had wanted to show her all those blueprints of the new buildings they were going to build in 2012. When she got back down to the room, Aunt Elner was sitting there with the remote in her hand, busy flipping back and forth from channel to channel on the television set up above her head. "Hey, Norma," she said, "I don't think they get cable here. I was hoping they got the Discovery Channel, but I can't find it."

Norma sat with Elner while she ate her lunch, and Elner was as happy as a lark. She had ordered three Jell-Os and two orders of ice cream, and for some unknown reason they had brought it. Nevertheless, Norma watched Elner carefully for signs of anything unusual, but she seemed perfectly normal, chatting away with every Tom, Dick, or Harry who came into the room. Norma was beginning to feel a little better, but just to be on the safe side, when they were alone, she asked, "Aunt Elner, now you're *sure* you didn't tell anybody else about your . . . little trip?"

Elner looked at her. "No, honey," she said. "Just you."

Norma was relieved for a moment, until Elner added, "And those people that just took my deposition."

Norma said, "What? Oh my God. What people?"

"Just some redheaded lawyer and a girl."

"When?"

"Just now, while you were gone," she said, still flipping the channels. "But don't worry, I didn't tell them about seeing your mother or Neighbor Dorothy, I just told them about floating over the hospital roof and seeing the shoe."

Norma cringed. "Oh my God." Norma suddenly was afraid that something like this could hit the papers, and then the entire family could wind up as tabloid fodder. "Oh my God," she thought, "they could be checking for family skeletons right now," and she started to hyperventilate and ran over to the sink and threw cold water in her face.

Elner looked over at her. "Well, Norma, the girl made me swear to tell the truth, the entire truth, and nothing but the truth. You didn't want me to outright lie, did you?"

"Yes! Oh . . . no. Oh Lord."

Norma excused herself and quickly ran up to Franklin Pixton's office, while doing her deep breathing, and asked Miss Hampton if she could see him right away.

As she walked into the room, her knees were shaking. "Mr. Pixton, I'm so sorry to have to bother you, but . . ." She looked around the room and lowered her voice. "This is a little embarrassing, but I wanted to speak to you about that . . . deposition?"

Pixton pretended he did not know what she was talking about.

"Deposition?"

"Yes, my aunt said your lawyer just came in and took her deposition?"

"Oh, that," he said. "Oh, yes, I forgot. It was just a quick little thing for our records, nothing to be alarmed about."

"Yes, well, I just wanted to explain to you that my aunt . . . Well, she may be just a little bit confused, and anything she might have mentioned about, uh, floating around in the sky and seeing strange shoes or anything . . . I just hope it won't be used against her or get out in public."

Franklin was quick to reassure her. "Oh, of course not, Mrs. Warren. That deposition is *strictly* a confidential matter, and as far as anything she may have mentioned about floating, don't think a thing of it. NDEs are a fairly common occurrence."

Norma said, "I'm sorry?"

"Oh, I'm sorry. NDEs. 'Near-death experiences.' Reports of people experiencing a floating sensation, seeing white light, speaking with dead relatives, religious figures, and so on and so forth. Quite common."

Norma was somewhat relieved. "So, it's not unusual?"

"Not at all. It's sort of a hallucinatory experience, caused by oxygen suddenly leaving the brain, certain endorphins being released. But as far as we are concerned, it's completely unimportant."

"I see, and so it won't be on public record or get in the papers or anything?"

"Oh no, never, and frankly, Mrs. Warren, I see no reason why we shouldn't just strike anything of that nature out of the deposition. I'll call Winston and take care of it right away, so you have nothing to worry about."

"Oh, thank you so much. I was a little concerned."

"Rest assured it will be taken out."

Norma thanked him profusely and left feeling much better.

Franklin didn't know what was in the deposition, and he didn't care. All he knew was that Winston Sprague thought the old woman was as nutty as a fruitcake, and he was beginning to wonder about the niece, as well.

A New Kitty

3:10 PM

Linda Warren had been able to get back to her office and at
least work half a day. When she walked into her house,
her daughter, Apple, was waiting and ran to greet her all excited and asked, "Where's my kitty?" The au pair looked at
Linda and said, "All she's talked about since you've been gone
is that cat." Linda felt terrible. In the rush of the past forty-
eight hours she had completely forgotten she had promised to
bring Apple a cat. In the past Linda had always felt that she
was far too busy with work and raising a child to have to take
care of a cat, but she was stuck now, she had promised. She
told a disappointed Apple that tomorrow they would go to the
Humane Society and find a cat. After all, Aunt Elner always
said that everybody should have a cat. Later, as she started
dinner, Linda suddenly had a brainstorm. She was in charge of
the AT&T corporate community outreach program and had
been wondering what their next project should be. Not only
would she and Apple get a cat, tomorrow she would declare
April Adopt a Cat Month. With over eight hundred fifty em-
ployees, a lot of people would be getting a cat. Aunt Elner
would be pleased to think that her falling out of a tree would

be the reason an awful lot of cats were about to find good
homes!

⌁

Macky had arrived back at the hospital from the airport at
around three-thirty that afternoon, and he and Norma had
stayed with Elner until around six. As they drove home, Macky
was happy, and said, "I think she's doing just fine. Don't you?
She told me she never felt better in her life."

Norma was unusually quiet, and did not reply.

He looked over. "Don't you think she's doing great? No broken bones, no brain damage."

Norma sighed. "I'm not so sure."

"What do you mean?"

"Well . . ."

"What do you mean 'well'?"

"I didn't want to say anything, Macky, but the truth is I'm
just worried to death."

"Why?"

"Macky, if I tell you something, will you *swear* to God not
to repeat it?"

"Of course. What?"

"Aunt Elner thinks she took a trip to heaven."

"What?"

"Yes. . . . She told me that yesterday, while we were downstairs in the waiting room, she got up and went down the hall
looking for somebody, then got on an elevator that zigzagged
her over to another building."

"Another building?"

"Wait, Macky, it gets worse. She said she went down this
long white hall and Ginger Rogers walked by, wearing a feather
boa and carrying a pair of tap shoes."

"Ginger Rogers? You're kidding."

"Yes, then she said she saw Mother sitting behind a big desk at the end of the hall."

Macky was suddenly finding this extremely interesting. "And then what?"

"Mother took her up some glass stairs to heaven, but it was really Elmwood Springs fifty years ago; and then she went over and had a visit with Neighbor Dorothy, and some man named Raymond."

Macky laughed.

Norma looked at him. "Don't laugh, Macky, she said mother knew all about Tot doing her hair and makeup. How would she know that?"

"Oh, Norma, for God's sakes . . . it was just a dream. And if your mother was in it, it was a nightmare."

"I told her it was just a dream, but she said no it wasn't, it really happened. She swears she talked to Ernest Koonitz and met Thomas Edison and that this Raymond person told her that the egg comes before the chicken, and something about a flea, and gave her all kinds of messages to bring back."

"Messages? Like what?"

"Oh, stupid cliché stuff. You know. Be happy. Smile . . . silly stuff. I couldn't make any sense out of it, everything was all jumbled around, but she's convinced it really happened, she said she even ate a piece of cake while she was there."

"Don't worry about it, Norma, it was just a dream."

"Are you sure?"

He looked at her. "Of course I'm sure, Norma. The woman was knocked out cold. Who knows what medication she was on, people do that all the time. Remember when Linda had her tonsils out and dreamed there was a pony in her room?"

"Do you think that's all it was?"

He nodded. "Of course. She'll probably forget all about it in a day or so, you wait and see."

"I hope you're right, but I'm still afraid she'll tell everyone she meets that she's been to heaven. You know how she likes to talk. . . . Let's just pray she doesn't tell anybody she saw Ginger Rogers or we'll never get her out of that hospital."

After they drove awhile, Macky asked, "What kind of cake?"

"She didn't say."

Then he laughed again. "Raymond? Where does she come up with this stuff?"

"I don't know, but, Macky, you don't think there's *any* way Mother knows that Tot did her hair, do you? I couldn't hurt Tot's feelings, I don't know what else I could have done under the circumstances. . . ."

Macky looked over at his wife, who was busy twisting a Kleenex to death. "Norma, you need a good night's sleep."

Nurse Boots

7:19 PM

Before she went off duty that night, Ruby Robinson's nurse friend, Boots Carroll, stopped by Elner's room to check on her. "Is there anything you need before I go?" she asked.

Elner said, "Not a thing, honey, everybody is taking real good care of me."

"Well, you try and get a good night's sleep, and I'll stop by in the morning."

Boots was the oldest working nurse at Caraway, and the only reason she was still on duty was because of the terrible shortage of nurses. It was not like it used to be when she and Ruby had entered the profession. They had both been influenced by the movie *Women in White,* and when they were young girls, nursing was thought of as almost a noble profession, a true calling to serve humanity, one step below a nun, as her Catholic friends had said at the time . . . but things had changed. A lot of the new crop of nurses were just in it for the money. They now had the unions and were always going on strike, or threatening to. Never mind about the poor patients. All the nurses who had walked out on strike hated her because she had crossed the picket line, but with Boots her patients were her first priority. Nursing was no longer just a career for young girls. The profession was now full of men, and she resented it. In her day it had been the male attitudes that had kept most women from becoming doctors, and now they were horning in on her profession. Some were serious and did a good job, but there were also a lot of sissy boys who had taken up nursing. She couldn't care less about their so-called sexual orientations, but there was one in particular who had lied about her to the head of the hospital; told him she had made mistakes when she hadn't. He had caused her to be demoted. She also did not like the way he talked. He thought it was funny to refer to all his female patients as "that bitch in room 304" or "that fat bitch" or that "skinny bitch." He clearly did not like females, and it irritated her. A good nurse does not notice gender. She had never referred to any of her patients as bastards or bitches, and throughout the years she'd had her share of both. Plus, he was always standing around in the hall, talking about his sex life, spreading rumors about movie stars he had never met, and to hear him tell it, he had been propositioned by every man he ever said hello to. But the real reason she had no use for him was that he was a mean-spirited vicious little gossip who should not be in nursing. Boots had lost part of her right leg to cancer in 1987 and wore a false leg, and so when she overheard him calling her "The Goody One-Shoe old bitch" behind her back, it was not so funny to her. He had no idea how much she hurt each night from walking those halls all day, or how long and painful it had been to learn to walk again. He may not know it, but she had feelings. "I may be a nurse," she thought, "but I'm a woman too!"

Welcome Home

8:48 PM

When Norma and Macky drove up to their house, they saw that Norma's car was parked in the driveway, with a note on the windshield. Merle and Verbena had driven it over from Elner's house for them. And when they went to the front door, there were six or seven notes that friends had taped to the door. All saying how happy they were Elner was alive. As she went in, Norma was exhausted, but there were so many messages asking about Elner on the answering machine, it had run out of tape. Norma was not surprised by any of this. Aunt Elner knew everybody and was the only person Norma knew who didn't hide from the Jehovah's Witnesses. After Norma had called everybody back and cleared the machine, she came into the den and sat down by Macky. "Linda called, she got home all right and said they were going to get a cat tomorrow."

He nodded. "That's good."

After a while she looked over and said, "Did I mention that she said she walked through a button?"

"No. What kind of button?" he asked.

"A big mother-of-pearl button with a door in it."

Macky roared with laughter.

"Well, you can laugh all you want, Macky, but thank heavens I got to Mr. Pixton in time about the deposition. They could have carted her off and we would never have seen her again!"

"Norma, if anybody gets carted off, it will be you for believing such a thing."

Norma looked at him with alarm. "I'm not saying *I* believe it, Macky, I said she believes it, and you're right, I'm so tired I don't know what I'm thinking. . . . I swear, if one more thing happens—"

There was a knock on the door. "Who in the world is that?" she said. When Norma opened the door, Ruby Robinson stood there with a gun in her hand and announced, "I tried to call, but your line was busy. I found this in the bottom of Elner's dirty-clothes basket and I didn't know if you'd want me to put it back or not."

Norma thought about fainting again but was just too tired.

"Oh, come on in, Ruby," she said. "Macky will have to deal with this. I've got to go lie down before I fall down."

When Macky came into the bedroom a little while later, Norma was lying flat on the bed with a cold rag on her head.

"What fresh hell now?" she moaned.

"Oh, it's nothing, Norma. Ruby found it in Elner's dirty-clothes basket and got all freaked out, that's all."

"Just tell me that was not a real gun. If it is, don't even tell me. I can't handle it."

"No, it's not a real gun," said Macky, unbuttoning his shirt. "It's just a little starter pistol, like they use at the stock car races. It probably belongs to Luther Griggs. I'm sure she was just keeping it for him. Just go on to sleep."

"I don't care if it's fake or not, it obviously scared poor Ruby to death! Tell Luther to quit leaving stuff like that at her house;

first that truck, and now a gun. She could have hurt herself with that thing."

"No, she couldn't. It only shoots blanks."

"I don't care what it shoots, it has no business being in her dirty-clothes basket. I swear, if it's not one thing it's another, you have to watch her twenty-four hours a day."

After Norma had gone to sleep, Macky lay there wide-awake. He had lied to Norma. The gun was not a fake, or a starter pistol. Ruby knew it, and he knew it, and he wondered what the hell Elner was doing with a loaded .38 in her dirty-clothes basket? After a while he decided that the only possible explanation was Luther Griggs, and what in the hell was he thinking leaving something that dangerous at her house? He knew thinking was not one of Luther's strong points, and he liked Luther, but nevertheless, he was going to kick his butt from here to Wyoming and back. Macky wished that Ruby had not brought it over, because Norma was looking for any excuse to try to get Elner into that damned assisted living place, and Elner was not helping matters. First falling out of a tree, and now the gun. Tomorrow he would get up early and ride over and throw the thing in the river and get rid of it. He was not worried that Luther had shot or robbed anybody with it. Luther was too stupid to do anything and not get caught; when he had broken into his father's trailer, he had left a note saying that he was the one who had done it.

Another New Day

4:00 AM

Norma woke up very early, and Macky was snoring. She pushed him over onto his side and tried to go back to sleep, but it was no use. No matter how tired she was, once she was awake, she could never get back to sleep. As she lay there, she began to have anxious thoughts about what Aunt Elner had told her about seeing her mother and all the rest. True, it had obviously been some kind of a dream—walking around in the sky and going through a giant button, you would have to be an idiot to think otherwise—but still, there were certainly a lot of strange and unusual things that had taken place. They said that she really had been dead, and they had checked all the machines and they had been working just fine, and after all, as the doctor said, Aunt Elner did survive a fall that would have killed most people; then there was the fact that she could suddenly hear without her hearing aid. Could she possibly be telling the truth? Oh, dear. Last night she had been so sure, but as usual, now she was scared she might be wrong. Maybe Aunt Elner had not been dreaming. The longer she thought about it, Norma began to wonder if maybe this might be the sign, wonder, or miracle she had prayed for. Wouldn't it be wonderful if it were true? Maybe there really was an afterlife. She got up out of bed and quietly picked out her clothes and tiptoed out of the bedroom.

She put on her makeup and got dressed and left a note on the coffeepot for Macky.

> Honey, couldn't sleep, so I have gone to the hospital to see Aunt Elner. Call you later at work.
>
> Love, Me

Before she drove out of town, Norma decided to run by Elner's house on the way and pick up her hairbrush and a few other things she might need while she was still in the hospital. It was still dark when she arrived, and when she opened the front door and turned on the lights, she was astonished at how neat the place looked. She would have to thank Tot and Ruby for doing such a nice job of cleaning up. While she was in the bedroom, she stopped for a second and seriously thought about taking down that photograph of those hideous little rats jumping around in the sand that Aunt Elner had cut out of a *National Geographic* magazine and Scotch-taped to the wall above her bed. She had been able to get rid of that *robe,* and now was probably her only chance to get rid of this, but she didn't do it, and it took every ounce of strength not to. She went over and opened the dresser and got out two of the new nightgowns she had given Elner for Christmas and picked up her hearing aid as well, better safe than sorry. Aunt Elner could hear fine yesterday, but you never know.

And as far as Norma was concerned, that was the main problem with life. You never knew what was going to happen from minute to minute, and more than anything in this world, Norma hated a surprise. As she headed toward Kansas City, she realized that if someone had told her a few days ago that she would be on her way to the hospital this morning to see Aunt Elner, she would not have believed it. Why did this have to happen now?

Just when she had finally finished decorating her new town home, had gotten through menopause without murdering anybody, had dropped five pounds, and after forty-three years of marriage, her and Macky's love life was exactly like she had always wanted it to be—on schedule, once a week, every Sunday afternoon at around four or five, depending on what else was going on. She liked that it took place on Sunday; it lifted it up out of the ordinary, into a more spiritual event, more in keeping with the marriage vow, rather than just doing it on the whim of the moment, like Macky wanted to.

Being an organized person, she liked to know exactly what was going to happen, and when. She wanted to have time to take a nice hot bath, put on some pretty music, and make a real occasion out of it. After all, Macky was still a good-looking man who had most of his sandy-colored hair, but he had never understood why she had not wanted to just drop everything and jump into bed without any advance notice or warning. He wanted to be "spontaneous," he had said. Of course, when they were younger she had gone along with it, just to keep him happy; men can get their feelings hurt so easily. She had no idea what other people did or how often they did it. That was a subject she would never discuss with anyone, and she had been so relieved when she'd learned that by the time Linda had reached that certain age sex education was being taught in high school, and she did not have to have the birds and the bees conversation.

When she was growing up, people did not talk about their sex life the way they do now, and she preferred it that way. Even though she leaned toward being a little prudish on the subject, she was not frigid by any means—a fact that delighted Macky, but embarrassed her and still made her blush. "You don't have to talk about it, Macky," she would say whenever Macky would compliment her about how sexy she was. But it did please her, and every once in a while she would take her special bubble bath on a Wednesday or Thursday just to surprise him; unlike her, he did not need to be forewarned. She supposed all men were like that, but she certainly was not going to ask. Norma and Macky had been going steady since the seventh grade and married at eighteen. Norma had never dated another boy so her knowledge of the opposite sex was limited to Macky Warren and that was fine with her. She liked her life exactly as it was right now, and wouldn't you know it, just when she finally had everything under control, Aunt Elner picked this very time to have some crazy near-death experience and get her all confused!

Norma arrived at the hospital in time for breakfast. The orderly had just placed Elner's breakfast tray on her table.

"Well, hey!" said Elner when Norma walked in. "How did you get here so early?"

"I decided to try and beat the traffic. How are you this morning?"

"My bites are itching a little, but other than that I'm fine. Have you come to take me home?"

"I don't know yet. I hope so, but I haven't talked to the doctors."

"I hope so too, I'm ready to go home. Look at this," said Elner, holding up a biscuit. "Hard as a rock. Oh well, the scrambled eggs are pretty good, but all they give you here is apple jelly. Have you had your breakfast?"

"No, not yet."

"Don't you want some of this?"

"No. You eat it all, you need your strength. Everybody at home sends their love, I think some of the girls might be coming over later. Did you sleep all right?"

"Oh, sure, except they kept waking me up all night giving me shots and taking all my vitals. They sure keep an eye on you here, too much so, if you ask me." She showed Norma her cup. "Look, this coffee is not very strong. Maybe later on you'll get me some from somewhere else."

"I will, but I had something I wanted to ask you."

"What?"

"Well . . . about what you told me yesterday . . . about your . . ." She looked around, and whispered, "Visit?"

"I thought I wasn't supposed to talk about it?" Elner whispered back.

"You can talk to me, just not anybody else. Tell me again, exactly, what were the messages you were supposed to deliver?"

"Well, let's see . . . Raymond said, 'The world is getting better all the time,' and things of that nature."

"Uh-huh . . . and what did Neighbor Dorothy say again?"

"She said that life is what you make it, and what you make it is up to you. Smile, and the world is sunny."

"And that was it?"

"Pretty much so. Why?"

"Oh, I don't know, I guess I expected something a little more profound, more complex, than 'Life is what you make it.' "

"Me too, but I think that's the good news, life is not as complicated as we thought."

"Are you *sure* that's all they said? Did they say anything about the end of the world?"

"Not specifically, but Raymond did say to hang in there. I think that's a positive message myself."

"Oh, yes, but positive thinking is not all that new. I was hoping for something with more of a revelation, something we haven't heard before."

"Well, Norma, just because you've heard it before doesn't make it wrong."

"No, I understand that, but—"

The door suddenly swung open and a nurse said, "Mrs. Shimfissle, we have a radio station calling, wanting to do a live feed with you . . . somebody named Bud?"

Elner's eyes lit up. "Oh, it's the Bud and Jay show! Can I tell them about the chicken and the egg? I won't say where I heard it."

"Oh my God," thought Norma, "Aunt Elner, you are *not* going on the radio, let me talk to them."

A few minutes later Bud of the Bud and Jay show said to his listening audience, "Well, folks, just spoke to Elner Shimfissle's niece in Kansas City, and she says Mrs. Shimfissle can't come to the phone quite yet but that she's fine, and sends us all her regards. And now, Mrs. Shimfissle, if you are listening . . . here's a song just for you this morning. . . . Here's Miss Della Reese singing 'What a Difference a Day Makes.' "

When she came back in, Norma sat and stared at Elner like she was a bug, trying to observe her actions to see if she could tell if she seemed to be in her right mind, but with so many people in and out of her room, it was hard to tell. But so far she seemed normal, if you *could* call Aunt Elner's regular behavior normal.

The Visitors

11:30 AM

Around late morning a group of the ladies from Elmwood Springs met downtown in front of the newspaper office, then they all piled into Cathy Calvert's station wagon and headed over to the hospital to see Elner. They were all in a good mood, happy to be going to the hospital instead of the funeral parlor, where they all might have been that day.

Irene said, "Can you believe it? Here she is alive and kicking, and I had already made three green bean casseroles and three Bundt cakes."

Tot, who sat in the backseat by the window because she was the only one who smoked, said, "I was too stoned out on my pills to cook."

Neva added, "Well, I practiced her gospel songs."

Ruby Robinson said, "I cleaned out her refrigerator and almost took that nasty old cat home."

"Merle and I sent her a plant, and he went over and killed her snails. I just hope she doesn't find out, you know how she is about her snails," said Verbena.

Cathy Calvert said, "Well, girls, I think I have you all beat, I already wrote her obituary!" And they laughed all the way to Kansas City.

When the ladies walked into Elner's room, they all declared how well she looked, considering. Then Tot looked over and said to a pale Norma, "But you look terrible, you look just plum wore out."

"Well, I am a little tired, I got up pretty early," said Norma.

Then Tot turned to Elner. "You have just put us through the ringer, girl, we all thought you were a goner."

"So did I," laughed Elner.

"When are you coming home?" asked Irene.

"I don't know yet, I'm still being observed."

"For what?" said Tot.

"I don't know that, either . . . to see if I'm still in my right mind, I guess."

Verbena stood staring at her. "How do you feel now? Do you have a headache? Wasp stings give me a headache."

"No, no headache, but I feel like a big old pincushion. They've stuck me with so many needles and looked at me from every which way, inside and out, from top to bottom. I think I had every test they could think of, and some twice. You can't accuse them of not being thorough."

Tot plopped down on a chair beside the bed. "Let's cut to the chase. What I'm dying to know is, how did it feel to be dead? Did you go through a white tunnel or see anybody interesting?"

Norma held her breath, but Elner, a woman of her word, answered, "No, I didn't go through any white tunnel."

"Well, shoot," said Tot, "I was hoping you'd have a lot to report, some words of wisdom."

"Yes," added Neva. "Did you have any insights, or revelations or anything?"

"Yeah," said Verbena. "I heard people that died and came

back could cure things, I was hoping you could help me with my arthritis."

Elner, looking at Norma, said, "All I can tell you is that you better live each day like it was your last, because you never know. Take a lesson from me, one minute I'm picking figs, the next minute I'm dead."

While the rest of the ladies were still visiting with Elner, Ruby Robinson went down the hall looking for her friend Boots, to have a chat and see if she could find out anything more about what had happened.

Ruby asked where she was and found Boots down in the nurses' room taking her break. Boots was very happy to see her, and confided, "I've been given orders not to discuss it, but I'll tell you this much." She looked around to see if anyone was listening. "They've checked and rechecked everything and they still don't have a clue what went wrong. My friend Gwen was in ER at the time and she swears Elner was dead."

"It's odd, isn't it?" said Ruby.

"In all my years of nursing, I've never seen anything like it."

When Ruby came back into the room, Elner called out to her, "Cathy just read me my obit, and it was a good one. I'm sorry now that she didn't get to run it in the paper."

The ladies stayed until around three, and then left for home so they could beat the traffic.

After the ladies left, Elner said to Norma, "Ruby said they tried to call Luther, but he was out of town. He's gonna be sorry he missed the excitement, won't he?"

"Frankly, I think he's better off, you know what a big baby he is."

"Yes, that's true. Neva said my funeral was going to be one of the biggest ones ever, and to hear Irene tell it, you and Macky were in for a lot of good casseroles. Now, aren't you sorry I didn't stay dead? You can freeze those, you know. I'll bet you and Macky could have probably eaten off of them for a good year."

"Oh, Aunt Elner. Good Lord," said Norma. "I can always make a casserole, for heaven's sake. You don't have to die for us to get a casserole."

"Well, anyway, I just hope Dena and Gerry didn't buy one of those nonrefundable tickets to get to my funeral, but if they did, I guess they can just keep it and use it the next time, don't you reckon?"

Norma looked at her. "Aunt Elner, if you die again any time soon, I swear . . . I can only handle so much."

That night when Elner was having her dinner of liver and onions, she waited until the nurse left, and then said to Norma, "This liver is way too dry, not near as good as they make it over at the Cracker Barrel."

Norma looked over at it. "No, it doesn't look that good."

"When am I getting sprung out of here, do you know? I need to get home."

"I'm not sure, maybe they will let us know something tomorrow."

"Norma, I hate you having to drive all the way here and back home again, you probably have a lot more important things to do than sit with me all day."

"Don't be silly. The most important thing to me is making sure you're all right." Norma reached over and took her hand. "You know, I would just die if anything happened to you."

"Well, that's mighty sweet of you, honey."

That evening after Norma went home, when Elner was alone, she had a chance to think more about her trip. She wished Norma had believed her about seeing everybody and how wonderful it was, but she couldn't make her believe if she didn't want to. Of course, Elner had been happy to see her friends and relatives again, everybody had been so nice. And she certainly wouldn't have hurt Norma's feelings for anything in the world, but Elner found herself a little sad to be back. She understood that Raymond and Dorothy must have had their reasons for sending her home, but she longed to go back. She had been so disappointed not to get to see Will. It was difficult, because it was certainly a feeling you had to keep to yourself. You couldn't very well tell your loved ones you would rather be dead, and not expect them to have their feelings hurt. But still she couldn't help but wonder why she'd had to come back. Oh, well, it was just one of those mysteries and only they know the answer. She lay there for a moment, and then broke out in song again. "Ah, sweet mystery of life. At last I've found thee . . . At last—"

The worried night nurse rushed in.

"What's the matter, Mrs. Shimfissle? Are you in pain?"

"No, I feel fine, thank you."

"Oh, I'm sorry. I thought I heard you moaning in pain."

"No. I was just singing." Then she laughed. "I guess I sing about as well as Ernest Koonitz plays the tuba, but at least he's getting lessons."

"Well, sorry to have disturbed you. Good night."

"Good night, and next time, when I feel a song coming on, I'll be sure and warn you."

"Please do, give me a chance to stuff my ears with cotton."

"I will."

The nurse left the room smiling and said to her friend at the desk, "That woman in 703 is a real character. I'm going to be sorry to see her go home. You should have heard her earlier, she was telling a bunch of us all about her seven orange cats named Sonny."

"She has seven cats named Sonny?"

"No, not all at once. Each time she gets a new cat, she names it Sonny, and she said when she gets out of here she is sending us all fig preserves and a copy of a picture of some kind of mice jumping around in the desert."

"Good God, she sounds nuts to me."

"Probably, but she's a funny nut. Good-humored at least. Quite a relief from the sourpusses I usually get stuck with."

"Speaking of that, that jerk lawyer Winston Sprague was here earlier, throwing his weight around, talking to everybody like they are dirt. He made one of the girls cry, he was so rude snapping his fingers at her, ordering her around. Who died and made him king, is what I want to know."

"Yeah. What a little snot he is. I just hope he gets knocked off his high horse someday and I'm there to see it." She looked around to see if anyone could hear, then said, "I'll bet he powders his private parts with a powder puff. Don't you?" The other woman screamed with laughter as softly as she could, considering where she was. Then she said, "You know he does. What a jerk."

Still Confused

6:58 PM

As Norma drove home from the hospital that night, her mind was spinning. She was *still* not sure whether to believe Aunt Elner or not. Mr. Pixton said that what she had described had been a very common near-death experience. She had heard about that kind of thing before, so she knew that was certainly a real possibility. And of course Macky was certain that everything Elner thought had happened had been nothing more than a dream, and he could be right, but still Norma wondered. She knew Aunt Elner's story was insane and probably not true, but she wanted so much to think that there was something or somebody at least checking up on us from time to time, even if it was somebody named Raymond. She had worked so hard at trying to believe. The first thing she did every morning was read the card she had received in her newcomers packet at the Unity Church. She had taped it on the mirror above the bathroom sink.

GOOD MORNING!
This is God.
I am going to handle

All your problems today,
So go in peace.
Have a good day!

Every day she tried to go in peace, turn all her worries and problems over to God, but every day by nine or at least by ten, she would forget he was supposed to be in charge and she would take them back. Why couldn't she hold out for at least one day, and if He were really there, why didn't He just say so and quit making it so hard? It's not like the believers in the world were all nice. They had been killing one another for years. Her own mother had been a Presbyterian and was not very nice—even now that she was dead, according to Aunt Elner. And although he didn't believe in God, Macky was one of the nicest people in the world. "Oh Lord," she thought, "no wonder so many people are either drunk or on dope."

The Jerk

7:03 PM

Winston Sprague sat in his expensive condo with the top-of-the-line television, stereo system, appliances, and personal workout room, paid for by indulging in dubious ethical behavior, and stared at the wall. After Winston had taken the old lady's deposition, he had returned to his office and had dismissed it as being no big deal. But as the day wore on and he reread the deposition over and over, something about what the old lady said still nagged at him. She had been so damn specific about that damn shoe. He knew she was probably as crazy as a loon, but he had decided just for the hell of it to go back over to the hospital and go up on the roof and take a look around. When he got there, he went up and opened the door to the roof and walked all over the entire area, checked every corner. Nothing but a dead pigeon, and just as he had expected, no shoe. He was halfway embarrassed that he had even checked. As he stood there looking out over Kansas City, he laughed out loud when he thought of the old woman thinking she had floated over the roof and back into the hospital. As he was leaving, he glanced over at the old annex building, where the laundry facilities were now located, and figured while he was at it, he might as well go over and check out that roof as well. But when he got to the top landing of the other building, the door leading up to the stairs to the roof was locked. He had to go back down and find one of the janitors to go up with him and unlock the door.

"Is this door always locked?" he asked.

"Yes."

"Have you been up here lately?"

"No, not lately. The last time I can remember was when we had a couple of leaks and a company came and hot-mopped around that ledge."

"When was that?"

"Three or four years ago."

"Other than that, nobody's been up here that you know of?"

"No."

After the janitor unlocked the door for him, Winston walked up the narrow flight of stairs and pushed against the last door leading to the roof. It was either stuck or locked, he did not know which, but he kept pushing and shoving it until he was finally able to open it far enough to step out onto the roof. This building faced the south, and the sun was blinding as it reflected off of the light gray gravel that covered the entire roof. The afternoon heat was rising from the floor as he walked around and looked behind every chimney, but the only thing he found was an old mop handle. He walked around to the other side and glanced over behind the chimney closest to the ledge of the building. Nothing. He walked around the other side and looked. Suddenly he felt the hair on the back of his neck stand up and started to break out in an ice-cold sweat. Lying on its side, wedged between the ledge and the chimney, was one brown golf shoe with cleats. Jesus Christ!

He closed his eyes and opened them again to make sure he

was not hallucinating. He looked again. No. It was there, all right, exactly as she had described it. Sprague's clothes were now wringing wet and sticking to him. He forced himself to walk over closer to it. He stood there looking down at it. Finally, after a moment, he cautiously nudged the shoe with his foot as if it were a snake that might bite. It did not move. He kicked it again. It still did not move. He crouched down and tried to pick it up, but still it would not budge. Half of the shoe was stuck in the black tar surrounding the chimney. He had to work at it for about five minutes with sweat pouring off of him, pulling it back and forth until it finally came loose in his hand. But now that he had the shoe, he stood there and wondered what the hell he was going to do with it, and how was he going to get the thing downstairs without anyone seeing him? He propped it up by the side of the door and ran down to the next floor and found a brown paper bag with half a sandwich inside in a trash can. Winston emptied the bag and ran back up and put the shoe in it, and then carried it under his arm. He went down the emergency stairs all the way to the basement, crossed over to the main building, and ran into the bathroom. He scrubbed as much of the tar off his hands as he could and hid the sack behind a door, and wondered why he was feeling like a criminal. He then ran back upstairs to Franklin Pixton's office, ducked into the office, closed the door behind him, and stood against it, out of breath and sweating.

A surprised Pixton looked up at him. "What are you doing here? Why is your face so red? Have you been running?"

Sprague said, "A shoe on the roof!"

"A shoe on what roof?"

"In the deposition . . . the old lady, Mrs. Shimfissle . . . swore . . . she saw a shoe on the hospital roof."

"So?"

"You d-don't understand," he sputtered. "She said she was floating around in the air up over the hospital and saw a shoe on the roof . . . and when I went up there, there was a shoe on the roof!"

"Are you making this up just to irritate me?"

"No. I'm telling you the truth, the shoe was exactly where she said it was."

"Oh, come on, Winston, pull yourself together. It's probably just a coincidence."

"A coincidence? That it was in the exact spot she said it was, that it was a brown leather shoe? Not only a brown leather shoe, but a golf shoe!"

"She said it was a golf shoe?"

"Yes. A damn brown leather golf shoe and that's exactly what it was. I'm telling you there is no way she could have seen that thing, unless she was really dead or something."

"Oh, for God's sakes, Winston, let's not get crazy. We have enough real problems without adding all this voodoo-hoodoo out-of-body near-death crap."

"Well, it may be voodoo hoodoo to you, but I'm telling you, Franklin, the shoe was there!"

Franklin got up and walked over to the door and locked it; then he walked over and poured Winston a drink.

"Here, just calm down and tell me again what she said."

"She said she saw a brown leather shoe with spikes lying by a chimney on the roof, and that's exactly where it was."

"OK. Something's not adding up, I'm beginning to smell a rat here."

"What do you mean?"

"Who's to say that they didn't plan this entire thing? That the shoe thing is some sort of scam, that she didn't plant the thing up there herself?"

"How? When? The nurses swore she never left the room."

"Maybe it was the niece or the niece's husband, or maybe they are in cahoots with someone who works here and they put it up there. Maybe they hired a small plane and flew over and dropped it on the roof, or a hot-air balloon."

"Why? For what reason?"

"Money, a book deal, or to get on *Oprah*."

"Oh right, Franklin, an eighty-nine-year-old woman deliberately sticks her hand in a wasps' nest, gets stung seventeen times, falls twenty feet out of a tree, and knocks herself out cold, just to get on *Oprah*? Besides, the door was locked, and nobody has a key but the janitor."

"What other logical explanation could there be?"

"None! That's what I'm telling you."

"Is it still there?"

"No, I took it."

"Why?"

"Why? Why? Because I don't know why, it just scared the hell out of me."

"Where is it now?"

"I hid it in the bathroom. Do you want to see it?"

"No, I don't want to see it. But listen, if the Warrens try to pull anything, we'll just say, be our guest, have a look on the roof if you like. In the meantime, we never saw any shoe, right? If this gets out, we'll be overrun by every nut job in America camping out in the parking lot."

Winston nodded. "I guess you're right, but what should I do with the shoe?"

"Get rid of it. Forget about it."

"Wouldn't that be illegal?" asked Sprague.

"Good Lord, man, you're the lawyer. No, you found a shoe . . . it's trash . . . you got rid of it. End of story."

After Sprague left the office, Pixton sighed. With all his other problems, now his lawyer had flipped out over some weird co-incidental shoe sighting. He had no patience for that sort of thing, all the so-called miracles: statues crying, crop circles, the Loch Ness Monster, Bigfoot, each and every one proven to be hoaxes and scams. It never ceased to amaze him just how gullible people really were. They would pray to a can of green beans if they thought it was going to cure them or get them into heaven. "God," he thought, "when are people going to crawl out of the dark ages of ignorance?" Franklin had minored in philosophy at Yale, and if he had his way, every school in America would begin teaching kids Diderot, Kant, Nietzsche, Hegel, and Goethe. The current lack of education alarmed him. Most of the young people he dealt with nowadays could hardly string a proper sentence together, much less think for themselves. He was afraid we were going to wind up a nation of knuckle-dragging Neanderthals. Thank goodness Sprague was a Harvard man, and underneath it all, a man of reason.

A Troubled Sleep

8:03 PM

When Norma got home from Kansas City, Macky had a mushroom and chicken casserole on the table waiting for her. Mrs. Reid had brought it over with a note. "Didn't want it to go to waste, enjoy." Norma was glad she did not have to cook, and sat down and started eating. Macky wanted to know how Elner was doing, and after they talked for a while, Norma was so exhausted, she went to bed at nine-thirty and fell asleep immediately. But as tired as she was, it was a troubled sleep. Something that Aunt Elner had said that day was bothering her, and she kept running it over and over in her mind. Even in her sleep. At around three AM Norma suddenly sat straight up in bed and announced in a loud voice, "Oh my God. It's a Johnny Mathis song!"

Macky was startled awake. "What? What are you talking about?"

" 'Life Is What You Make It.' Remember?" Then she sang, " 'Life is what you make it, if you can take it, it's worth a try.' "

Macky reached over, turned on the light, and looked at her. "Norma, have you lost your mind?"

"No, just listen to the lyrics, Macky." And she continued

singing, " 'Smile the world is sunny . . . your Easter bunny . . . when even sad turns to funny.' Don't you remember it?"

"No, *I* don't remember. For God's sake, Norma, it's three o'clock in the morning."

"Well, I do. Linda had the record and used to play it all the time. Aunt Elner is channeling an old Johnny Mathis song. And Sonny is the name of her cat. Don't you see? And the crystal stairs? That's right out of her gospel song. She dreamed the whole thing, Macky. She no more went to heaven than I did!"

"I told you that yesterday. Now go to sleep."

Macky turned off the light, and Norma lay back, relieved she had finally figured out why it had sounded so familiar to her. Then a few seconds later an unexpected wave of sadness hit her when she realized that Aunt Elner's trip to heaven *had* just been a dream. It had not been a sign, a wonder, or a miracle, after all. That tiny little glimmer of hope had been dashed. Now she was right back where she'd started two days ago and her old doubts came creeping in again. She felt scared and all alone in the universe without a purpose again, and tomorrow would be just another day, just another twenty-four uneasy hours to try to get through. As she lay there, tears ran down her face, and she realized that maybe Macky was right after all, and people were nothing more than an accident caused by spontaneous generation started millions of years ago. We were all just a bunch of tadpoles that had crawled out of the water and started walking around, and yet, she still hated to think that when we died we would just fall into a black hole and disappear into nothing. What would be the point of living? With her anxiety she desperately needed to believe that at least some small part of her would continue on, and if there was no heaven . . . Maybe she would start trying to believe in reincarnation like Irene Goodnight. Irene had sworn on the Bible that her Pekinese dog Ling-

Ling was her late husband, Ralph, come back to haunt her. She said they snored exactly alike and had the same way of looking at her. It wasn't much to go on, but it was something at least. Then another thought hit Norma. If there was such a thing as reincarnation, and she did come back, she just hoped to God she wouldn't wind up in a third world country, where she couldn't get fresh produce, or have access to good skin products, because if she couldn't get her Merle Norman cold cream, she would just rather not come back at all. She reached over and got a Kleenex, wiped her eyes, blew her nose, and went back to sleep.

The Report

7:00 AM

Early the next morning, Franklin Pixton sat and listened to the entire report. No machine malfunction. All the attending nurses in ER depositions corroborated Dr. Henson's testimony. Every fact had been checked and rechecked. According to all legal and medical requirements, the woman had been for all intents and purposes clinically dead. Franklin sniffed and adjusted his glasses. "So, Dr. Gulbranson, what is your official explanation?"

Dr. Gulbranson looked up. "Damned if I know, Franklin. I'd have to say it was just a fluke."

Franklin slowly turned his chair around and looked out the window. "A fluke? I see. So I am to tell the head of my board that she was officially dead, and the fact that she sat up and started talking several hours later was a fluke. Or should I get up and sing three choruses of 'It was just one of those things'? Which would you suggest?"

Dr. Gulbranson shook his head. "I don't know what to tell you, Franklin. Sometimes things just can't be explained."

The Unexplained

The very first day Elner had been brought to the hospital, La Shawnda McWilliams, a heavyset woman with freckles and skin the color of coffee with cream, had been the orderly on duty on Elner's floor. At around four that afternoon of April 1, it was getting close to the end of her shift and she was glad; she had been on duty for twelve hours, and just like every other morning, La Shawnda had gotten up at four AM and fixed her mother's breakfast, left it on the table for her, then ridden two buses across town, in order to arrive at the hospital by five-thirty. Just as she was about ready to leave for home that evening, she had received the call to come down and collect some personal effects for a patient. A nurse in ER had gathered Mrs. Shimfissle's clothes, which in the excitement of the moment of her sudden awakening had been thrown on the floor.

When La Shawnda got there, the nurse quickly handed her a pair of maroon felt house slippers wrapped up in a brown plaid robe, and on top was a pair of large white cotton underpants. "Here," the nurse said, "this goes with Shimfissle." La Shawnda took the items and inquired, "No jewelry?" "No, this is all," the nurse said as she hurried down the hall to take care of another patient who had just come in. La Shawnda looked at the small pile, not much, and figured by the looks of that robe the patient must be a charity case, poor lady. She didn't know that the underpants almost hadn't made the trip to the hospital either. Earlier that morning, Elner had even debated whether or not to put them on, but figured since she was going up a ladder, she'd better.

La Shawnda took the things and went into the utility room and pulled out a large white plastic bag that said PERSONAL EFFECTS, and in the process of refolding the robe she felt something soft in the pocket. She reached in and pulled out whatever it was, wrapped in a large white napkin with the letters D.S. embroidered in gold thread. She opened the napkin and saw the lump was a big piece of cake. "Huh," she thought, "that poor lady must have put it in her pocket before she left home." She poked it with her finger and it was still light and moist, like it had just come out of the oven. "It's not stale yet." She stood there wondering what to do with it. She knew they would not let the lady eat it while she was a patient. The hospital dietician, Miss Revest, was dead set against anything made with white flour or sugar. But still, La Shawnda hated to throw out a perfectly good piece of cake. And after all, it wouldn't be stealing, they were instructed to throw out any old food, so she went over to the drawer and pulled out a Ziploc bag and slipped it inside. Her mother would just love to have that piece of cake. Her poor mother had been so sick lately, and hardly ever got out of bed. La Shawnda had had to bring her to Kansas City from her home in Arkansas. She knew her mother was unhappy having to live in a small apartment in the city, but she had no choice. She carefully folded the underpants and the robe, each smelling like fresh-baked cake. For a second there she was tempted, and thought about eating that cake herself, but didn't. She placed the old lady's things in a white plastic bag and took them down-stairs and gave them to the woman's niece.

When La Shawnda arrived home that night, she found her mother asleep in the living room, still in her nightgown. La Shawnda looked at her and thought, what a way for her to wind up, old and riddled with arthritis, with no insurance and not a dime to her name. Thank heavens the hospital had let her put her mother on her policy, or she would not have been able to af-ford any of her medications. Her poor little mother had worked as a domestic all her life, had raised five children by taking in washing and ironing after she got home from work and on weekends, and had never made more than seventy dollars a week in her entire life. Her only joy had been attending her church, but now she was too weak and feeble to go anymore, and it was all La Shawnda could do to get her to eat and keep her strength up. Her mother had brought up all her children in the church, but now with them all scattered across the country, only one sister still went. La Shawnda didn't go anymore. No matter how much her mother insisted that God was good, she didn't see it. It seemed to her that any so-called God that would let one of his so-called children suffer was not a God she cared to know. After she put her things down she went straight to the kitchen and took out a plate from the cabinet, pulled out a clean fork from the dishwasher, and walked back into the living room. "Momma," she said, shaking her gently. "Wake up, honey. I have a surprise for you." Her mother opened her eyes. "Oh, hey, baby. When did you get home?"

"Just now. Did you have much pain today, Momma?"

"Not too bad."

"Look what I have for you."

The old lady looked over and saw the piece of cake and said, "Oh, doesn't that look good. And it smells good too!"

The next morning the alarm went off as usual at four AM and La Shawnda forced herself to get up and get ready for another day. After she dressed and went to the kitchen, she got the surprise of her life. The light was on and her mother was standing at the stove cooking. "Momma," she said, "what are you doing up?"

Her mother said, "I just woke up, and I felt so much better this morning I thought I'd get up and do you some eggs."

"Have you taken your medicine?"

"No, not yet. I had me the bestest dream last night. I dreamed I looked down and saw hundreds of little tiny golden hands rubbing all over me, and it felt so good, when I woke up I felt tingly all over. I tell you, honey, I think that cake must have cheered me up. I've been sick so long I forgot how good home-made cake is. I think it done woke up my taste buds. I've been thinking about making us some good old corn bread. What would you think about that?"

"Corn bread?"

"Yes. Maybe you could find some collards or turnip greens, or maybe some butter beans. Wouldn't that just hit the spot?"

The Recipe

7:20 AM

Three days after finding the cake, La Shawnda was on the bus headed for work, and was amazed at how much her mother's health had improved. Last night her mother had even fixed that pan of corn bread! She made up her mind to find the lady who the robe had belonged to, and tell her just how much her mother had loved that cake, and how it had cheered her up so. She might even see if she could get the recipe.

At around seven-twenty AM on Thursday she knocked on the door to Elner's room and saw that the white-haired lady was sitting up and awake.

"Mrs. Shimfissle? May I come in?"

"Sure," said Elner, "come on."

"How you feeling today?"

"Just fine, thank you," said Elner, looking to see if the woman had a needle in her hand.

"Mrs. Shimfissle . . . you don't know me, but I'm the one who packed up your personal effects."

"My what, honey?"

"Your robe and house shoes."

"Oh, yes. I was hoping somebody had done that. I was wondering what happened to them."

"I gave them to your niece the night you came in."

Elner's face fell, and she said, "Uh-oh. There goes my robe. Norma has just been itching to sling it out for years. Oh well. That's what I get for not minding her, I guess."

La Shawnda came closer to the bed and said, "Mrs. Shimfissle, on Monday night when I was folding up your robe, I found a piece of cake in your pocket."

Elner's eyes lit up. "Oh, good. I was hoping it made it back."

"Yes, ma'am." La Shawnda looked around to see if anyone was coming in. "I was supposed to throw it out, but I didn't."

"You didn't?" said a hopeful Elner, who was happy to think she might get it back. She could stand another piece of Dorothy's cake right now.

"I hope you don't mind, I took it home to my mother. She grew up way out in the country, and I thought a piece of homemade cake would cheer her up."

"Oh. I see." Elner was somewhat disappointed but said, "Well, bless her heart. I grew up in the country too, so I know just how she feels, and if they weren't going to let me have it, I'm glad she got to enjoy it."

"Oh, she did, because the next morning she felt better than she has for a long time."

"It was good cake, all right."

"I wanted to ask you where you got it. Did you make it?"

Elner laughed. "No, I didn't make it, mine don't turn out near that good."

"Where did it come from?"

Elner looked at her and smiled. "Honey, if I told you, you wouldn't believe me."

"Did you buy it at a bakery?"

"No, it's homemade all right, a friend of mine made it."

"That's too bad. I was hoping I could get the recipe from you . . . she sure loved that cake."

"Oh, I'd be happy to give it to you. Just give me your address and I'll send it to you. I have the recipe in the Neighbor Dorothy cookbook at home. . . . Oh, and here's a tip: make sure to always check your oven and make sure it's preheated to the right temperature. Dorothy told me that was the secret to a good moist cake."

La Shawnda quickly jotted down her name and address on a piece of paper and handed it to Elner.

"I sure appreciate it, Mrs. Shimfissle." Then La Shawnda looked over at the door and whispered, "And I sure would appreciate it if you didn't tell anybody about me taking that cake home the other night, or I could lose my job. They're just looking for excuses to fire people around here."

"Ahh, I see. Well, no, I promise I won't mention it. But tell your mother I said I'm glad she's feeling better, OK?"

As La Shawnda said good-bye, a nurse wearing rubber gloves and pushing a tray came in and said with a big smile, "Good morning, Mrs. Shimfissle," and from her smile Elner knew she was in for something she wasn't going to like.

Going Home

After the nurse had checked and rechecked Elner, Dr. Henson, her emergency room doctor, was handed the report. He had come to visit with Elner several times a day since she had been there, and the more he got to know her, the better he started feeling about the human race. All findings had cleared him of any negligence, he was not being fired, and evidently the hospital was not being sued and his patient was doing great, and he was in a great mood.

He opened the door and walked into her room with a big smile. "Good morning, Sunshine."

"Well, hey," she said, happy to see him.

"I hate to tell you this, because we wish we could keep you, but I'm sending you home today, young lady!"

"You are? Is my niece coming to get me?"

"Nope. We just called her and told her not to come, because there is someone here who wants to escort you home in style."

After the nurses packed her up, they put her in a wheelchair and Nurse Boots Carroll and Dr. Henson rolled her to the elevator and downstairs, through the lobby, and then through the big double glass doors. And parked right out in front was a long shiny black limousine. When Franklin Pixton had reported to Mr. Thomas York, the head of the hospital board, about the old lady who fell out of her tree, Mr. York had been fascinated and had replied, "Now, there is someone I'd like to meet." And so when the chauffeur opened the back door, a distinguished-looking older man stepped out of the back and said, taking off his hat, "Mrs. Shimfissle, I'm Thomas York. I wonder if you might allow me the privilege of accompanying you home?"

"Well, sure," she said.

Elner and Mr. York chatted away as they drove toward Elmwood Springs, and she found out that even though he was a retired CEO of a bank, he had a fondness for chickens as well. His grandfather had been a chicken farmer. They had a grand time all the way home discussing the superior qualities of the Rhode Island Red versus the blue speckled hen. As they neared Elmwood Springs, she looked out the window. "I just hope Merle's out in his yard to see me come driving up in a limousine. I don't remember the trip to the hospital, but I sure am enjoying the trip home. I never dreamed I'd ever get to ride in the back of one of these things."

When they drove down her street, she asked if the driver could slow down so maybe some of her other neighbors would see her. When they pulled up to her house, Norma and most of her neighbors were waiting for her, and she was so happy to see that Louise Franks and her daughter, Polly, had come to town to welcome her home as well.

After Mr. York had come up on the porch and eaten a piece of welcome home Bundt cake and visited for a while, and before he left, Cathy Calvert took a picture of him and Elner standing by the limo to put in the newspaper. When the limo drove off,

Elner turned around and said to Norma, "Where's old Sonny? I can't wait to see that old fool."

"He's inside," Norma said. "I locked him in, I knew you'd want to see him the minute you got home."

Elner walked in and Sonny was in his spot on the back of the couch. She went over and picked him up, and sat down and petted him. "Hey, Sonny, did you miss me?" But Sonny acted as though he didn't even know she had been gone, and after allowing himself to be petted a short while, he jumped out of her lap and headed to his dish for a snack. Elner laughed. "Cats, they don't want you to know they care a thing in the world about you, but they do."

That first night home all the members of the Sunset Club gathered in her side yard with their chairs, and it was a particularly beautiful sunset that evening. Verbena remarked, "Elner, I think that's the good Lord's way of saying welcome home!" And Elner was glad to be back home again, until the next morning when she opened up her dirty-clothes basket and looked in.

"Uh-oh." Never in a million years did she figure someone would go rooting around in there. "Now what?"

Elner walked over to Ruby's house and knocked on the door. "Yoo hoo."

"Come on in, Elner," Ruby said from the kitchen. "I'm still doing my dishes."

Elner walked back and said, "I just came over to thank you again for feeding Sonny and the birds and straightening the house and all."

"Oh, you're more than welcome, honey. Glad to do it."

Elner nodded, then as casually as she could, she inquired,

"You didn't happen to find something in my dirty-clothes basket, did you?"

"Like what?" asked Ruby.

"Oh, nothing . . . just something."

"No, I didn't find anything but clothes. Why?"

"I just wondered."

"Oh."

"Well, OK, then."

Ruby hated to lie, but she and Macky had made a pact. And as a registered nurse and a good neighbor, she knew it was for the best. Old people and firearms do not mix. Old Man Henderson who used to live up the street shot half his lip off fooling around with a loaded weapon.

As she walked back home, Elner was worried. If Norma had found it, she was in big trouble again.

Luther Comes Home

5:03 PM

That afternoon when Luther Griggs drove back into town after his Seattle run, he wondered if anybody had missed him at the funeral. He had felt terrible about not being able to go, but there had been nothing he could do about it. He thought about driving past Elner's house before he went home, but changed his mind. It would be too sad not to see her out there on the front porch. He would go home, and after he had a nap and a bath, he would go over to Mrs. Warren's house and tell them why he had not been at the service, and find out where she was buried. He knew where to get some nice flowers for her grave. He had seen a bunch of different arrangements the last time Bobbie Jo had dragged him through Tuesday Morning right next to the picture frames. He would get some as pretty as the ones he put on his own mother's grave, nicer even, he thought. After all, she had been nicer to him than his own mother. But as he turned off the interstate and approached Elmwood Springs, he changed his mind and decided he would drive by her house. He realized that as fast as they were tearing down all the older houses in town, he better go by before it might be too late. As he came down First Avenue, he was relieved to see the house was still standing. He was thinking that he might try to buy the old house himself; he had saved some money over the past couple of years. He was thinking this when Elner Shimfissle walked out onto her porch with a watering can, and waved at him.

"Goddamn it, Luther!" yelled Merle. Luther had just run his eighteen-wheeler truck up over the curb, had almost run Merle over, and had taken out almost all of Merle's prize hydrangea bushes. Merle ran up to the truck and banged it with his green and white plastic lawn chair, but Luther was so badly shaken up by seeing Elner on her porch that he wouldn't get out of the truck. By this time Elner had walked across the street, and she stood looking up at him in the cab of his truck, which had landed in a ditch in Irene Goodnight's yard.

"Hey, Luther," she said. "What are you doing?"

Macky had just walked in from work when Norma met him at the door, with her car keys in her hand. "You are not going to believe what just happened. I was just getting ready to call you."

"What?"

"That crazy Luther Griggs didn't know Aunt Elner was still alive and ran his truck up in Merle's yard and took out all his shrubs, and half of Irene Goodnight's. They just called Triple A to come over and pull him out of the ditch."

"Good God, was anybody hurt?"

"No, evidently just the shrubs. He was just scared to death I guess but we better go over there and make sure everything else is all right. What else is going to happen?"

They drove up in time to see the truck being lifted and pulled across Irene's yard, taking out most of her rosebushes.

Irene was standing beside Cathy Calvert, who had walked down with her camera. "Dammit," said Irene. "Why couldn't they have pulled that truck back across Merle's yard? His yard was already ruined. He isn't even a Triple A member! I'm the one who called, and they take out my yard!"

Poor Luther was still shaken up pretty badly and was over at Ruby's porch. Ruby had just brought him a shot of whisky. Elner sat with him and said, "I'm sorry to have given you such a fright, honey."

He shook his head, almost in tears. "Whew. I had you dead and buried, and then to see you come out of your house like that . . . Man . . . it almost scared me to death."

After Macky had walked over and surveyed the damage to both yards, he told Merle and Irene to come out to The Home Depot garden shop in the morning and he would make sure to replace what he could. Then he walked back over to Elner's and sat on the porch.

After a while, when Luther had pulled himself together and was able to talk without bursting into tears, Macky said, "Luther, let's take a little walk, OK?"

"Sure, Mr. Warren."

"Excuse us, ladies," he said. As he walked Luther around to the side of the house, Macky said quietly, "Let me ask you something, Luther. Did you leave a gun at Elner's house?"

Luther seemed surprised. "A gun?"

"Yeah, a gun. I'm not going to turn you in or anything. Just tell me if you left a loaded .38 at her house."

"No, sir. I'd tell you. I'm on probation. I can't have a gun. I took a shotgun from Daddy's trailer but they got that back."

"Do you swear to God?"

"Yes, sir. I wouldn't ever do that to Miss Elner, not in a hundred years. I was going to marry Bobbie Jo Newberry because Miss Elner wanted me to. I think the world of that lady, I'd never give her no loaded gun!"

Macky believed him, and if it wasn't Luther's, then whose gun was it?

The Nose Has It!

8:03 AM

The next morning when Norma woke up, Macky had already left for work. She yawned and went to the bathroom and was reading her "Good morning, this is God" message when she happened to glance at herself in the mirror. "MY GOD!" There were bright red spots all over her nose! Oh God. Well, here it was. The day had finally come, she had nose cancer. She immediately sat down on the floor of the bathroom, so she wouldn't faint and hit her head. Oh no, they would probably have to remove her entire nose. She was going to be disfigured. "Why me, dear God? Why my face?" Norma thought. In high school Norma had never had a hint of acne, not one bump. Now she was being punished for it. She pulled herself up and looked again. They were still there! Not only was she going to lose her nose, it probably meant chemotherapy. There went all her hair! Oh God. "Be brave," she thought. In times like this she tried to remember little Frieda Pushnik, who had been born with no arms and legs and had been carried around all her life on a pillow, but it did not help. She was terrified as she called the dermatologist, made an appointment, got dressed, and drove over to the beauty parlor and ran in. "Tot, give me one of those Xanax. I may have to have my nose removed!"

Later, as Dr. Steward the dermatologist stared at her nose with a magnifying glass, Norma felt as if she were going to throw up. As she continued to look, the doctor asked, "Tell me, Mrs. Warren, do you blush easily?"

"What? Oh, yes."

"Uh-huh," said the doctor as Norma's heart pounded away. "And do you have any allergies that you know of?"

"No, other than maybe Chinese food. . . . My face gets sort of hot and red, but . . ."

The doctor turned around to wash her hands, and Norma heard herself ask in a raspy voice, "Is it cancer, Doctor?"

The doctor looked at her. "No, what you have is rosacea."

"What?"

"Rosacea. It's very common with English and Irish or other light-skinned people. Blushing easily is one of the symptoms."

"It is? I thought I was always just embarrassed or shy. But what are these bumps?"

"You're having a break-out."

"But why?"

"It could have been triggered by a number of things . . . heat, sun, or stress. Have you been under any unusual stress lately?"

Norma said, "Yes, I have. My aunt just fell out of a tree and . . . well, I won't go into detail, but, yes."

As Norma drove to the drugstore, she realized that her entire image of herself had been wrong. Whenever someone told a dirty joke or she had been embarrassed, she had always thought it was because she was shy, but it had just been a skin condition all along.

Norma stood at the counter waiting for her prescription for Finacea, and was convinced that the stress of worrying about her aunt had caused her nose to break out. It was no telling what would be happening to her next. She looked over at the blood pressure machine in the corner of the drugstore and she thought about going over and seeing if hers had rocketed sky-high in the last week, but decided against it. If it had, she didn't want to know. Hopefully she would just drop dead in her tracks, without having to be scared to death by all kinds of tests, and maybe before she had to undergo a complete heart transplant and wind up in a power chair herself. This was all the more reason why Elner should go to Happy Acres, where professionals could keep an eye on her, and Norma wouldn't have to worry herself into the grave about her. Norma would wait until after Easter and then have a serious talk with Elner.

"Here you go, Norma," said Hattie Smith, a cousin of Dorothy Smith's late husband, Robert Smith. But of course, according to Aunt Elner, Dorothy was now married to a man named Raymond. "Rub a thin layer on your nose, twice a day, and that should do it."

As Norma walked out with her ointment, Irene Goodnight walked in, and said to Hattie, as she held out her hands, "Hattie, look, are these freckles or old-age spots."

Hattie looked at the seventy-three-year-old woman's hands and lied.

"Honey, those are freckles."

"Well, good," said Irene. She turned around and left, happier than when she came in.

Hattie had knocked herself out of a sale, but "What the heck," she thought, "old age is hard enough. What Irene doesn't know won't hurt her."

Ask Me No Questions

Macky waited until a few days after she was home to broach the subject of the gun with Aunt Elner. On the fourth morning, they were sitting on the back porch as usual watching the sun come up, having coffee, and talking before he went to work.

Elner was saying, "There was the prettiest sunset last night, Macky, it's getting later and later. Pretty soon we will be able to sit out until seven-thirty. I didn't come in last night until a little past seven."

"Oh yeah, summer is definitely on its way." He then looked over at her and said, "Aunt Elner, did you know that there was a gun in your dirty-clothes basket?"

"There was?" she said as innocently as possible.

"Yes, you know darn well there was."

Elner looked out into the backyard at the cat who was stalking around. "I think old Sonny is getting fat, don't you?" she said, trying to change the subject. "Look at him, he just waddles anymore."

"Aunt Elner," Macky said, "you're busted so you might as

well tell me where it came from. Luther said it wasn't his. Was it Uncle Will's gun?"

She didn't answer for a while, then said, "Macky, all I can say is, ask me no questions, and I'll tell you no lies."

"Aunt Elner, this is serious. Now listen, I didn't tell Norma it was a real gun, I covered for you."

"Thank you, honey," she said.

"You're welcome, but you need to be honest with me. I need to know where that gun came from."

"All I can say is that it wasn't Will's gun." She looked up at the ceiling. "I'm gonna have to take a broom to those corners, look at those spiderwebs."

"So, you're not going to tell me where it came from."

"Honey, I would if I could."

"All right, just tell me this then. You haven't done anything you shouldn't have, you haven't shot anybody, have you?"

She laughed. "What a question. Good heavens."

"Well, wherever it came from, it's long gone now. I took the damn thing out and threw it in the river. You know I have never fussed at you before, but I love you too much to take a chance on you hurting yourself or somebody coming in here and finding it and shooting you with it."

She sat there looking chagrined. "Where in the river?"

"Never you mind where, just promise me that from now on you will keep away from guns."

"OK. I promise."

He felt bad he had to be stern with her and walked over and kissed her. "Well, all right then, let's just forget about it, OK?"

"OK."

"I've got to go to work. I love you."

"Love you too," she said.

She had learned a lesson that day that very few people on earth have a chance to find out firsthand and after the fact. When you are dead, people go through all your things, so if you have anything you don't want found, you better get rid of it before you go!

Elner hated not being able to tell Macky what he wanted to know, but she had certainly never stolen anything or killed anybody. True, she may have been guilty of hiding and withholding evidence from the police, but what the heck. Besides, some people just needed killing. She remembered when her husband, Will, had had to shoot a rabid fox. Nobody is happy about it, you hate to do it, but you have to protect your chickens, and you can say self-defense until you are blue in the face, but sometimes it just doesn't work. She periodically asked herself if she had it to do over again, would she? The answer was always yes, so her conscience was clear. Besides, Raymond hadn't said a word about it, so she figured she was home free on that count.

Beauty Shop

8:45 AM

After things settled down a little, Norma was able to get back to normal again, and on Wednesday morning she was back in the chair at Tot's Tell It Like It Is beauty shop having her hair rolled up, and listening to Tot say the same old things she had been saying over and over again for the last twenty years.

"I tell you, Norma, I'm so sick of all these whiners saying how society made them into criminals. My hind foot. Being poor is no excuse to rob people. Hell, I was poor, I pulled myself up by the bootstraps; you know what I came from, Norma, just plain trash and you didn't see me run out and rob people . . . and there's no shame anymore. People will just come right out and tell how they cheat on their taxes, and are proud of it! And when they film all those people on television looting, they just smile and wave at the camera. And if they do get caught, they get a free lawyer, and hot and cold social workers telling them they are victims of society, boo-hoo, and aren't responsible for their behavior. And don't tell me there are no jobs out there. Anybody can work if they want to. Dwayne Junior thinks he's too good to get a job. He sits at home on welfare and his disability, while his sister and me work our fingers to the bone. Even his sorry, no-good daddy worked. Granted, it was only between drunks, but at least he made an effort." Tot took a drag off of her nonfiltered Pall Mall. "Poor James, as much as he aggravated me to death, I hated that he ended up like that. The last time Darlene and I heard from him he was living in some old flophouse hotel. A couple of months later he died in the lobby watching reruns of game shows. Died watching *The Price Is Right*. He had a bad beginning and a bad end. He was no Prince Charles but he was human, I guess, and he was not a whiner. I'm so sick and tired of all the whining and bellyaching about stuff that happened in the past, and God help you if you happen to be a white person, you can't say a thing without somebody jumping down your throat calling you a racist. Everybody's so damn sensitive anymore, you have to tiptoe around everything. Those Political Correctors are lurking in every corner just waiting to pounce. . . . Next they'll be making us sing, 'I'm dreaming of a multicolored Christmas.' I tell you, I'm scared to open my mouth anymore and voice an honest opinion."

"Oh, if that were only true," thought Norma as Tot continued her weekly tirade.

"Like that time that black girl came in here looking for a job. Norma, you know I don't need anybody, I can barely afford to pay Darlene as it is, and I told her so, in a nice way too, but the next thing I know, she's calling me not only a racist but a homophobe! How was I supposed to know *she* was a *he*? I remember when this whole stupid thing started, everybody that had a black jockey boy statue had to paint them white, do you remember?"

Norma nodded. She did remember. Her mother had refused to paint her jockey boy and someone had knocked its head off.

Tot continued, "It's not my fault I'm not a minority. And how about my rights? I don't see anybody standing up for me. I pay my taxes and I don't expect anybody to take care of me, but do I complain?"

"Every week," thought Norma, but she said nothing.

"Anyhow, all you hear on TV is how bad white people are. Frankly, Norma, I don't know whether I'm a racist or not anymore. I hope not, but I don't know why I even bother to worry. They say we are all going to be speaking Spanish in the next five years anyway. It used to be just black and white, but now it seems like the whole world's gone some sort of brown color. Speaking of that, have you seen the bathtub Madonna the Lopez family has in their front yard?"

"No. What's a bathtub Madonna?"

Tot laughed. "Well, they took an old claw-foot tub, turned it sideways, and buried it halfway in the ground. Then they painted the inside of the tub blue and stuck a statue of the Blessed Mother in it."

Norma cringed. "Oh my God, and it's in the front yard?"

"Yeah," said Tot, taking another drag off her cigarette. "But it's kinda pretty, really. You know those Mexicans are artistic, you have to say that for them. He keeps that yard as neat as a pin."

That afternoon Norma thought that Tot might be right. Things were changing right there in southern Missouri. Where it used to be mostly Swedes and Germans, more and more nationalities were moving in, and when Norma had walked up to Aunt Elner's porch that morning, the radio had been blaring Mexican music out into the yard. Aunt Elner had tuned in to some new Spanish station from Poplar Springs.

"Why are you listening to that?"

"What?"

"That Spanish station?"

"Is that what it is? I wondered, I thought maybe it was Polish."

"No, honey, it's Spanish."

"Well, whatever it is, I like it. I don't understand what they are saying but the music is real cheerful and happy, don't you think?"

Thank-You from Cathy

2:18 PM

The male nurse who had informed Gus Shimmer about the potential lawsuit against the hospital was very disappointed when Gus Shimmer informed him that the old lady's niece would not sue. He had hoped to make a lot of money on his cut of the settlement, but he figured out another way he might be able to get something for his information. He picked up the phone and called his friend and got the number of a tabloid newspaper that would pay for stories of an unusual nature, and he had one.

That afternoon Norma had run into the Piggly Wiggly supermarket to pick up a few things to bring over to Aunt Elner's house for Easter dinner, and was at the checkout counter when she glanced over and saw the headline on the front page.

MISSOURI FARM WOMAN, DEAD FOR FIVE HOURS
SITS UP AND SINGS STAR SPANGLED BANNER!

Norma felt herself starting to faint and sat down on the floor before she hit the ground. Thankfully Louise Franks and her daughter Polly happened to be in line behind her and helped her up. The manager came over and they took her to the employee bathroom and sat her down on a chair and gave her a glass of water. When she could talk, she grabbed Louise's hand and said, "I knew it. We're ruined. We're probably going to have to move out of the country now." She wailed, "There goes my daughter's career!" and sat sobbing in the chair. When Louise came back to the bathroom with the paper, and showed Norma the large photograph of the woman on the front page, she was thrilled to see the woman in the photo was NOT Aunt Elner!

After the male nurse had called in the story, the reporter from the tabloid assigned to cover it had called the local paper trying to get all the details, and had informed Cathy Calvert that she was willing to pay a lot of money for any cooperation Cathy could offer. After hearing the amount of money the woman was offering, Cathy had quickly and happily agreed to supply her with not only a story but a photograph of the woman as well. All the reporter had to do was agree to change the name of the woman and the town, and Cathy would give her the information for free. The reporter didn't care about exact details or the validity of her sources. After all, *The Inquiring Eye* wasn't *The New York Times,* and the reporter didn't mind getting paid for work she did not have to do. Not only that, the gal wrote a hell of a good story to boot. That part about the old lady's claiming she had been transported to another planet where all the women looked just like Heather Locklear was a great touch!

Finally after all these years, Cathy had found a way to pay Elner back for loaning her the thousand dollars. She had also spared Elner and the town from being overrun with all the crazies and the curious. The woman in the photo on the front page was Cathy Calvert's grandmother on her father's side, Leona Fortenberry, who had been dead for years, and had stayed dead as far as Cathy knew.

Norma recovered and went home, but in the excitement she forgot her sack of groceries. She was too embarrassed to go back and get them.

Easter at Elner's

Elner and everyone else in town were so happy she had made it home in time for Easter. And this Easter turned out to be one of the best ones ever. The entire family flew in to spend it with her. Dena and Gerry flew in from California, and Linda and Apple came in from St. Louis. As usual, the day before Easter, Elner and Luther dyed over two hundred fifty eggs, and by sunrise on Easter morning, the two were out in the yard hiding them. Elner walked around the yard with the golden egg and thought about where she might hide it.

Norma got up early and ran out to the cemetery to put flowers on her parents' grave, and when she got back, they all headed over to Elner's house. The Easter egg hunt always started around twelve, but this year people had arrived with their children even earlier, and everyone was waiting in the front yard at 11:45 ready to go. When it was time, Elner stood on the porch and rang the old school bell, and about eighty little children with baskets along with Polly, Louise's forty-two-year-old daughter, ran screaming and running at breakneck speed through the yard, while the grown-ups sat in lawn chairs and watched them. Sonny the cat had to run up a tree before he was trampled to death by the rushing hordes, and he sat there very unhappy-looking for the next hour. Louise Franks and Elner watched Polly as she ran giggling from place to place, along with five-year-old Apple by her side. As it turned out, one of Tot's grandchildren found the golden egg, but as usual, Polly Franks received the biggest prize, a large stuffed rabbit that Elner and Louise had picked out the week before. Later that afternoon, after all the children except little Apple and Polly had gone home, Macky and Gerry set up the big folding table out in the yard and they had their Easter dinner under the fig tree. Reverend Susie Hill was with them and said grace, and then they started passing out the food. Elner sat happy as a lark eating her food and drinking her big glass of iced tea. She turned to Dena and said, "You know, this is about one of the best Easters I remember, and if you think about it, I had my own little Easter already, didn't I? I sort of rose up from the dead myself. And I'm mighty glad I did, I wouldn't have missed this ham and these deviled eggs Louise brought over for anything." She called out down the table, "I think they're the best deviled eggs you ever made, Louise!"

Louise Franks laughed and said, "Elner, you say that every year."

Elner said, "Well, then it must be true."

Susie, the Weight Watchers leader, helped herself to a second helping of the sweet potatoes with the marshmallows on top, and added, "Everything here is delicious."

Elner looked at the assortment of pies and cakes at the end of the table and said, "I can't wait to hit the coconut cake and that lemon icebox pie, can you?"

"No," confessed Susie, "me either."

The next morning when Linda came to pick up Apple, who had spent Easter night with Elner, Sonny the cat was hiding under the couch, and couldn't wait until she left. He was tired of being picked up and almost squeezed to death by the little girl. It wasn't until they were on the plane flying home that Linda noticed something on her daughter's hand. "What is that on your thumb?"

Apple proudly held it up. "Aunt Elner took my fingerprint. Did you know that nobody in the whole world has one just like it?"

Falling in Love Again

5:48 PM

Aunt Elner's near-death experience had a profound and un-expected effect on Macky. Almost losing one person you love shines a bright spotlight on life, and suddenly strips you of everything but your real feelings. And after the close call with Aunt Elner, for the first time, Macky saw the true facts as clearly as if a fog had suddenly been lifted. He realized that what he had felt for Lois had never been real love. Not the deep-down-in-your-bones-and-marrow love he had for Norma. Lois had been an infatuation, an ego boost, a last grab at youth fantasy. Over the years Norma had become so much a part of him that he had almost forgotten that she was his whole life. What the hell had he been thinking, for one second to even seriously en-tertain the idea of going off with a stranger? He had come so dangerously close to wrecking his life. Some great act of fortune or luck or something had saved him. That afternoon Norma walked in the door, exactly as she had a thousand times, but this time he really saw her and she was as beautiful to him as she had been at eighteen.

"What are you looking at, Macky?" she said as she put the mail down on the hall table. "Are you sick?"

"No," he said. "Have I told you lately that I adore you?"

She put her purse down. "What?"

"Did you know that you are more beautiful than you ever were?"

"Me?"

"Yes, you."

Norma looked at herself in the mirror. "Me? How could you think that, with my gray roots and wrinkles and old tired saggy body, and now these red things on my nose? I've just fallen into a heap."

"Maybe so, but you're my heap, and you don't look old to me."

Norma said, "Well, don't ever get your glasses changed, because you are obviously losing your eyesight, because I look just like the wreck of the hespers."

He laughed. "What are hespers?"

"I don't know, but that's what I look like."

"Well, you look like a million bucks to me, and I just want you to know that you are and always will be the only girl for me."

She walked over and put her hand to his forehead. "Macky, you're not sick are you? Is something wrong and you're not telling me?"

"No."

"Have you been to Dr. Halling behind my back?"

"No, I've never felt better in my life. How about we pretend it's Sunday?"

"Sunday? Why . . ." Then it dawned on her what he meant. "Oh, for heaven's sake, Macky, it's only Tuesday." And she looked back at him. "Do you really think I still look OK, or was that just a come-on?"

"Norma, of all the women in the world, to me you are the best-looking. And I can see fine, just like Aunt Elner says . . . all the way to the moon."

Norma sat and stared at him for a moment, then said, "You know what?"

"What?"

"I think I just heard church bells. . . . Did you?"

"What?" Then it dawned on him what she meant. "Oh, yeah. I hear them."

"Let me go and have my bath. Can you hold that thought for thirty minutes?"

"Barely, but I will."

As he sat waiting, he thought, "Marriage. Isn't it great? Each time you fall back in love with your wife, it gets better and better."

As she sat in the tub, Norma was so relieved and happy. She knew Macky like the back of her hand, and she could tell by the way he looked at her that he was finally once and for all over that Lois. He thought that she hadn't known about it, but she had.

The Letter

A few days after Easter, Elner went to the mailbox and pulled out a letter, postmarked Kansas City. She did not recognize the handwriting. She opened it, and read what was written.

> Dear Mrs. Schrimfinkle,
> I want to thank you for that mighty fine cake recipe you sent to my daughter. I enjoyed it to the highest.
> > Yours truly,
> > Mrs. Teresa McWilliams

Elner laughed at the way her named was spelled, and sat down and wrote her a note back.

> Dear Mrs. McWilliams,
> I am so happy you are enjoying the recipe. If you are ever over close to Elmwood Springs, please drop in and see me.
> > Sincerely,
> > Elner S.

A Surprise for Linda

6:31 PM

A few months later, Linda Warren was making dinner for herself and Apple when the phone rang. She almost didn't get it. When the phone rang at dinnertime, it was usually a telemarketer, but it kept ringing.

When she picked it up, a man's voice asked, "Is this Linda Warren?"

"Yes?"

"Who works for AT&T?"

"Yes?"

"Oh, well, I don't know if you remember me or not, it's been a while, but I was one of your aunt's doctors, Brian Lang the neurologist. I spoke to you when she was in the hospital?"

"Oh yes, of course."

"How is she doing?"

"Just fine."

"I hope you don't mind me calling you like this, but I was just transferred to St. Louis, and . . . well, I wondered if I could take you to dinner or lunch . . . or something."

"I see, well, I think that would be very nice."

After they had set a date for that Friday night, she hung up and was strangely excited. Of course she had remembered him. She remembered thinking that he would be someone nice for Apple to get to know. He was one of the best-looking Chinese men she had ever seen. She wondered if he knew she had a Chinese daughter.

Of course he knew. Elner had told him. Besides, when he'd first met Linda, he'd thought she was one of the best-looking girls he had ever seen.

A daddy for Apple. What a happy thought.

He sat in the phone booth at the airport and thought, "I hope she likes me."

She thought, "I liked him right away."

He thought, "Maybe I'll find out what area of town she lives in, and get an apartment nearby."

She thought, "I need to lose three pounds before Friday." It would be hard. It was already Thursday.

He thought, "I liked her right away."

She thought, "Don't get excited, it's just dinner."

He thought, "I've been looking so long, maybe she's the one." Maybe they were supposed to meet.

Someone knocked on the door of the phone booth.

"Are you finished?"

"Sorry," he said, and he picked up his bag and walked out, thinking, "I could be just starting." He looked around the St. Louis airport. It suddenly looked so nice. June was suddenly bursting out all over!

"Oh, dear," he thought, "I am in trouble."

Going on a Trip

5:00 AM

Elner had a plan: she knew better than to ask Norma if she could go, so she left a note on the front door.

> Norma, have gone with Luther and Bobbie Jo to get married. Will call when I get home.
>
> Love, Aunt Elner

At around twelve that afternoon when Norma found the note, she called Macky immediately. "Macky! Aunt Elner's gone off with Luther to get married. Did you know she was going?"

"She said something about it."

"Why didn't she tell me?"

"She didn't want you to worry."

"Where did they go?"

Macky chuckled. "Dollywood."

"Dollywood! My God, that's all the way to Tennessee. She's gone all the way to Tennessee in a truck! And you let her go?"

At five o'clock that morning Luther and Bobbie Jo had picked her up in his eighteen-wheeler truck and they had hit the road headed for Tennessee. Bobbie Jo had always wanted to be a June bride, and Miss Elner had always wanted to go to Dollywood, so Luther thought it was a fine idea to be married in the little chapel on the grounds, and kill two birds with one stone.

The next day Bobbie Jo, a happy new bride wearing a tank top and shorts, stood holding her wedding certificate and her free corsage the folks at the chapel had given her, watched as Luther and Elner rode on Thunderhead, the largest roller coaster at the theme park. That night at a wedding dinner at the Cracker Barrel, Elner was beaming as she ate her liver and onions. "I'm so happy for the two of you, I just don't know what to do."

When the waiter came up and asked if they would be wanting to order dessert, the new bridegroom said, "Does a cat have a tail?" Bobbie Jo thought it was about the wittiest thing she had ever heard.

When Elner got back home a few days later, she called Norma, and as she expected Norma was upset.

"Aunt Elner, why would a woman your age want to get in a truck and go all the way to Tennessee?"

Aunt Elner said, "Norma, that's just *it*. At my age how many more chances to get to Dollywood do I have? I just figured I'd better go while the going was good, don't you think?"

Norma Puts Her Foot Down

4:32 PM

The next day as she drove over to Elner's house, Norma was determined to put her foot down once and for all, but when she walked up onto the porch, before she could say a word, Aunt Elner hit her with a question.

"Hey, Norma, do you think that woman on that beeper commercial is an actress or a real person?"

"What woman?"

"The one that's fallen and can't get up."

"Oh, that one. I'm sure she's an actress."

"She didn't look like an actress to me, she could be a relative, don't you think?"

"A relative? Whose relative?"

"Of the beeper people. She could be a family member, couldn't she?"

"I suppose so, Aunt Elner, but speaking of that, I want to talk to you about something, and I want you to listen to what I have to say and not interrupt me."

"Uh-oh," thought Elner. From Norma's tone she knew whatever she had to say was not something she wanted to hear.

Macky was in the kitchen chewing on the pimento cheese and celery sticks she had made to tide him over until dinner when Norma got back home from Elner's.

He looked at her. "What did she say?"

Norma sighed and put her purse on the counter and washed her hands.

"*Exactly* what you said she would say. She won't go."

"You can't force her, Norma. Everybody wants to be independent for as long as they can. I'm sure when the time comes—"

Norma interrupted him. "When the time comes? Macky, if you knock yourself out falling out of a tree and think you've just seen Ginger Rogers and orange and white polka-dotted squirrels and then you run off to Dollywood, I would say the time has come, wouldn't you?"

"I know, but I think for her to have to go to a place like that would be terrible."

"Well, I don't know what's so terrible about assisted living. Personally, I can't wait to have somebody assist me. I'd go early if I could. I understand why people want to be movie stars, it must be nice to have people waiting on you hand and foot, catering to all your whims, is all I can say."

"No, you wouldn't. You'd hate not being in charge of everything."

"I would not, and what would you know about it anyway? You've had assisted living all your life. First your mother, then me. You'll sail on into it and not miss a beat. I'm telling you, Macky, I am one step away from checking myself into a room over there at Happy Acres for good, then you and Aunt Elner can be independent for as long as you like."

Macky said, "They may call it an assisted living facility, but it's still an old folks' home no matter what fancy name you give it."

"And what's the matter with an old folks' home? She is old. *How* old, we will never know, thanks to Mother."

Back in Kansas City

10:48 PM

Winston Sprague had finally been knocked off his high horse, not by a person, but by a shoe. The lawyer sat staring at the golf shoe he now kept under his bed, and pondered the same old question that had nagged at him for the past weeks: "How in the hell had she known it was there?" Franklin Pixton had been sure there was a logical explanation, but Winston had not been as sure, and had done a little investigating on his own. He had spent hours going through the old hospital archives and had discovered that at one time, before the new hospital building and trauma center had been built, there had also been a helicopter pad on top of the building. He had searched through the data they had on microfilm and had found out that between the years 1963 and 1986 the old hospital had flown in over nine hundred and eighty patients suffering from heart attacks. Three hundred and eight had been flown directly from the many golf courses around the area, including six cases of men who had been struck by lightning while playing golf. So it was certainly possible that in the rush to get them off the helicopter and onto a gurney, one of the three hundred and eight golf players might have lost a shoe. But still . . . the question remained, "How could the old lady have seen it?"

Norma Gives Up

11:14 AM

The day after Elner refused to go to Happy Acres, Norma made a phone call to their family physician. Maybe Tot had the right idea, she took tranquilizers.

"Dr. Halling," she said, "I wonder if you could give me something for stress?"

"Stress?"

"Yes. A few months ago I broke out with rosacea, and the dermatologist said it was caused by stress."

"I see. Well, why don't you come in and let me take a look at you?"

"No, I really can't do that right now. My nerves are just too bad. If there is something seriously wrong with me, I really don't want to know."

Dr. Halling said, "All right, but come in and let's at least talk about it."

Dr. Halling knew Norma well, and he knew he would never get her to come in if he threatened her with any tests. She was the biggest hypochondriac he had ever encountered in all his years of practice.

The next day Norma sat in Dr. Halling's office as far away from him as possible. Even though he had promised no tests, she was still nervous.

He looked at her over his glasses. "So, other than rosacea and your hair falling out, any other symptoms?"

"No."

"Are you still walking thirty minutes a day?"

"Yes, well, I try. I used to go to the mall and walk twice a week with Irene Goodnight and Reverend Susie, my minister, but I haven't gone in a while."

"I see. Well, you need to do that. What is your average day like?"

"Oh, nothing much. I get up and clean the house, do the laundry, visit a few friends."

"Any outside activities?"

"Besides church and Weight Watchers? No, not really."

"Hobbies?"

"No, not really. Other than cooking, taking care of the house, and trying to look after Aunt Elner, of course."

"Well, I'm going to give you a prescription for something to help you sleep, but I think your main problem is that you have too much time on your hands, too much free time to worry. Have you ever thought about going to work?"

"Work?"

"Yes, have you ever worked?"

"No, not outside the home. There was one day I worked as a hostess at the pancake house, but I hated that so I quit."

"I see. Well, I think you should consider getting a job. Maybe a part-time job?"

"A job? At my age? What kind of job?"

"Oh, I don't know. Something you might enjoy. What do you like to do?"

As Norma walked out to the parking lot, she kept thinking, "What do I like to do? What do I like to do?" At one time she had considered opening her own Merle Norman cosmetics store. But that was only because she had been afraid they would change the original cold cream formula. When she got to her car in the parking lot, she looked and read the bumper sticker she had on her back fender: I BRAKE FOR OPEN HOUSES. And it came to her. Real estate! That's what she liked to do. Every weekend she and Irene Goodnight went to all the open houses. And she never missed *House Hunters* on the Home & Garden television channel. Her friend Beverly Cortwright had even said she should go into real estate with her.

For the first time since Linda had come home from China with her little girl, Norma was excited.

She drove across town and pulled up in front of Beverly's office and went in.

Beverly walked out of the back with an armload of flyers.

"Hey, Norma, how are you?"

"Fine. Listen, were you serious about me going into real estate?"

"Well, sure, why?"

"Because I've been thinking about it."

"Oh, well, sit down and let's talk about it."

The Sunset Club

9:02 PM

That night everyone had gone home after watching the sunset, except Tot and Elner, who were still sitting in the side yard talking about the good old days. Elner asked Tot, "Do you remember that maple syrup that used to come in a little tin house, looked like a cabin?"

"Oh yeah. And remember that three-in-one rainbow, pink and blue and white coconut candy? And that brown bread that came in a can?

"Hell," said Tot, "I'm so old I still remember learning to read from those little Dick and Jane books they used to have. I guess old Dick and Jane are headed for the old folks' home now . . . along with Nancy Drew, and the Rover boys. Little Orphan Annie must be a hundred and eight by now."

Elner looked over. "Hey, Tot, I have a question for you. Do you ever have any regrets in life?"

Tot looked at her as though she had just lost her mind. "Regrets? Me? Oh, other than having an alcoholic for a father and an insane woman for a mother, marrying James Whooten, the biggest fool on the earth, and breeding two mutants, then marrying another man who dropped dead on our honeymoon . . . no, why?"

Elner laughed. "No, honey, I mean things you always wanted to do and didn't do. I realized I never got to go to Dollywood and I was sad about it, but then, when I had the chance, I went, so now I can die without any regrets."

"Well, it's too late for me," Tot said, taking another sip out of her beer. "My ship has sailed and sunk a long time ago."

"Now, Tot, that's just not true, honey. It's never too late. Look at Norma, starting a brand-new career late in life."

"I don't want a brand-new career. I hate the old one, why would I want a new one?"

"You know, Tot, I haven't told anybody else this, but being dead sort of puts things in perspective, and you need to try and enjoy your life and do things you always wanted to do before it's too late. Take it from me."

"I would, but there's not anything I always wanted to do."

"Oh, I'll bet there is, Tot. You just wait and see. One day you'll find something."

"Well, it won't be some man, I can tell you that. You were lucky. Will Shimfissle was a sweet man and just crazy about you. Everybody could see that. My James was just plain crazy."

Learning the Ropes

3:28 PM

Beverly Cortwright and Norma were riding around about
twenty miles south of town, looking for property, when
Beverly spied an obviously homemade HOUSE FOR SALE sign
nailed to a fence. Beverly's eyes lit up. "Look at that, Norma."
She quickly turned the car around and drove back up to the
fence and stopped. Down a long driveway and set on a pretty
pine tree lot stood a little neat brick house that looked to be in
pretty good shape. Beverly was excited. This house must have
just gone on the market in the last few days, because it had not
yet appeared in the multiple listings book. Beverly read that
thing every morning like a racing form. She knew the details of
every property listed, and most of the time had seen the place
before the realtor's open house. She was a master at getting in to
see the listings before anyone else, and today was no exception.
Norma was still a greenhorn and still a little uncomfortable
barging into people's homes, but not Beverly. Before Norma
knew it, Beverly had driven up the driveway, stopped in front of
the house, and was busy rummaging through her large purse for
her tape measure and camera. She always had the purse with her

wherever she went in case of an unexpected real estate spotting. Beverly was always prepared.

"Come on. We need to see this, Norma," she said as she got out of the car.

"But shouldn't we call first?" said Norma as she reluctantly got out of her side of the car.

"No, I find it's best not to," Beverly said as she walked up and pushed the doorbell. "You'll find out soon enough, Norma. In this market, you can't stand on ceremony."

She pushed the bell again and leaned down and looked through a window.

"Oh, here comes somebody."

An older man opened the door, and they could hear the sounds of a football game on the television set inside the house.

"Can I help you?" he said.

Beverly immediately flashed her two-in-one surefire real estate smile, apologetic yet friendly at the same time. "Hi. I'm Beverly Cortwright and this is my friend Norma. We are so sorry to bother you, I know this is a terrible thing to do to you on a Saturday, but if it's at all possible, we would just love to take a quick peek at your house. I said to Norma, this is one of the cutest houses I've seen. It is just adorable, and if you will just let us run in and take a look, I promise we won't be but just a few minutes."

The man was hesitant. "Well, it's kind of a mess right now, and my wife is not home."

But Beverly, the old pro, had already stepped inside the door. "Oh, don't you worry about that, we're used to that, we just want to see the layout, and take a few pictures."

The man reluctantly said, "Well, if you want to, I guess it's all right."

"Oh, thank you so much, you just go back to your game and don't pay any attention to us," she said as she headed toward the kitchen.

"Don't you want me to show you around?"

"No, you just get on back to what you were doing."

"All right, then," he said.

Beverly was a woman on a mission; within ten minutes they had covered the entire house and taken pictures of each room. After Beverly had finished measuring the second bedroom, she said to Norma, who was taking notes, "Twelve by ten, small closet, wall between could be knocked out." After she had flushed the toilet and run the water in the bathtub, shower, and bathroom sink, she said, "Water pressure's good but I don't like that tile." As she walked, she threw comments over her shoulder at Norma. "Hate the fake wood paneling. Nice double-hung windows throughout. Original floors. Kitchen needs updating." When they were ready to leave, Beverly stuck her head inside the den and addressed the man in the BarcaLounger. "We're done, but can I ask you a few quick things?"

The man turned down the volume and said, "Sure."

"Are you on septic or sewer?"

"Septic."

"When was the house built?"

"1958."

"How much land do you have here?"

"About five acres."

"Ah, and do you know if it could be subdivided or not?"

"No, ma'am, I don't."

"Well, thank you so much. Oh, wait a minute, I almost forgot the most important thing, how much are you asking?"

The man looked puzzled. "For what?"

"The house."

"The house? This house isn't for sale."

Now Beverly was confused. "Has it already sold?"

"No."

"Then why do you still have the sign up?"

"What sign?"

"The sign on the fence out there."

The man looked at her kind of funny and said, "Lady, that sign says HORSE FOR SALE."

As they drove out, they took another look at the sign. It did in fact say HORSE FOR SALE.

Norma was horrified at what they had done. "Oh my God, that poor man, he must have thought we were crazy, running through his house like that. Here we tromped all through his house, opened closets and everything. Flushed the toilets, opened all the kitchen drawers. It's a wonder he didn't call the police on us."

Beverly said, "I guess I was in such a real estate frenzy I'm starting to hallucinate. But look at it this way, Norma, at least he has my card and if he ever does decide to sell, we got the jump on RE/MAX."

"Still, I feel terrible, that poor man. He was so nice."

"Yes, he was, but he can afford to be, he's not in the real estate business. You know what they say, don't you, Norma? Real estate agents never die, they just remain in escrow forever. Isn't that a good one? I made that up myself."

No two ways about it, Norma was learning the business from the bottom up.

A Visitor for Elner

12:48 PM

Over the past months, Mrs. McWilliams, La Shawnda's mother, and Elner had written each other several times, and today La Shawnda had driven her mother all the way to Elmwood Springs for a visit. When they arrived at Elner's house, she was waiting on the front porch to greet them.

"Hey, Mrs. McWilliams, you made it," she said to the small black lady, who scurried up the sidewalk toward her, grinning from ear to ear and carrying a large black-and-white striped hat box with a caramel cake inside.

"I did," she said, "and I made us a cake!"

They had a nice long visit and between the three of them ate most of the cake that the old lady had made, and it was almost as good as Dorothy's.

Later, as they were sitting out on the porch, Mrs. McWilliams said to Elner, "I'm so glad we got to come out today. I'm going to be moving back home tomorrow, back to Arkansas, but I wanted to meet the cake lady before I went."

"Well, I'm so glad you did too. Us old country women have to stick together. These youngsters don't know what it's like to wake up and hear the birds, do they?"

"No, they don't. . . . All the young want is to listen to all that nasty hippity hop music and run their cars up and down the road day and night." She looked over at her daughter and said, "I'll miss my baby here, but I'll be so glad to be home."

La Shawnda said, "I'll come and visit you, Momma."

"I hope you do."

Mrs. McWilliams looked out in the side yard and remarked, "That's a mighty fine fig tree you got out there, Mrs. Shim-fissle."

Elner looked at it and smiled. "It is, isn't it?"

As the two visitors got up to leave, Mrs. McWilliams said, "I hope I get to see you again someday."

"Oh, you will," said Elner.

Going Professional

Six months later, after Norma had passed her real estate exam and gotten her license, Beverly told Norma that they needed a picture to put in the office brochure. A few days later Norma brought in the picture she had had made at Wal-Mart, where she was wearing her bright red jacket with the emblem and a black turtleneck sweater.

Norma thought it looked very professional, but Beverly looked at it and said, "This is nice, but you don't want just an ordinary pose, you need a photo that will grab people, a gimmick, a hook, something to set you apart." Beverly had her photo made with her in a picture hat, holding her two pet ferrets, Joan and Melissa, with the caption "Let Us Ferret Out a New Home for You."

But Norma was at a loss. She told Macky, "I'm as dull as a dishwasher," as she flipped through the multiple listings looking for ideas for a professional picture. A lot of agents had their pictures taken with them talking on a phone, one had her picture with a cello, a lot had their dogs, another one was standing by an antique car, and somebody named Wade had his picture made at a castle somewhere. It could have been made at Disneyland. It was that picture that sparked the idea for Norma. The next day, wearing her red jacket, she went over to Aunt Elner's yard with Macky and she stood by the birdhouse that Luther had made Aunt Elner, and smiled.

LOOKING FOR A HOME?
CALL NORMA

Tot Still Telling It Like It Is

As busy as she was on Wednesday, Norma was in her chair as usual and had braced herself for another tirade from Tot.

"I'm telling you, Norma, entertainment has gone from bad to worse. With all that violence and sex stuff they put in the movies now, no wonder people around the world don't like us, if they think that's what we are like."

"It could be," said Norma.

"Why don't they make movies about nice people like they used to? I don't mind a little cussing, I do my share, but it seems like every movie I see, every other word is the *F* word. I'm not a prude, my God, I've been married twice, but what ever happened to love stories? Nowadays, it's hello, how do you do, let's have sex—and I'm not so sure they even stop to say hello. Oh, it's everywhere, even the nature shows want to show you animals having sex, and you know it's men that are filming those shows. You sit in your own living room with your grandchildren to watch television and here comes an ad for Viagra. Good God, just what we don't need, more men with more erections. It's disgusting. And then they say right out loud for the whole world to hear, if you experience an erection lasting over four hours, you need to seek medical attention. Can you imagine? And wouldn't that be a pretty sight coming into the hospital. Wasting the doctor's time with that silliness. What idiot thought that pill up ought to be shot, and you *know* it was a man. The number one problem in the world is overpopulation and now they're inventing pills to help make it worse. I tell you . . . men and their sex. Why don't they work on curing cancer or some other diseases, and just leave well enough alone. Let sleeping dogs lie, I say. If any of my husbands had ever tried that, I would have run him off with a stick."

She slammed a bobby pin into Norma's scalp.

"They say our morals have just slid to the gutter and everybody has just gone criminal anymore, and we'll be back in the jungle with bones in our noses and sticking each other in pots, if we don't watch out. I'm thinking about moving to a gated community and getting a gun myself. They say the barbarians are at the gate."

"Oh, Tot," sighed Norma, "you need to stop staying up all night listening to all that hate radio. It just keeps you upset."

"It's not hate radio, it's the truth!"

"Well, I think if you can't say something nice, then don't say anything."

Tot looked at her in the mirror. "Norma, I tried being nice and it didn't get me anything but a bad back, a bad marriage, and two ungrateful children, plus a nervous breakdown. I'll tell you, Norma, it's a good thing I don't work for the suicide prevention hotline, because in the mood I'm in, I'd tell them to just go on and do it."

As the weeks went by, Norma realized she could no longer go to the beauty parlor without getting upset at having to listen to Tot rant on and on, and with the stress of the new job, she was afraid of having another break-out on her nose, so she made a hard decision and drove over to Tot's house.

She walked in and said, "Tot, I came over to talk to you about something. You know I love you. I've known you since I was born, but you have to know something. I've been struggling with an anxiety disorder."

"Oh, who hasn't?" Tot said. "You'd be crazy not to be anxious these days. The best thing for you is to get yourself some Xanax and have a drink once in a while, that's what I do."

Norma said, "Well, that's fine, but the truth is I'm trying to do it without drugs. Or alcohol."

"Why?"

"Well, I'm trying to eliminate all the negative influences from my life, and as much as I don't want to, I'm going to have to cancel my future hair appointments."

Tot looked at her in disbelief. "Why?"

"Because I work so hard all week to keep myself positive, and by the end of my appointment with you, I start to feel bad and get anxious all over again. You may not realize it, Tot, but you are very negative, and it makes me feel bad."

"Oh but, Norma, that's just talk, that shouldn't make you anxious."

"I know it shouldn't, but it does. It's not your fault, it's mine. I'm probably too sensitive, but I just wanted you to know."

After she left in tears, Tot was flabbergasted. She had never lost a customer before, and it shook her to the bone.

For the next few days Norma was wondering if she had done the right thing. She would certainly miss Tot. It was hard to think of anyone fixing her hair but Tot. She couldn't face even looking for someone else. When she had been in Florida, not having her own hairdresser had been very hard on her. They had not done her hair right for two years.

The following Wednesday, Norma sat in the kitchen looking at the clock, wondering if Tot had filled her spot yet, wondering who was sitting in the chair, having her hair rolled up. Down at the beauty shop Tot sat over in the corner staring at the empty chair. She could no more have put anybody else in Norma's appointment spot than fly to the moon. That afternoon, Tot drove over with her shampoo and rollers in a large bag and knocked. Norma, looking somewhat frazzled, came to the door and was surprised to see Tot standing there.

Tot said, "Honey, I've come to apologize, and if you will take me back, I promise not to talk about anything but positive things from now on. I thought about what you said, and you're right. I just got myself into a bad habit of being negative and I didn't even know it, but I'm going to try and kick it. Can I come in?"

"Oh, Tot, of course you can," said a relieved Norma.

"Whew," Tot said. "The thought of anyone else doing your roots just made me crazy. I couldn't bear to think of you going out to Supercuts: they don't know you and they don't know your hair."

Tot washed Norma's hair in her kitchen sink, and after she finished rolling it up she felt like a hundred-pound weight had been lifted off her chest.

As she left she said, "Norma, I've been thinking, when you come in next week, I want us to go a little lighter with your color. I have a new product for us to try, if you're up for it."

"Sure, whatever you want, Tot," she said. She was so happy to be going back, she would have let Tot dye her hair green if she had wanted to. Both her escrows were closing on time, and she had Tot back. All was right with the world again.

A Very Nice Cat

8:40 AM

Every year on the same day Macky picked Sonny up and took him to the vet's office for his annual checkup and shots. This morning Aunt Elner was in the living room waiting for Macky, and Sonny was already in his cat cage ready to go.

When he walked in, she said, "Ohhh, Macky, is he mad at me. He knows where he's headed and he's not happy about it either."

Macky picked up the box. "How did you catch him?"

"I tricked him, I opened up a can of cat food and when he tried to eat it I threw a towel over him."

He looked inside and he could see Sonny was not glad to see him.

"I'll see you later, Aunt Elner," he said as he picked the cage up.

"OK, tell Dr. Shaw hey for me."

When Macky brought Sonny back that afternoon, Aunt Elner was out on the porch to greet him, happy to have Sonny back home.

"How did he do?"

· 327 ·

Macky handed him over. "Just fine, he's good to go for another year."

"Did he bite anybody?"

"No, not that I know of."

"Well, good, they say he's hard to pill."

Early the next morning Norma was in the kitchen trying to pull together a home inspection and a termite report on the old Whatley place when the phone rang. When she picked it up, it was Aunt Elner.

"Norma, you are going to have to get Macky to come up here and take this cat back over to Dr. Shaw."

"Why?"

"It's not my cat."

"What do you mean, it's not your cat?"

"It's not my cat. He's a very nice cat, but he's not my cat."

"Of course it's your cat."

"No, it's not."

"What makes you think it's not your cat?"

"I can just tell. You know your own cat, Norma."

"Well, maybe he's still traumatized from having to go to the vet, give him a day or so and he'll be back to his old self."

"I'm telling you, Norma, this is not my cat. This cat's hair is fuller around the face than Sonny's was, and his personality's not the same."

"Honey, Dr. Shaw has treated Sonny for years, he would know if it was the right cat or not. What possible reason would he have for giving you the wrong cat?"

"Maybe they gave Sonny to some other person, and I got their cat by mistake. I don't know, but I do know this is not my cat."

Norma hung up and called Macky out at The Home Depot.

"Macky, Aunt Elner thinks the cat you picked up yesterday is not Sonny."

"What?"

"She's convinced that the cat you brought back is not her cat."

"What makes her think so?"

"Oh, I don't know, Macky. What makes her think anything, but you better go over there and talk to her."

"Have you called Dr. Shaw? Who knows, maybe they did give her the wrong cat."

"You saw the cat, Macky, didn't it look like Sonny to you?"

"Yes, but all those orange cats look alike to me, I couldn't tell one from another."

Norma felt like a fool but she made the phone call anyway just to be on the safe side.

Dr. Shaw was in the back busy clipping Beverly's new ferret's toenails, so Norma spoke to his wife, who worked in the office.

"Abby, it's Norma, let me ask you a silly question. Did you happen to have more than one orange cat over there the other day?"

"Other than Mrs. Shimfissle's cat?"

"Yes?"

"Gosh, I don't think so, why?"

"Oh, she has some crazy idea that the cat Macky picked up yesterday is not her cat."

"Huh . . . well, let me check it out and make sure, but I don't remember and I was here. Hold on. . . . No, no other orange cats were here."

⚬⚬⚬

"Aunt Elner, I just spoke to Abby. Honey, that had to be Sonny, she said they didn't have any other orange cats over there."

"Well, I don't know what to tell you, but this is not my cat. It's too bad cats don't have fingerprints or I could prove it to you once and for all. Like I say, he's a very nice cat but he's not my cat."

"Well, what are you going to do?"

"What can I do, just keep him, I guess. I've gotten used to him now. I just hope whoever has Sonny is sweet to him."

"Ironic," thought Norma. They had switched cats on her in the past and she had not noticed, and now, when she really did have the right cat, she thought she didn't. Go figure.

Something's Wrong

6:30 AM

After the cat incident, they should have been concerned about Aunt Elner, but Macky just laughed, and for the past year Norma had been so busy with her real estate, they had not thought any more about it. However, in early March they suddenly started to notice she wasn't hearing as well, and she began to be confused about who people were. As the months went by she would often call Norma, Ida, and sometimes would call Macky, Luther. Soon, other little things started to happen. She started forgetting conversations and would call three or four times and repeat the same things over and over, and after a while she started to become confused as to where she was, as though she were back on the farm again. Then a few weeks later, when Macky went over for coffee, he walked into the kitchen and found she had left the stove burner on, but was not in the house. He went next door to Ruby's, looking for her, but she was not there. He then walked out into the back field behind the house and found her wandering around, lost and confused. When she saw him, she said, "The barn's gone, I can't find the barn, and I've got to feed the cows." Macky knew something was wrong. After he told Norma what had happened, she said, "It's just not safe for her to be alone anymore, Macky. I'm afraid she's liable to burn the house down. We are going to have to put her out at Happy Acres for her own good, before she hurts herself." As much as he didn't want to, he had to agree. The time had come. They had the initial meeting, and as they walked down the hall on a tour of the place, it almost killed Macky. On every door the management had placed a photograph of the person so they could find their room. As he went by he saw face after face of someone who used to be young. It was so sad to think that a woman as bright as Aunt Elner would wind up in a place like this. The room they did pick out for her was one with a nice view, at least. He knew she would like that. As they were driving home, they said nothing for a while, then Macky asked, "Who's going to tell her?"

Norma thought about it. "I think you should, Macky, she'll listen to you."

The next morning he walked up the steps thinking he would rather cut off his own arm than have to tell her what he was going to have to tell her. Fortunately, today was one of her good days and she was perfectly lucid.

He waited until they were sitting out on the back porch, then he said, "Aunt Elner, you know Norma and I love you very much."

"And I love you too," she said.

"I know you do . . . but sometimes we have to do things we don't want to do, things that . . ." He struggled for the right words. "Things that seem . . . but in the long run are really . . . You know Norma worries about you living all alone, and she thinks maybe it would be best if you were in a place where there were people around to look out for you."

Elner looked out into the yard, but did not say anything.

Macky sat there feeling sick.

After a while she looked over at him. "Do you think I should go on out there, Macky?"

He took a deep breath. "Yes."

"Oh," she said. "Well, if you think it's best."

"I do, honey."

They sat saying nothing for a while, then she asked, "Can I take Sonny?"

"No, I'm afraid not, they don't allow pets."

"I see, well, like I say, he's a nice cat, but he's not my cat, but you will find a good home for him, won't you?"

"Of course."

"When do I have to go?"

He looked at her. "When do you want to go?"

"Can I wait till after Easter?"

Easter was only a few weeks away, so Macky said, "Sure."

Getting Ready

9:30 AM

In the following few days, they helped Elner pack up the few things she wanted to take: her glass paperweight with the Empire State Building inside, a few photographs of Will and of little Apple, and her picture of the dancing mice. She had given most everything else away. A lot went to neighbors, and she gave her five bulldog doorstoppers to Louise Franks, who had always admired them.

Two days after Easter, the day they were to pick her up and drive her out to Happy Acres, Macky woke up with a pit in his stomach, and even though she knew it was for the best, Norma felt the same way. Ruby was going out with them to help get Elner settled in, but still Macky felt like a hundred-pound weight was on his chest. After Elner had agreed to go, she had surprised both of them at how she had accepted the inevitable. Macky almost wished she had fought it more; her being so accommodating and trying not to make them feel bad only made him feel worse. He was shaving and Norma was running her bath when the phone rang.

"That's probably her, Macky, tell her we'll be there by ten."

He wiped off his face and walked into the bedroom and picked up the phone.

Norma turned the water off and stepped into the tub and sat down. She did not hear Macky and called out, "Honey, was that her?"

But he did not answer. "Macky?"

Macky was still sitting on the bed, and he smiled as he thought, "Well, the old gal got what she wanted after all." He stood up and went to the bathroom to tell Norma that they would not be taking her to Happy Acres after all.

And although nobody but Elner knew it, the wish she had wished for on the first star every night for so many years had finally come true. Ruby had just informed him that when she went over to Elner's house a few minutes ago, she had found that Elner had died peacefully in her sleep, at home in her own bed.

A Final Good-bye

A day after Elner died, Cathy Calvert ran the same obituary in the paper that Elner had read at the hospital and liked so much, and it pleased Cathy to know she had gotten a chance to see it. Only the date had been changed.

When Verbena Wheeler called the Bud and Jay show to tell them that Elner Shimfissle had died, Bud listened politely and said, "Thank you very much for calling, Mrs. Wheeler." But he did not announce it right away. He said to Jay, "I'm giving it a week, to be on the safe side."

True to her word, Norma did not hold a funeral, but a few weeks later, according to Elner's wishes, her ashes were scattered out behind her house at sunset, and also according to her wishes, Luther Griggs stood with the family during the ceremony. When it was over and Norma turned around she had been surprised to see what looked like the entire town quietly gathered in the yard, all come to say good-bye to Elner. She would be missed, that was clear.

As it turned out, a few months later, Luther and Bobbie Jo wound up buying Elner's house and got Sonny the cat in the deal. At first the neighbors were horrified to think about that big truck sitting in the yard, but they needn't have worried. Bobbie Jo made him sell the truck and stay home. Luther went to work out at The Home Depot with Macky in Automotive Parts, and did quite well. Nine months later Luther and Bobbie Jo had a little girl and named her Elner Jane Griggs. Sonny the cat was not happy there was a baby in the house. Babies grow up to be children.

The Family Bible

2:18 PM

The winter after Elner died was one of the coldest ones on record, and Mr. Rudolf called and told Norma the bad news. Norma had grown up in what was still considered the prettiest house in Elmwood Springs. Because Norma's father had been a banker, Ida had insisted he build a house to reflect his standing in the community and had hired an architect from Kansas City to build them a large redbrick bungalow, but after Norma's father died and Ida moved to Poplar Springs, Ida donated the house to the local garden club for safekeeping. Ida told a disappointed Norma, who really would have liked to have the house not for herself and Macky but for Linda, that giving the house to the garden club was the only way she could ensure the future of her English boxwoods. After all these years, the house and the gardens were still there, including her mother's "ugly English boxwoods," as they were referred to privately by Norma and her father. Growing up, there had been times when both she and her father had suspected that her mother had cared more for her English boxwoods than she had for them. But unfortunately the boxwoods were now no more. That January freeze had killed them and they all had to be dug up and re-

· 338 ·

placed with a much lesser plant, the dreaded pittosporum, as her mother called it. Norma thought that it was a good thing her mother was not still alive, because she would have died anyway, if she knew.

A few days later Norma heard a knock on the door. When she opened it, there stood Mr. Rudolf, the head gardener for the garden club. He said, "Mrs. Warren, the boys were digging around in the garden and they found this. We opened it up and I think it might have belonged to your mother, so I wanted to bring it over." He tipped his hat and handed her a large plastic Tupperware container; inside, she could see still half wrapped in cotton and Saran wrap a large black Bible. Norma thanked him and went to the living room and sat down and opened it. It was the old Nuckle Knott family Bible that had belonged to her grandparents. Norma's hands were shaking as she opened it and saw the names listed.

KNOTT

Henry Clay   born Nov. 9, 1883 died 1942
Nancy Nuckle   born July 18, 1881 died 1919

CHILDREN

Elner Jane   born July 28, 1910
Gerta Marie   born March 11, 1912
Ida Mae   born May 22, 19

Her mother's birth year had been scratched out completely, of course, and so the exact date of her mother's birth had followed her to her grave, and beyond. But now Norma knew that Aunt Elner had lived to be almost ninety-six years old. "Good Lord," Norma thought, with that kind of longevity in her family, she was not too old to start a new career after all.

However, as it so happened, the old Nuckle Knott family Bible was not the only thing that had been buried away by one of the sisters. Elner Shimfissle had a secret as well, and after she died, there was only one person on earth left who knew exactly *what* it was, *where* it was, and *what* had happened.

What Had Happened

Elner's friend and old neighbor out at the farm, Louise Franks, had not had an easy life. She had worked hard for years, and had had her first and only child late in life. When her daughter, Polly, was born and they were told she was a Down syndrome baby, the news had been difficult for Louise, but it had been devastating for her husband. A year later she woke up one morning and he was gone. He left her the farm and a few thousand dollars in the bank, but that was it. It was just her and Polly from then on. Thank heavens, for the most part Polly was a happy child, and as long as she could sit and color in her coloring books she was content for hours, but even though at that time Polly was twelve years old, Louise usually did not leave her daughter alone in the house. However, on that one fateful day, Polly had been so preoccupied and busy coloring in her new Casper the Friendly Ghost coloring book that Louise had figured she could leave her while she ran into town and back, and Polly would be fine. She was a good child, and always minded her mother, and she promised not to leave the kitchen until she returned. It was a pretty fall afternoon when Louise walked out and told her hired man, who was chopping wood in the back, that she had to run into town to pick up a few things, and to watch the house while she was gone.

"Yes, ma'am," he said, tipping his hat. As had been his pattern on other farms, he had been waiting for this opportunity for weeks, and now was his chance. He continued chopping wood and watched until Louise's car was out of sight, then he threw down the hatchet and headed into the house to find that girl. "She may be ugly," he thought, "and older than most of the other little girls on the farms before, but she is too stupid to tell anybody anything." Besides, he was ready to move on, and as usual, he would be long gone by the time the mother got back. He came up onto the porch and threw open the kitchen door. Polly was still sitting at the table coloring. "Come here, little girlie," he said as he unbuckled his pants. "I've got something for you."

When Louise drove up to the house, she thought it was odd that the hired man had not finished chopping the wood, but the second Louise walked in the door, she knew something terrible had just happened. The kitchen was in complete shambles, things knocked over, chairs and dishes broken and scattered everywhere. Polly was still sitting at the table coloring right where Louise had left her, with her face all wet and beaten up, rocking back and forth. Louise screamed, dropped her groceries, and ran over to her daughter. "Oh my God, what happened?" Polly only repeated over and over "Hurt, Momma" and then pointed across the room to over by the sink. Louise looked over to where she was pointing, and to her horror she saw a man naked from the waist down with a mop bucket on his head, sitting propped up against the wall. Louise was terrified and immediately grabbed Polly and pulled her up out of the chair and ran with her to the bedroom, and quickly locked the door behind them. She wanted to call someone for help but her only phone was in the kitchen, so she sat on the bed frozen with fear and prayed that he would not get up and break the door down.

At that very moment her closest neighbor and friend, Elner Shimfissle, drove up the driveway, completely unaware of what had just taken place. She was just stopping by to bring Louise and Polly a freshly made pecan pie, before she drove the other pies over to the church. Elner got out of the truck and opened the kitchen door, calling out, "Hey, girls, I've got a—" then stopping dead in her tracks. The first thing she spotted was the naked man sitting on the floor with the bucket on his head.

"Good Lord," she said, dropping her pie. "What's going on? Louise, Louise!"

Louise heard her and called out, "Oh, Elner. Help me, help me." Then Elner ran past the man to the bedroom in the back. Louise let her in and Elner saw that Polly had blood on her face. Immediately Elner ran over and helped Louise take Polly into the bathroom to clean up the cuts on her head and her lip, and Elner tried to calm Louise down enough so she could tell her what had happened.

"Who's that naked man?"

"I don't know."

"What's he doing with a mop bucket on his head?"

"I don't know," said a frantic Louise. "He was here when I came in. . . . I should have never left her, it's all my fault."

When Elner had sized up the situation, she said, "You stay here. I'll be right back."

"Don't go in there!" screamed Louise. "He's liable to kill you!"

"Not if I get to him first," she said. "The very idea of him doing such a thing . . ."

She then looked around for something heavy, and picked up a lamp. "Lock the door behind me," she said, and walked back into the kitchen, ready for a fight. But the naked man had not moved from where he had been. Still, Elner took no chances. She knew he could be playing possum and jump up at her, so she picked a rolling pin up off the counter. And now, armed with a lamp and a rolling pin, she walked over slowly, but the man did not move. She nudged him with her foot, and he fell over onto his side with the bucket still on his head and just lay there motionless. Satisfied it was safe, she then reached down and pulled the bucket off the man's head and recognized him as Louise's hired hand. He was not a pretty sight. No wonder Polly had put a bucket over his head. Elner walked over and pulled the tablecloth off the kitchen table; she did not care to look at a naked man dead or alive. After she had covered him up, she went back into the bedroom. Polly had evidently put up a pretty good fight, because she had not been raped, and other than being roughed up, she was not too badly hurt. After they got her into bed with her doll, Elner said in a calm, matter-of-fact tone of voice, "Louise, when you get her to sleep, could I see you in the kitchen for a minute?"

When Louise came back to the kitchen, she was still shaking all over. Elner was sitting at the kitchen table calmly drinking a cup of coffee and eating a piece of her own pecan pie.

"Is he still here?"

"Oh yes." Elner nodded over at the man underneath the red and white tablecloth. "Polly may be retarded, but she's a good shot, I'll say that for her. Got him right between the eyes."

"What?"

"That's your hired hand over there."

Louise looked over at the covered-up body. "Oh my God. Is he dead?"

"He sure is. As far as I can figure, he must have pulled a gun on her and she somehow got it away from him." She indicated a gun lying on the table beside her. "I found it on the floor near the sink."

Louise looked down at the gun, then gasped. "Elner, that's my gun! Do you think he shot himself with it?"

"It's not likely he could shoot himself between the eyes, throw the gun across the room, and then put a bucket on his head."

"Then who shot him?"

Elner said, "I think it would be safe to say that it was Polly."

"But how did she get the gun?"

"I don't know. Where did you have it?"

She ran over to the door of the pantry. "I kept it in here." When Louise opened the door, she saw that inside the pantry there were cans and broken jars strewn all over the floor. "I kept it right here, on the second shelf behind the beans," she said, pointing.

Elner got up, walked over, and looked in at the mess. "Well, Louise, she must have run in here trying to get away from him, and it got knocked off the shelf, and she picked it up and pulled the trigger. She might have thought it was a cap pistol. I don't know."

"Oh my God. We have to call the police right away and let them know somebody's been shot."

Elner looked at her and said, "We could do that, but let's take a minute before we do anything."

"But what about him, I mean, don't we have to call right away?"

"Oh, don't worry about him, he's not going anywhere."

Elner stepped inside the pantry with Louise, closed the door behind her, and said, "Now listen, Louise, I've been thinking. The fact that he's shot between the eyes could be looked on by some people as a murder."

"Murder!" Louise said loudly, then lowered her voice. "But he was trying to rape her. It was self-defense, an accident. She didn't mean to kill him."

"Self-defense or not, the police are going to have a lot of questions, there may even be a trial, and it would be in the newspapers. You don't want poor little Polly dragged through that, it would scare her to death, she probably doesn't even understand what happened yet."

"You're right, she would be terrified." Louise started wringing her hands. "I know, I'll just say I did it! I came in and saw what he was trying to do and I shot him."

"Louise, honey, think. Again, no witnesses. I've seen this kind of thing on *Perry Mason,* and if something does go wrong, who will take care of Polly for the rest of her life? You don't want her to wind up in that awful state institution, do you? Remember how awful it was when we went over there?"

"Yes, it was horrible, and I promised her she would never have to go."

"Yes, and after what all you went through to get to keep her at home? I'm just afraid if they find out she shot a man, they could take her away from you, and put her out there for good."

Louise burst into tears. "I'm so confused. I don't know what to do."

Elner cracked the door open a little and looked over at the large lump underneath the red and white checked tablecloth for a moment, then closed the door again and said to her friend, "You know, Louise, normally I'd say that everybody deserves a decent funeral, but any man that would try and rape a little re-tarded girl, well, that's just a horse of a different color."

"Oh, Elner. I just don't know what to do."

"I know you don't, Louise, so listen to me. Nobody knows about this but us, and Polly's not going to say anything. By the way, who is he, anyway?"

"Just a drifter looking for work, as far as I know. I don't even know his last name."

Elner looked out at him again. "Well, it's not like he's a fam-ily man and will be missed, and who's to say he hasn't done this before or what he might have done to some other poor girl in the future."

"What are you saying?" asked Louise.

Elner closed the door. Twenty minutes later when the two women came out of the pantry, they had a plan.

As soon as the sun went down and Polly was sound asleep, they moved into action.

About ten minutes later Louise came back into the kitchen with all of the hired man's things in a duffel bag.

"Did you get everything?"

"Yes."

Elner then walked over and leaned down and picked the man up by his arms. She stood him up against the counter and then heaved him up over her shoulders. "Open the door, Louise."

"Can you carry him all by yourself? Don't you want me to help?"

"Honey, I'm a big strong farm woman, just open the door . . . and get the shovel."

Louise looked over at the table. "Should we bury the gun with him?"

"Good Lord, no. If somebody does find him, we don't want your gun to be with him. Leave it and I'll get rid of it later."

After Elner had thrown the hired hand into the back of her truck and they had driven him a good distance away, back to the very end of Louise's property, Elner and Louise got out and dug the hole. When they finished, Elner heaved him over the side and they started filling it back up with the loose dirt.

"What if they catch us?" asked a nervous Louise. "What if somebody comes looking for him?"

"If anybody does, just say he left. You don't have to say he left feet first."

When they were driving back to the farmhouse, Elner said, "Just promise me one thing, Louise."

"What?"

"Be careful about who you hire from now on. People may act nice, but you never know."

As Elner's husband, Will, always used to say, "Think what you want, but some days luck is just on your side." Being so far out in the country, nobody heard the shot out at the Franks farm, except a few men shooting quail in a field about two miles away, and they figured it was just other hunters. Nor did anyone ever ask about the hired hand, whose fatal mistake had been trying to drag Polly to the bedroom. Polly may have been retarded, but that day all she knew was that her mother had told her not to leave the kitchen under any circumstances, and she hadn't. No matter how hard that man had tried to drag her out, she was not going. It had been sheer plain old good luck that in the struggle in the pantry the gun had landed next to her. Poor Polly didn't know the difference between a Roy Rogers cap pistol and a real gun, and pulled the trigger. Another piece of good luck: she had shot somebody who was not well liked, or even missed, for that matter.

The night of the shooting, after she'd helped Louise clean up the mess, Elner had taken the gun home and had hidden it in the henhouse. She figured if someone ever did find the body, she would call the police and confess that she had done it and show them the murder weapon. She didn't want to go to jail, but if it would keep poor little Polly at home with her mother, she'd do it. Now that she was a widow, all she had was a cat, and she figured Sonny could do without her a lot easier than Polly could do without her mother. A few years later, when Elner sold the farm, she stuck the gun in her purse and brought it to town with her, just in case.

The Repercussions

Elner Shimfissle had been told that everything that happened, happened for a reason. Of course she couldn't have known it at the time, but the repercussions of her having fallen out of the fig tree turned out to be many and varied.

A few years later, Polly Franks died of heart failure. After her daughter passed away, Louise Franks sold their ten-acre farm to a developer for a small fortune. Norma handled the sale. Louise sold it all, except for one small half acre of land way out in the back of the property. Norma thought it was odd, since she was not going to live there, but Louise explained, "Norma, I have an old beloved pet buried out there, and I just don't want that land developed." Louise moved into town and used the money she made on her property to build and staff a school for the developmentally handicapped, and named it The Elner Shimfissle Center.

After his encounter with Elner, Dr. Bob Henson changed his mind about people and became much happier in his work.

And as fate would have it, a year later the slip-and-sue ambulance-chasing lawyer, Gus Shimmer, fell over in court with a major heart attack. He had to be rushed to Caraway Hospital, and it was Dr. Bob Henson who worked on him for over three hours, literally saving his life. The same Dr. Henson he would have sued if Norma had let him.

However, when Franklin Pixton found out that Dr. Henson had saved Gus Shimmer's life, right in the middle of a lawsuit against his hospital, he was not happy. "Where is malpractice when you really need it?" he mused. But he needn't have worried about Gus Shimmer. After Dr. Henson saved his life, Gus made a vow to God never to sue another hospital or doctor again. Not only was Gus a changed man, his informant at Caraway Hospital was gone for good as well.

The male nurse who had been Gus's informant, the same one who had caused Ruby's friend Boots Carroll to be demoted, had finally called the wrong woman "bitch." Mrs. Betty Stevens, a very wealthy and generous widow—her husband had invented Johnny Cat, one of the best kitty litters—was in for gallbladder surgery and overheard the male nurse referring to her as "that old rich bitch" behind her back. Considering she had given millions to the hospital fund and was a close friend of Mrs. Franklin Pixton's, the nurse was fired on the spot, and Boots was back in her old job as head supervisor. It was not that Mrs. Betty Stevens objected to being called rich or a bitch. It was the "old" part she'd objected to. After all, she was still a good-looking woman of sixty-four.

From the day the lawyer Winston Sprague found the shoe on the roof, he was never quite the arrogant know-it-all, some said "snotty young man on the rise," again. He had gone from thinking he was smarter than everyone else in the world, to someone who was now not quite so sure. To some this may have been a bad thing, however, in Winston's case it proved to be the best thing that ever happened to him. The girl he had been in love with for so many years, the one who had assured him she wanted to get married, just not to him, happened to see him out in a crowd of friends, and noticed that there was something different about him. He sat alone and had a faraway look in his eye. When she walked over to speak to him, and asked how he was, he told her he had just quit his job, and was headed for a two-week stay at an ashram in Colorado.

"An ashram? Hmm," she thought. "That's interesting. This guy may not be such a jerk after all." So instead of leaving, she sat down.

Six months later, after the girl had agreed to marry him, she said, "Winston, I don't know what happened to you, it's almost like you're not the same person anymore." And she meant that as a compliment.

Winston did not tell her about finding the shoe, the event that had changed him, but a few days later, after his yoga class, he drove across town to the trophy shop and walked in with a brown paper bag under his arm and said to the man behind the counter, "I'd like to have something bronzed, do you bronze shoes?"

"Yes," the man said. "We do baby shoes."

Winston opened the bag, pulled out the golf shoe, and put it on the counter. "Can you do this?"

The man looked at it. "This? You want this bronzed? Just one shoe?"

"That's right, can you do it?"

"Well, I guess so, do you want a plaque on it or anything?"

Winston thought for a moment. "Yes. Just put 'The Shoe on the Roof.'"

"The shoe on the roof?"

"Yes," he said with a smile. "It's sort of an inside joke."

But Winston's was not the only romance that resulted in marriage. On June 22 at the Unity Church in Elmwood Springs, Reverend Susie Hill pronounced Dr. Brian Lang and Linda Warren man and wife. And although Verbena Wheeler swore she would *never* set foot in one of those "new age do-it-yourself" churches, she did.

But best of all, Linda Warren's corporate community project, Adopt a Cat Month, had been so successful that the idea had spread to other corporations, and thousands of cats all across the country were being taken home every day, and they didn't even know it was all because Elner Shimfissle fell out of her fig tree one April morning.

Another Easter

8:28 AM

As for Norma, her attention to detail served her well, and soon Cortwright Realty became Cortwright-Warren Realty and she was very happy about that. But as far as the other part of her life, sadly she never did receive a sign, a wonder, or a miracle, and she had pretty much given up even looking for one, until another Easter four years later.

Norma was out at the cemetery leaving the lilies on her parents' graves like she always did, trying not to let the plastic flowers that were now on almost every grave make her insane. But as she was leaving, she happened to walk by the old Smith plot on the south side of the cemetery where Neighbor Dorothy was buried, and for some unknown reason she stopped and read the two names on the large tombstone in the middle and was stunned when she saw what was written.

DOROTHY ANNE SMITH
Beloved Mother
1894–1976

ROBERT RAYMOND SMITH
Beloved Father
1892–1977

Norma's mouth flew open. *Raymond?* She never knew Neighbor Dorothy's husband was named *Raymond*! Suddenly that tiny little flicker of hope that had almost burned out started up again, and she smiled and stood there looking up at the blue sky. And it was such a pretty day too.

The following Sunday, also for some unknown reason, Macky got up and said to Norma, "I think I'll go to church with you today and see what it's all about." Norma didn't know what had brought this on, but she was so glad he picked that day to go, because the text of Susie's sermon that Sunday was:

> There Lives More Faith in Honest Doubt,
> Believe Me, Than Half the Creeds.
>
> —ALFRED, LORD TENNYSON

And everyone said it was the best one she had ever given.

Gone Native!

M acky going to church was a surprise, but perhaps the most surprising event took place in May of the following spring.

Verbena picked up the phone and called Ruby.

"You will not believe what has happened to poor Tot."

"Oh Lord, what now?" said Ruby, sitting down to hear the bad news.

"I just heard from her . . . hold on to your hat . . . Tot has gone native!"

"What?"

"Gone completely native overnight! She says she doesn't know how or what happened to her, but the minute she hit Waikiki and got to her hotel room, she threw off her clothes, underwear and all, put on a muumuu, stuck a flower behind her ear, and says to tell everybody good-bye, that she's never coming home."

"What? She's a white person, she can't just go native!"

"She said that's what she always thought, and it came as a total revelation to her. She said she hadn't even wanted to go to Hawaii, but when she got off the plane, something just took her over! She says she thinks she might have been a Hawaiian princess in another life because she is as happy as a bird and feels right at home."

"Well, what is she doing?"

"That's just it, she's not doing a thing . . . except floating around on the beach all day taking hula lessons. She sounds awfully happy and cheerful."

"That's not like Tot."

"No, it's not, and it just makes me wonder if she might not have found herself a boyfriend over there."

"Did she say so?"

"No, but it stands to reason, don't you think? And I wonder if he's not a Hawaiian?"

Ruby sighed. "Oh, I just don't know anymore, Verbena. The world has gone so crazy, it could be a Hawaiian *woman,* for all we know."

"Well, I hope she's wearing sunscreen, she's going to ruin her skin running around in that hot sun. She's liable to get skin cancer."

"That's right, when they take off part of her nose, she won't feel so native, I can tell you that."

"I don't think she cares one way or another. She said she's just glad she made it to social security."

"Tot is the last person in the world I ever dreamed would go native."

"Me too. I'm telling you, the longer I live the more surprised I am at people. You just never know from one minute to the next what will happen."

And so, contrary to the sign she had up in her beauty shop, OLD HAIRDRESSERS NEVER RETIRE, THEY JUST CURL UP AND DYE, Tot did in fact retire. She took the advice Elner had given her and was living every day as if it might be her last. And as Tot sat on her lanai that evening enjoying the warm tropical breeze and sipping her piña colada, she glanced over at her new companion, who sat beside her, and she suddenly remembered the old travelogs they used to show at the movies.

She closed her eyes, and soon the soft strains of Hawaiian music began to play and she could almost hear a familiar man's singsong voice saying,

"And as the golden sun sets, once again, over beautiful Waikiki Beach, we bid all of you, Aloha and good-bye. . . . until we meet again."

Epilogue

When Elner Jane Shimfissle got off the elevator, she looked down at the end of the hall, and saw a smiling Dorothy and Raymond standing outside the door, waiting to greet her. She was overjoyed to see them again. But just before they went inside, she stopped and whispered to Dorothy, "This is the real thing, isn't it? It's not another short visit, is it?"

Dorothy laughed. "No, honey, it's the real thing this time."

Raymond smiled and said, "Come on in, you've got a lot of people anxious to see you." The big door swung open, and there stood a large group, including her mother and daddy, her sisters Ida and Gerta, and a lot of other relatives she had only seen in old family photographs. Ginger Rogers and Thomas Edison stood behind them, waving and smiling at her. It was at that moment that she found him. There, standing right in the middle of the first row, was her husband, Will! He stepped forward wearing a big grin, with his arms wide open, and said, "What took you so long, woman?" She ran to him and knew she was home for good.

Recipes

Neighbor Dorothy's Heavenly Caramel Cake

PREHEAT OVEN TO 350 DEGREES.

1¾ cups cake flour (sift before
  measuring)
Resift with 1 cup brown sugar
Add:
½ cup soft butter
2 eggs

½ cup milk
½ teaspoon salt
1¾ teaspoons double-acting
  baking powder
1 teaspoon vanilla

Beat for 3 minutes. Bake in greased pan for ½ hour.

CARAMEL FROSTING

2 tablespoons cake flour
½ cup milk
½ cup brown sugar
½ cup sifted powdered sugar

1 teaspoon vanilla
¼ cup butter, softened
¼ cup shortening
¼ teaspoon salt

Mix cake flour and milk. Cook to a thick paste over slow flame.
Cool. Cream sugars and vanilla with butter and shortening. Beat

until light and fluffy. Blend in salt. Mix in cooled paste. Beat until fluffy. Blend. Should look like whipped cream.

Mrs. McWilliams' Corn Bread

4 cups cornmeal
2 teaspoons baking soda
2 teaspoons salt

4 eggs, beaten
4 cups buttermilk
½ cup bacon drippings, melted

Preheat oven to 450 degrees. Combine dry ingredients and make a well in center. Combine eggs, buttermilk, and bacon drippings, mixing well; add to cornmeal mixture and beat until smooth. Heat a well-greased 12-inch cast-iron skillet in the preheated oven until very hot. Pour batter into hot skillet; bake for 35 to 45 minutes, or until a knife inserted in center comes out clean and top is golden brown. Yield: 6 to 10 servings.

Louise Franks' Deviled Eggs

1 dozen hard-cooked eggs
1 5-ounce jar pasteurized
   Neufchâtel cheese spread
   with olives, or pimiento-
   flavored
2 tablespoons mayonnaise

2 tablespoons minced sweet
   pickles
2 tablespoons minced sweet
   onion
½ teaspoon salt

Peel eggs and cut in half lengthwise. Mash yolks; blend with cheese spread and mayonnaise. Stir in remaining ingredients. Refill egg whites. Yield: 2 dozen halves.

Irene Goodnight's Bundt Cake

1 package yellow cake mix	*¾ cup water*
1 package instant vanilla	*4 eggs*
pudding mix	*¼ cup sugar*
¾ cup butter-flavored oil	*½ cup chopped nuts*

Combine cake mix and pudding mix with oil, water, and eggs in mixer bowl. Beat at medium speed for 8 minutes. Mix sugar and nuts. Sprinkle half of that mixture into well-greased Bundt pan. Top with half the cake batter. Add the remaining nut mixture, then the remaining cake batter. Bake at 350 degrees for 50 minutes.

Aunt Elner's Liver and Onions

1 pound calf or beef liver	*2 large onions, peeled and*
salt	*thinly sliced*
pepper	*2 tablespoons all-purpose flour*
all-purpose flour	*¾ cup plus 2 tablespoons beef*
¼ cup plus 2 tablespoons	*broth*
butter or margarine	*¾ cup sour cream (optional)*

Sprinkle liver with salt and pepper and dredge well in flour. Cook in 2 tablespoons melted butter in a large skillet until liver loses its pink color and is lightly browned. Remove from skillet and set aside.

Melt ¼ cup butter in skillet over medium heat. Add onions and sauté until tender and lightly browned. Sprinkle flour over onions, stir well, and cook 1 minute, stirring constantly. Add beef broth; cook, stirring constantly, until thickened and bubbly. Add liver to sauce; cover and simmer 10 minutes. Remove from heat; transfer liver to a serving platter. Stir sour cream into skillet and pour sauce over liver. Serve with hot buttered noodles or rice. Yield: 4 servings.

Irene Goodnight's Green Bean Funeral Casserole

1 10¾-ounce can cream of
    mushroom soup, undiluted
½ cup milk
4½ cups cooked and drained
    cut green beans

½ cup slivered almonds, lightly
    toasted (optional)
1 cup crushed saltines
1½ cups (6 ounces) shredded
    cheddar cheese

Preheat oven to 350 degrees. Combine soup and milk. Arrange half of green beans in bottom of a greased shallow 1½-quart baking dish. Spread half of soup mixture over beans; sprinkle with half of almonds, saltines, and 1 cup cheese. Repeat bean, almond, soup mixture, and saltine layers. Bake, uncovered, for 25 minutes; sprinkle with remaining ½ cup cheese and continue baking 5 minutes longer. Yield: 6 servings.

Norma's Pimiento Cheese

3 cups (12 ounces) shredded
    mild cheddar cheese
1 cup mayonnaise
2 tablespoons grated
    onion

2 to 3 teaspoons Worcester-
    shire sauce (optional)
¼ to ½ teaspoon red pepper
2 4-ounce jars diced pimiento,
    drained

Combine first 5 ingredients in a food processor; pulse until blended and cheese is processed as fine as you want it. Add pimiento; pulse just to blend. Store in covered container in the refrigerator. Yield: about 3 cups.

Aunt Elner's Pecan Pie

½ *cup butter or margarine,*
   melted
1 *cup firmly packed light*
   brown sugar
1 *cup light corn syrup*

4 *eggs, beaten*
2 *teaspoons vanilla extract*
⅓ *teaspoon salt*
1 *unbaked 9-inch pastry shell*
1½ *cups pecan halves*

Preheat oven to 325 degrees. Combine first 3 ingredients in a small saucepan and cook over medium heat, stirring constantly, until butter melts and sugar dissolves. Cool slightly. Beat eggs, vanilla, and salt in a large bowl; gradually add sugar mixture, beating well with a wire whisk. Pour into pastry shell and scatter pecans over top. Bake for 50 to 55 minutes. Serve warm or chilled. Yield: one 9-inch pie.

ABOUT THE AUTHOR

FANNIE FLAGG began writing and producing television specials at age nineteen and went on to distinguish herself as an actress and writer in television, films, and the theater. She is the *New York Times* bestselling author of *Daisy Fay and the Miracle Man, Fried Green Tomatoes at the Whistle Stop Cafe* (which was produced by Universal Pictures as *Fried Green Tomatoes*), *Welcome to the World, Baby Girl!, Standing in the Rainbow,* and *A Redbird Christmas*. Flagg's script for *Fried Green Tomatoes* was nominated for an Academy Award and a Writers Guild of America Award, and won the highly regarded Scripters Award. Flagg lives in California and in Alabama.

ABOUT THE TYPE

This book was set in Sabon, a typeface designed by the well-known German typographer Jan Tschichold (1902–74). Sabon's design is based upon the original letter forms of Claude Garamond and was created specifically to be used for three sources: foundry type for hand composition, Linotype, and Monotype. Tschichold named his typeface for the famous Frankfurt typefounder Jacques Sabon, who died in 1580.